A SCOURGE OF VIPERS

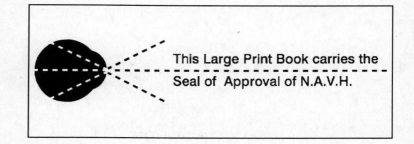

This Large Print Book carries the
Seal of Approval of N.A.V.H.

A SCOURGE OF VIPERS

BRUCE DESILVA

THORNDIKE PRESS

A part of Gale, Cengage Learning

GALE
CENGAGE Learning·

Farmington Hills, Mich • San Francisco • New York • Waterville, Maine
Meriden, Conn • Mason, Ohio • Chicago

LIBRARY OF CONGRESS CATALOGING-IN-PUBLICATION DATA

DeSilva, Bruce.
    A scourge of vipers / by Bruce De Silva.
        pages cm. — (A Liam Mulligan novel) (Thorndike Press large print crime scene)
    ISBN 978-1-4104-8044-6 (hardcover) — ISBN 1-4104-8044-5 (hardcover)
    1. Journalists—Fiction. 2. Providence (R.I.)—Fiction. 3. Large type books.
I. Title.
PS3604.E7575S37 2010
813'.54—dc23   2015010354

Published in 2015 by arrangement with Tom Doherty Associates, LLC

Printed in Mexico
1 2 3 4 5 6 7 19 18 17 16 15

For Blackie, the car-chasing, chicken-killing mutt my mom and dad gave me for my fourth birthday, and for all the pooches I've loved since then. But especially for Brady, my gentle Bernese mountain dog, and Rondo, his goofy mixed-breed best bud, whose joyous approach to life sustained me during the long slog of writing this novel. Nothing keeps your head straight like the companionship of a great dog.

AUTHOR'S NOTE

This is a work of fiction. Although a few of the characters are named after old friends, they bear no resemblance to them. For example, my old high school chum Bruce McCracken never worked as a private detective. A handful of real people, including New Jersey Governor Chris Christie, are mentioned in passing, but they have no speaking parts in the story. Although I borrowed the colorful nickname of a former Rhode Island attorney general, the fictional and real Attila the Nun are nothing alike, and the character's actions and dialogue are entirely imaginary. References to Rhode Island history and geography are as accurate as I can make them, but I have played around a bit with time and space. For example, Hopes, the newspaper bar where I drank decades ago when I reported the news for the *Providence Journal,* is long gone, but I enjoyed resurrecting it for this story.

1

A snake — that's what Mario Zerilli had called me. And now, just an hour later, something was slithering across my cracked kitchen linoleum. It was three feet long with lemon racing stripes twisting the length of its brown body. I watched it slide past the wheezing fridge and veer toward the kitchen table where my bare feet rested on the floor.

It raised its head and froze, its forked tongue flickering. It had caught my scent.

I pushed back from the table, got down on my knees, and studied it. A pretty thing. I flashed out my right hand and pinched it just behind its head. It writhed, its body a bullwhip. I was startled by its strength.

I carried the snake into the bedroom, opened my footlocker, and used my left hand to empty it, tossing a half-dozen New England Patriots and Boston Bruins sweat-shirts and a spare blanket onto the bed. Beneath the blanket was a Colt .45 that once belonged to my grandfather. I tossed that on the bed, too. Then I dropped the snake inside, slammed the lid, and started thinking about names.

Stop it, I told myself. The garter snake was probably an escaped pet, the property of someone else in the tenement building. How else could it have found its way into my second-floor apartment? When I had the time, I'd ask around, but if no one claimed it, I'd be heading to the pet store for a suitable cage.

I could hear the snake blindly exploring inside the footlocker, its scales rasping as they slid against the wood. I couldn't help myself. I started thinking about names again. Mario leaped to mind. But no, I couldn't call it that. I *liked* garter snakes. If Mario had sneaked it in, it would have been a copperhead or a timber rattler.

The trouble with Mario started a week ago when his great-uncle, Dominic "Whoosh" Zerilli, and I got together over boilermakers at Hopes, the local press hangout, to talk about the future. I was a newspaper reporter, so I didn't have one. Whoosh was contemplating retirement.

"The wife's still nagging me about it," he said. "Wants me to sell the house, turn my business over to Mario, and move to

10

Florida."

"So why don't you?"

"I'm thinkin' on it."

"And?"

"And *what*?"

"And what are you thinking?"

"I'm thinkin' I'm sick to death of fuckin' snow. I'm thinkin' the warm weather might be good for my arthritis. I'm thinkin' that if I move down there, I won't have to listen to Maggie *talk* about moving down there every fuckin' night."

"But?"

"But she's got her heart set on one of them retirement villages in Vero Beach or Boca Raton. Keeps shovin' brochures in my face. 'Look at this, honey,' she tells me. 'They got maid service, swimmin' pools, croquet, a golf course, horseshoes, craft rooms, shuffleboard. And have you ever *seen* so many flowers?' "

He made a face, the same one I once saw him make when he absentmindedly stuck the coal end of a Lucky Strike in his mouth.

"*Sounds* nice," I said.

"Oh, yeah? Then *you* move down there with her."

"What's wrong with it?"

"You shittin' me? Craft rooms? Croquet? And I *hate* fuckin' shuffleboard. No way

11

I'm wastin' whatever years I got left listenin' to a bunch of wheezers with bum tickers and colostomy bags pass gas and brag about the grandkids that never visit while they wait for the reaper to show up. Jesus Christ, Mulligan. Have you ever seen them fuckin' places? They're full of *old* people."

Whoosh was a few months short of eighty.

"Don't you dare laugh at me, asshole."

"I'm not."

"Yeah, but it's takin' some effort."

He waved the waitress over and ordered us both another round of Bushmills shots with Killian's chasers.

"Maybe you could compromise," I said. "Get yourself a beachfront cottage on Sanibel Island or a luxury condo in Fort Myers."

"Where the Sox have spring training? I already thought of that. Trouble is, ain't no way I can hand the business over to Mario."

"Why not?"

"Cuz he's a fuckin' moron."

Mario, just twenty-six years old, had already done state time for drunken driving and for using his girlfriend as a tackling dummy. Now he was awaiting trial for kicking the crap out of a transvestite who made the near-fatal mistake of slipping out of the Stable, Providence's newest gay bar, to smoke a cigarette. But he was Whoosh's

12

only living blood relative. The punk had inherited the title two years ago when his father was gunned down in a botched East Providence bank robbery. Mario's grandfather, Whoosh's only brother, fell to esophageal cancer back in 1997 while serving a ten-year stretch for fencing stolen goods.

Whoosh and Maggie did have an adopted daughter; but Lucia, a young mother who performed with a New York City dance troupe, was an unlikely candidate to take over his bookmaking business. My old friend and his wife never had any kids of their own.

"Wouldn't trust Mario with the business even if Arena gave a thumbs-up," Whoosh was saying. "Which there's no fuckin' way he's ever gonna."

"No?"

"He already said. The kid's unreliable. Draws too much attention to himself."

"So what are you going to do?"

"Find somebody I can trust," he said. "Ain't all that much to it, really. Take the bets, pay off the winners, collect from the losers. Keep half of the profits, and wire the rest once a month to an account I got down in the Caymans."

"Got somebody in mind?"

13

"Yeah. You."

"*Me?*"

"Why not? You been tellin' me how much you hate the corporate pricks who bought *The Dispatch.* You keep sayin' they're gonna fire your ass if you don't up and quit first. We been friends a long time, Mulligan. You've hung around me enough to understand how I do business. Anything you don't know, I can show you. How to write bets down in code. Which cops to pay off. How much tribute you gotta kick upstairs to Arena every month."

"Huh."

"So whaddaya say?"

I'd never had a moral objection to bookmaking, at least not the way Zerilli went about it. Unlike the officially sanctioned gangsters at the Rhode Island Lottery Commission, who peddled chump numbers games and scratch tickets to suckers, my bookie had always given me a fair chance to win. But I was reluctant to climb into bed with Giuseppe Arena. As head of the Patriarca crime family, his interests included truck hijacking, union corruption, prostitution, arson-for-hire, money laundering, and New England's biggest luxury-car-theft ring.

Still, I was growing anxious about how I'd

14

manage to pay the rent and keep my ancient Ford Bronco fed with gas and junkyard parts once *The Dispatch* was done with me. My young pal Edward Anthony Mason III — trust fund baby, son of *The Providence Dispatch*'s former publisher, and first journalist laid off when the paper's new owners took over last year — was dangling a reporting gig at his online local-news start-up, *The Ocean State Rag.* But the venture wasn't making any money yet, so the job didn't pay much. A standing offer to join my old buddy Bruce McCracken's private detective agency would pay better, but it wasn't journalism.

But bookmaking? Now *that* was real money. I could replace the torn sofa I'd found on the sidewalk, buy myself a new Mustang convertible, move into a luxury condo on the bay, start an IRA. Maybe even invest in some Red Sox T-shirts that weren't adorned with cigar burns and pizza grease.

"Have you broken the news to Mario yet?" I asked.

"Not yet."

"How he's gonna take it?"

"He's gonna be wicked pissed."

"He's still got that no-show Sanitation Department job, right?"

"Yeah."

"Probably doesn't pay much," I said.

"A couple grand a month. Chump change if you gotta work for it, which he don't, so what's to complain about?"

"He'll make trouble," I said, "unless you can buy him off with something else."

"Already on it. I been introducin' him to another line of work."

"What?"

"Somethin' that don't require a remedial course in junior high math. So are you in or out?"

I took a pull from my beer, tipped my head back, and thought about it for a moment.

"Can you give me some time to think it over?"

"Sure thing, Mulligan. Just don't take too goddamn long, okay? I'm havin' a helluva time holding Maggie off. She's fuckin' relentless."

I never learned how Mario found out about Whoosh's offer, but two days later the threatening phone calls started. The first one went something like this:

"You Mulligan?"

"The one and only. And you are?"

"I'm the guy who's gonna be your worst nightmare if you don't stop messin' with what's mine."

"You mean the redhead I picked up at Hopes Friday night?"

"What? No."

"Cuz you're welcome to her," I said. "She's a poor conversationalist, and the sex was below average. I got no plans to see her again."

"Stop kidding around, asshole. You know what I'm talkin' about."

"Let me think. Did my story about no-show sanitation jobs cause you some inconvenience?"

"I'm talkin' about my Uncle Whoosh's racket, you dumb fuck. You better hear what I'm saying, cuz this ain't no joke. Back off, or I'm gonna tear you a new one."

He called me daily after that, usually right around midnight. I should have stopped provoking him, but I didn't. Sometimes I just can't help myself. So after work last Friday, I found my Ford Bronco vandalized in the parking lot across from *The Dispatch,* although with all the old dents and rust, the new damage matched the décor. And tonight, before I came home and found the snake, Mario caught me staggering out of Hopes after last call and pointed a small nickel-plated revolver at me.

"Ain't laughing now," he said, "are you,

shithead?"

"You haven't said anything funny yet."

"My uncle's racket is supposed to go to me. I'm his blood. This is my future you're fuckin' with. I don't know what you got on Uncle Whoosh, but I'm warning you. Get lost. If you don't, I'm gonna bust one right through your heart, you fuckin' snake."

He was pointing the gun at my belly when he said it. I wasn't sure if he was confused about human anatomy or just a lousy shot.

Confident that he'd made his point, Mario brushed past me and pimp-walked away down the sidewalk. As I turned to watch him go, he shoved the pistol into his waistband and pulled his shirttail over it. I decided not to take any more chances. The next time we met, Mario wouldn't be the only one packing heat.

My late grandfather's Colt, the sidearm he'd carried for decades as a member of the Providence PD, used to hang in a shadowbox on my apartment wall. I'd taken it down and learned how to shoot a few years ago after my investigation into a string of arsons in the city's Mount Hope section provoked death threats. But Grandpa's gun had a hell of a kick and was too large for easy concealment. So the day after that encounter with Mario, I splurged three hundred bucks on a Kel-Tec PF-9 at the D&L gun shop in Warwick. The chopped-down pocket pistol was five and a half inches long, had an unloaded weight of just twelve and a half ounces, and tucked comfortably into the waistband at the small of my back.

Beyond ten yards, I couldn't hit anything smaller than Narragansett Bay, but I didn't figure on doing any sharpshooting.

2

It was just past eight A.M. when I stepped into *The Dispatch*'s third-floor newsroom and punched the time clock. The device was the latest employee-friendly innovation from General Communications Holdings International — GCHI to its closest friends — the bottom-feeding media conglomerate that had gobbled up the struggling newspaper last year. I'd never heard of a newsroom with a time clock, but there was no fighting progress.

"Mulligan?" the receptionist said. "The managing editor would like a word."

I plodded over to the aquarium, a glass-walled office where *Mister* Twisdale — who did not allow the staff to call him Charles and became apoplectic when addressed as Chuck or Charlie — sprawled in the black leather throne formerly occupied by my longtime boss, Ed Lomax. Lomax's passion had been to put out the best newspaper he could every day. Twisdale's assigned task was to wring as much money as possible from *The Dispatch* before it finally went belly-up.

He was a six-foot-three-inch, broad-shouldered thirty-two-year-old with a boy's regular haircut, a white dress shirt, and a red rep tie splattered with the Alpha Delta Phi fraternity emblem. Wrists thickened by weight lifting shot out of a navy-blue blazer he'd probably bought on sale at Men's Wearhouse. The smug bastard liked the way he looked.

I didn't, but I gave him a toothy good-morning grin and said, "What's up, Chuck?"

"Do I really have to tell you again?" he said.

"Tell me what, Chuck?"

"How to address your superiors."

I made a show of looking around.

"I don't see any of those here."

"Stop being such an asshole, Mulligan. When you win a Pulitzer, you can be an asshole."

"Really, Chuckie? When did you win yours?"

If he'd bothered to read my personnel file, he would have known that I *had* won a Pulitzer. Not that I gave a shit about that. It was a long time ago. I was more concerned about all the other things this former TV news producer from Oklahoma City didn't know about leadership, newspapers, Providence, or being human.

Over the years, I'd had my share of squabbles with Lomax, but I missed him. He'd been summarily dismissed because he possessed two qualities that our new owners could not tolerate — integrity and a hundred-and-twenty-thousand-dollar salary. Living on Social Security and savings now, he and his wife recently sold their big house in Cumberland and moved into a small condo in East Providence.

Twisdale glowered at me, then gave it up when he saw it wasn't working.

"You're late," he said.

"Just by five minutes."

"Which means you'll be docked an hour's wages. Company policy." He sucked in a deep breath and blew it out through his nose. "Do you know why I put up with you, Mulligan?"

"Not a clue."

"Because you're productive. You turn out twice as much copy as any of your colleagues."

"Do you know why, Chuckie-boy?"

"I suppose you're going to tell me."

22

"It's because you fired most of the paper's experienced reporters and replaced them with a skeleton crew of fresh j-school grads. Sure, they work cheap, but you get what you pay for. Most of them don't know the difference between a deadline and a chorus line."

Another glower.

"I *know* what you're up to, Mulligan."

"You do?"

"You're trying to bait me into firing you so you can join the rest of the moochers who live off food stamps and unemployment checks."

Chuckie-boy was on to me. If I quit, I wouldn't qualify for unemployment. If he let me go, I could live off Uncle Sugar while I figured out what the hell to do next.

"Well," he said, "it's not going to work."

"Oh, darn."

"There's a stack of press releases on your desk. Get cracking."

I'd never worked for anyone who said "get cracking" before, and I didn't like it. It made me want to crack his head. As I turned to leave, he pulled a bottle of Purell hand sanitizer from his desk drawer and shot a dab into his palm. Funny. I didn't remember us shaking hands.

The football-field-size newsroom felt hol-

23

low as I trudged to my cubicle past the handful of reporters and editors still employed there. Twenty-two years ago, when I hired on as a cub reporter, the place bustled day and night. The news department numbered three hundred and forty then, and they were the very best at what they did, making *The Dispatch* one of the finest small-city metros in the country. But decades of declining circulation and advertising revenue had taken a toll. By the time the local owners finally gave up and sold out last year, the news staff had already been reduced to eighty. At the time, it was hard to imagine it could get any smaller. Our new corporate overlords promptly cut it in half.

They accomplished this — yes, they trumpeted it as an accomplishment — by eliminating the copy desk, firing the entire photo staff, and giving cameras to the reporters, most of whom didn't know which end of the lens to look through. Now our stories, along with those from the chain's twenty-seven other piece-of-shit dailies, were e-mailed to GCHI's "international editing center," located in a strip mall on the outskirts of Wichita. There, junior-college dropouts with a tenuous grasp of English grammar checked them over and e-mailed them back. Because they had never laid eyes on Providence, thought Rhode Island was an island, and couldn't locate New England on a map, the chances of them catching our green reporters' mistakes were close to zero.

On today's front page, Aborn Street appeared as Auburn Street, State Senator Parker Smyth was identified as U.S. Senator Parker Smith, Burnside Park was rechristened Sideburns Park, and the Woonasquatucket River was spelled three different ways, each of them wrong.

Not much real journalism was getting done either. Gone were the days of aggressive political and criminal justice reporting, sophisticated science and religion writing, blanket coverage of all thirty-nine Rhode Island cities and towns, and blockbuster investigations that had sent scores of politicians, mobsters, and crooked businessmen to the gray-bar hotel. Now the news pages were filled with rewritten press releases, crime news cribbed from police reports, fawning features about our few remaining advertisers, and columns of clumsily cut wire copy. Meetings and press conferences were often covered by monitoring the local-access cable TV channel. Our reporters were seldom allowed out of the office, dispatched only when a three-alarm fire broke out or a grisly murder was committed — this thanks to our former TV producer's "if it bleeds it leads" news philosophy. On most days, the longest story in the paper was the list of corrections on page two. I used to be proud to work at *The Dispatch.* Now it was a freaking embarrassment.

Late that afternoon, I was rewriting a press release touting the Providence Place Mall's fabulous upcoming St. Patrick's Day celebration ("Fun for the whole family!") when Chuckie-boy summoned me again.

"Channel 10 is saying the cops have fished a body out of the Seekonk River just above the falls in Pawtucket."

"It's the Blackstone River," I said.

"Excuse me?"

"It becomes the Seekonk River *below* the falls. Above the falls, it's called the Blackstone."

"Whatever. It's close to here, right?"

"Less than ten miles."

"I need you to get out there ASAP."

"Soon as I find my sunglasses. I've been stuck behind a desk so long that my eyes are unaccustomed to daylight."

3

The Blackstone rises at the confluence of Mill Brook and Middle River in the old industrial city of Worcester, Massachusetts, tumbles southeast through a string of suburbs and rural villages, and enters Rhode Island at the decaying mill city of Woonsocket. Then it scoots south through the bedroom communities of Cumberland and Lincoln, mopes past the triple-decker slums of Central Falls, and finally rolls into the city of Pawtucket, where Samuel Slater erected the first water-powered cotton mill in America in 1790. There, forty-eight miles from its source, it spills over a low dam into the tidal Seekonk River.

In colonial times, the Blackstone was alive with Atlantic salmon and the lamprey that preyed upon them; but by the mid-1800s it had become an open sewer, running thick with effluent from textile mills, solvents and heavy metals from jewelry and woodworking shops, and human waste from the cities and towns along its course. In 1990, the Environmental Protection Agency branded it the most toxic river in America, and recent attempts to clean it up have been only marginally successful. Today it is designated a class C river, unsafe for swimming but suitable for boating and fishing if you don't mind the odor and have the good sense not to eat what you catch. That doesn't deter immigrant anglers who pull carp, one of the few critters hardy enough to survive in it, out of the murk and bring them home to poison their hungry children.

I cruised down Roosevelt Avenue past Pawtucket City Hall, a grotesque pile of masonry that gives Art Deco a bad name, and pulled Secretariat, my pet name for the Bronco, into the nearly empty Slater Mill Historic Site parking lot. There, a uniformed cop was waving away two Mystic, Connecticut, school buses crammed with middle-school kids who were too preoccupied with their iPhones to look out the windows. No field trip today, boys and girls. Take a rain check. The docents at the Slater Mill museum will bore the hell out of you with their looms and shuttles at a later date.

I grabbed my Nikon, climbed out of Secretariat, and flashed my press pass at the uniform.

"You're gonna have to wait over there," he said, pointing toward two TV vans and a clutch of reporters and photographers who didn't seem to be doing anything.

"No inglés," I said. I brushed past him and hustled toward a medical examiner's wagon and six Pawtucket police cars clustered beside a band of bare young maples that skirted the riverbank.

"Hey, bud! You hard of hearing?"

"No comprendo," I shouted and kept moving.

Before I got there, I was intercepted by a bespectacled young man wearing a cheap suit and tie under an unbuttoned cloth topcoat. He was carrying a clipboard.

"Excuse me, sir. Are you with the press?"

"¿Por qué?" I said.

And he said, *"¿Cómo te llamas?"*

The game was up. I didn't know any more Spanish.

"I'm Mulligan from *The Dispatch.* And who would you be?"

"My name is Kevin Muñoz," he said, stifling a laugh. "I'm the new press officer for the Pawtucket PD. I'm going to have to ask you to wait back there with the rest of the reporters. I'll have a statement for you in about an hour."

29

"Is Detective Sergeant Lebowski on the scene?"

"Yes, sir, I believe he is."

"Then trot on back where you came from and tell him Mulligan would like a word."

He raised an eyebrow. I raised one right back at him.

"Okay, sir. Please wait right here."

He scurried off and disappeared behind the meat wagon. Two minutes later, a detective with a head suitable for ten-pin bowling and shoulders borrowed from a silverback gorilla stepped from between two of the cruisers and waved.

"Mulligan? How the hell are you? Been so long since I seen you I was thinkin' maybe you croaked."

"My new boss doesn't let me out of the office much, Dude."

I'm not one of those assholes who calls everyone "dude," but I had to make an exception in this case. It was the detective's nickname, pinned on him when the Coen brothers film *The Big Lebowski* came out back in '98. I extended my right hand. Dude crushed it in his simian paw.

"So what have you got?" I asked.

"A floater," he said. "Couple of kids from Newport spotted it as they were lining up to get on their bus. They alerted their

30

handlers, who called 911."

"Male or female?"

"Male."

"Age?"

"Hard to say. The body took a beating from all the flotsam in the river. The M.E. says the carp chowed down on it, too. No wallet on him. Not much face left either."

"Mind if I have a look?"

He hesitated a beat, then said, "Yeah, okay. But don't touch anything. And no pictures."

He raised the yellow police tape, and I ducked under it. We brushed through the screen of trees and found Glenna Ferguson, an assistant state medical examiner, squatting beside the body. It looked to be about six feet long, clothed in a muck-smeared yellow and black Bruins sweatshirt and what once might have been blue jeans. With the loaded Boston hockey team poised for another deep playoff run and the rebuilding Celtics going nowhere, half the male population of Rhode Island was sporting Bruins gear this spring. I looked closer and saw that the corpse wore one mud-caked running shoe. The left shoe and sock were missing.

"A drowning?" I asked.

"Hey there, Mulligan," Ferguson said.

31

"Might have drowned unless he bled out from the gunshot wound in his neck first. Gotta open him up and look around before I can establish cause of death."

"How long was he in the water?"

"A day, maybe less."

I squatted for a closer look as she rolled the body to examine the exit wound.

"Looks like a large caliber," I said.

"Maybe. Hard to be sure yet with all the scavenger damage. It's through-and-through, so there's no slug."

"Damn thing could be anywhere between here and Woonsocket," Lebowski said. "No point in even looking, cuz we're never gonna find it."

"Give me a call when you get an ID?" I asked him.

"Sure thing."

"Thanks. I'd really appreciate it."

The Dude abides.

When I got back to the newsroom to write it up, Chuckie-boy had already punched me out. In doing so, he'd violated several state and federal labor laws, but I didn't hold it against him. He couldn't allow any overtime if he wanted to keep his job.

The story, which made me late for my evening feast of canned pork and beans, was worth just three paragraphs on an inside page of the metro section.

4

I spent the early part of the evening watching my snake explore every inch of the cracked twenty-five-gallon aquarium I'd snapped up at a big discount at Petco on North Main. Where he'd come from remained a mystery. A couple of neighbors thought he might have belonged to the meth addict who got evicted from the third floor last week, but they couldn't say for sure. I was going to name the snake Chara after the Boston Bruins' star defenseman, but when I mentioned it to Fadi, the Brown grad student who lived downstairs, he said it was a filthy word in Arabic.

"Eat up, Tuukka," I said, opening the aquarium top and dropping in one of the wriggling baby mice I'd bought. Tuukka Rask was the Bruins' quick-as-a-snake goaltender. Tuukka flicked his tongue at the mouse for a couple of minutes before unhinging his jaw and swallowing it whole.

Then he curled up for a nap and stopped being interesting.

I poured three fingers of Bushmills into a reasonably clean tumbler, fired up a cigar, and settled down to watch the second period of the hockey game on my twenty-four-inch TV. Moments after a David Krejci breakaway gave the Bruins a three-goal lead, "Confused" began playing in my shirt pocket. The tune by a San Francisco punk band called The Nuns signaled an incoming call from Fiona McNerney, a former Little Sisters of the Poor cenobite who was serving her second term as Rhode Island's governor.

"Attila the Nun," the handle a clever headline writer tagged her with because of her take-no-prisoners brand of politics, still attended mass every week, but her wardrobe and manner had become decidedly secular since she was released from her vows four years ago. The stern demeanor she'd adopted as a novice was gone now. Except for the graying hair, she'd reverted to the fun-loving, underage drinking partner I'd loved hanging out with in high school.

"Evening, Mulligan," she said. "What are you doing right now?"

"Watching the Bs kick the crap out of the Rangers."

"What are you wearing?"

"My clean pair of Boston Bruins boxers," I lied.

"Yum! I'll be right over."

"Time to finally shed your virginity?"

"It *is* a burden," she said, "but if I ever do the deed, it's gonna be with someone who can shower me with diamonds."

"Damn. That leaves me out."

"Sorry to disappoint."

"I take it the vow of poverty is history, too."

"Oh, *hell* yeah. That was just a phase. At the moment I'm sipping Dom Pérignon White Gold from a Waterford crystal goblet."

"Shall I come over and help you finish the bottle?"

"Please do. I'm making a major announcement in a couple of weeks, and I want to give you a heads-up."

"How major?"

·"I'll be unveiling my foolproof plan to solve the state's budget crisis."

"Oh, really? The last foolproof plan I heard about was when John Henry emptied his vault to create the greatest Red Sox team ever assembled."

"When they signed Carl Crawford, John Lackey, Nick Punto, and Adrian Gonzalez?"

"Yeah. Remember how that turned out, Fiona?"

"Not well."

"But *your* plan is foolproof?"

"Absolutely."

"This I've got to hear. I'll be right over."

Ten minutes later, Secretariat's chipped wiper blades slapped futilely at the mist gathering on the windshield, and his one working headlight bounced off a heavy fog that had descended on the city. As I crawled up Waterman Street, my cell played the opening bars of "Headline Hustler" by 10cc. — my ringtone for Chuckie-boy. I considered ignoring it, then reached for it and nearly sideswiped a parked car that materialized out of the gloom.

"Mulligan."

"It's Twisdale."

"What do you want, now, Chuck?"

"Channels 12 and 10 are reporting that a small plane has crashed in a residential area near Green Airport."

"Sorry to hear that, but I'm off duty."

"I know, but I need you on this."

"Are you authorizing overtime?"

'Come on, Mulligan. You know I can't do that."

"Then find somebody else."

A year ago, I wouldn't have hesitated. I

used to put in a lot of hours that I never got paid for. Back then, I was working for people who cared about the news more than they cared about money, so I did, too. It was different now.

"Look, do this for me and you can take tomorrow off."

"Tomorrow and the day after," I said.

"No way."

"Okay, then," I said, and clicked off. As I pulled away from the curb, Chuck called back.

"Yeah?"

"Okay, you win. Two days off. But make it tomorrow and Monday. I can't spare you two days in a row."

"Done. What's the address?"

I finished up with him and called Fiona.

"I need a rain check. Gotta go play reporter."

"That's a real shame." She sounded vaguely drunk. "Did I tell you that my announcement was major? Oh, and foolproof? Don't forget foolproof."

"I remember. But somebody tried to park a plane on a side street near the airport, so I gotta go take some pictures."

The plane had gone down on Brunswick Drive, less than a half mile south of the airport, in a neighborhood of modest brick and wood-frame houses in the Providence suburb of Warwick. I crept south on Post Road, turned left on Main Avenue, and ran into a police roadblock.

"The plane hit a house, and jet fuel is leaking into the basement," a uniformed officer told me. "We've got the whole neighborhood cordoned off, and we're evacuating everybody who lives within two thousand feet of the scene. It's a dangerous situation, bud. You need to get the hell out of here. And, hey, you got a busted headlight. Better get that fixed before you get a ticket."

I thanked him, turned around, worked my way down to West Shore Road, and parked the Bronco on a side street. Then I grabbed my camera and jogged a half mile to the scene, easily slipping by the police checkpoints in the fog.

The fuselage of a small plane was wedged in the wreckage of a red-brick two-story colonial. The aircraft's tail had snapped off and crushed the roof of a Ford Expedition parked in the driveway. The site looked chaotic with police cruisers, ambulances, and fire trucks parked at odd angles all over front lawns on both sides of the street. Some bore the insignias of the Warwick PD and

FD. Others were Green Airport security and rescue vehicles.

So far, nothing was on fire, but the damp air reeked of kerosene and, oddly, of french fries. That puzzled me until I remembered reading that jet fuel is sometimes manufactured by mixing distilled petroleum with recycled cooking grease from fast food joints. The street was strewn with what looked like tufts of cotton candy. I bent down, picked up a piece, and discovered that it was the house's fiberglass insulation.

As near as I could tell, I was the only journalist on the scene. With TV helicopters grounded by the weather, nobody else would have pictures by morning. The crash site was a news photographer's dream. Fog swirled around cops and firemen clawing through a tangle of shattered bricks and twisted metal. Everything was in silhouette, backlit by fire department spotlights. I wished my friend Gloria Costa, the great one-eyed photographer, could be here; but like the rest of *The Dispatch*'s photo staff, she'd been let go. Last time we talked, she was still looking for work. My photography skills were rudimentary, but I popped the lens cap and started shooting.

It was nearly a half hour before anybody noticed me. Then Oscar Hernandez, the

Warwick police chief, emerged from the wreckage carrying a blood-streaked black leather briefcase.

"Mulligan? Who the hell let you in here?"

"Nice to see you, too, Oscar. Whatcha got there?"

"Nothing that concerns you. We're dealing with a perilous situation here. I need you to leave right now."

"I've been in perilous situations before."

"Come on, get moving. One spark and this thing could blow."

"So you're saying I shouldn't smoke?"

"I don't have time for your jokes."

"If I refuse to leave, are you going to arrest me?"

He shook his head and sighed.

"If you insist on staying, I can't guarantee your safety."

"Nobody ever has. Can you spare a minute to fill me in on what happened here?"

"Walk with me."

We strode together down the street to his command car, where he placed the briefcase on the hood.

"The plane is a Beechcraft Premier I, a small twin-engine jet. According to the tower at Green, it took off from Atlantic City shortly after eight P.M. The flight plan had it coming straight up Narragansett Bay.

The pilot had already begun to descend when the fog rolled in. He was attempting a routine instrument landing, and there was no sign of trouble until the tower lost contact seconds before he was supposed to touch down."

"How many on board?"

"The pilot and one passenger."

"Dead?"

"Very."

"The bodies still in the wreckage?"

"Yeah. Gotta wet everything down to reduce the fire risk before we can cut them out."

"Anybody home when it hit?"

"A married couple and their three-year-old daughter."

"And?"

"The adults were watching TV in the family room on the other side of the house. They managed to climb out a window. Their daughter was in a back bedroom on the second floor. The father got a ladder from the garage, climbed up, broke a window, and found her cowering in her closet. Poor little thing was scared to death. He carried her down before the first responders got here."

"Any of them injured?"

"They're pretty shaken up, but they're all okay."

"What are their names?"

He gave me a stony look.

"Hey, I can always look it up in the city directory."

"Philip and Julia Correia."

"Philip with one *l* or two?"

"No idea."

"And the daughter?"

"Lucy."

"Where are they now? I'd like to talk to them."

"Some friends took them in, and no, you can't have the address. After what they've been through, they deserve a little peace tonight."

I nodded. They'd had a hell of a scare, and their house was so badly damaged that it would have to be torn down and rebuilt. I hoped their insurance was paid up.

"Have you ID'd the pilot and passenger?" I asked.

"Tentatively."

"And?"

"You know I can't give you that until next of kin are identified."

"How about off the record?"

He didn't say anything.

"Look," I said, "I just want to Google

them, see if I can find some background so I'll be ready when you release the names."

"Can I trust you on this?"

"Come on, Oscar. After what we went through together on the Kwame Diggs case? How can you even ask?"

"Okay, Mulligan. The pilot was Christopher Cox, age twenty-eight. He worked for Egg Harbor Aviation, a small outfit that flies high rollers in and out of Atlantic City."

"And the other victim?"

"Lucan Alfano, forty-four, of Ocean City, New Jersey, according to the passenger manifest."

"Anything more on him?"

"Not yet."

"The briefcase was his?"

"I managed to pry it from what was left of his lap, so I'm thinking yeah."

"What's in it?" I asked.

"Probably business papers, but maybe there's something in here to confirm the ID."

Hernandez slid a pocketknife from his pants pocket, used the blade to jimmy the lock, and raised the lid. Then he muttered, "Oh, shit," and slammed it shut.

"Did you see that?" he asked.

"I did."

"I should never have let you get a look at it."

"No, you shouldn't have, but I tell you what. Give me half, and I'll forget I was ever here."

The chief raised an eyebrow.

"Just kidding," I said. "Why don't we keep this between us until we figure out what it means?"

The briefcase was crammed with blue-banded bundles of hundred-dollar bills.

It was well past midnight by the time I got back to the newsroom. The place was deserted. Twisdale had left a note on my desk directing me to file something for our online edition, as if I needed to be told. I banged out a news story heavy on description, leaving out the cash and the names of the dead. When I was done, I shot Chuckie-boy an e-mail suggesting he have someone track down the Correias to get their account of surviving the crash. I figured *he* needed to be told. Then I spent a few minutes on Google.

I turned up a few routine business stories about Egg Harbor Aviation, a two-year-old item about Christopher Cox getting his pilot's license, and nothing at all about Lucan Alfano of Ocean City, New Jersey.

5

Next morning, my ringtone for Twisdale woke me at eight o'clock. I shut the phone off and went back to sleep. Around noon, I got up, made coffee, and popped a frozen sausage, egg, and cheese into the microwave. I snapped on the TV and ate standing up as I watched Logan Bedford, the blow-dried reporter for Channel 10, stand in front of the crash scene and paraphrase my story. He didn't have anything new. He rarely did.

I turned the cell back on, checked my messages, and found six, all from Twisdale. I didn't listen to them. Tuukka's water dish was dry, so I refilled it and dropped in another mouse. He startled, flicked his tongue at it, and turned away. Apparently still full from yesterday, he curled up to sleep. I considered joining him. Instead, I fired up my laptop, logged on to *The Dispatch*'s online edition, and was scanning the sports news when Twisdale called again.

"Where have you been?" he said. "I've been trying to reach you all morning."

"Where do you suppose I've been after working half the night, Chuck?"

"Well, shake off the cobwebs and get your butt in here."

"Have you forgotten already? You gave me today off."

"No, I haven't forgotten, but I need somebody who knows what he's doing to follow the crash story."

"Maybe you could hire back one of the veteran reporters you let go."

"Okay, okay. You've made your point. Now come on in. You can reschedule the day off for next week."

"No thanks," I said, and clicked off.

He rang back. I didn't answer. I was not about to spend the day under Chuckie-boy's thumb, but I couldn't leave the story alone either. He'd want me to chase the survivors for a feel-good human interest story. I wanted to find out who Lucan Alfano was and why he'd been hand-carrying tens of thousands of dollars in cash to Little Rhody.

I was trying to remember if I knew anyone in Atlantic City when my cell played the opening guitar riff of "Who Are You" by The Who, my ringtone for unknown callers.

"Mulligan?"

47

"Yeah?"

"It's Judy Abbruzzi."

"Hey, Judy. How have you been?"

"I'm good."

Judy had been *The Dispatch*'s night city editor before she got laid off a couple of years back.

"You working?" I asked.

"I am. I hooked on with *The Atlantic City Press* last November."

"As what?"

"Assistant metro editor."

"Glad to hear you landed on your feet."

"One of the few," she said. "I'm counting my blessings."

"So, Judy. I'm guessing this isn't just a social call."

"It's not. I hear that one of our South Jersey worthies got himself killed in Rhode Island last night."

"Two of them, actually."

"I know," she said, "but the one that intrigues me is Lucan Alfano."

"I thought the victims' names hadn't been released yet."

"They haven't. I got it from a source."

"So who was Lucan Alfano, and why are you intrigued?" I asked. "Other than the fact that he's dead, of course."

"Officially, he was the silent owner of a

48

string of New Jersey pawnshops and an Atlantic City payday loan company."

"And unofficially?"

"The state cops down here say he was a fixer for local gambling interests."

"That right?"

"That's what they tell me."

"What did he fix, exactly?"

"Whatever *needed* fixing," she said. "Zoning variances, wetlands exceptions, building permits, liquor licenses. That sort of thing. My sources say he was also the man to see in South Jersey if you wanted someone to disappear."

"He was a hitter?"

"No. They say he was to contract killers what Scott Boras is to Bryce Harper and Jacoby Ellsbury."

"Except that when ballplayers and their agents get paid," I said, "the only thing that gets hit is a baseball."

"Yeah. Except for that."

"Did Alfano have a record?"

"Uh-uh. The feds and staties dogged him for years, but they never came up with anything solid."

"How come *The Press* never published anything about him?"

"How do you know we didn't?"

"There's this new thing called the Internet," I said.

"We didn't because we could never prove anything. Whenever we started asking questions, his lawyers made noises about a libel suit. Maybe we could have found something if we'd put a couple of people on it for six months, but we don't have the resources for that kind of thing anymore."

"Any idea what was bringing Alfano to Rhode Island?"

"I was hoping you could tell me," she said.

"No idea."

I didn't tell her about the briefcase full of cash. No point in turning over my hole card until she had something more valuable to trade.

"You going to poke into this?" I asked.

"Got my best man on it, but I can only spare him part-time. Just a couple of hours a day."

"Let's stay in touch," I said. "If you learn anything, give me a call."

"And you'll do the same?"

"You bet."

After we signed off, I tidied up the kitchen and mulled over what I'd just heard. Then I called Chief Hernandez and asked if he could spare a few minutes.

The first thing that grabbed my attention

when I entered his office was his bulletin board. The pocked, ten-by-twelve-inch color photo of Joe Arpaio, the jowly Arizona sheriff notorious for harassing Mexican immigrants, had been taken down. In its place was a photo of Ted Cruz, the lunatic-fringe freshman senator from the great state of Texas. The darts that had once riddled Arpaio's image with holes rested beside the blotter on Hernandez's big mahogany desk. I snatched one up and flicked it, nailing an FBI poster of James T. Hammes, a Kentucky accountant wanted for liberating nearly nine million dollars from his corporate masters.

"Hit what you were aiming at?"

"Not even close."

Hernandez swept the remaining darts from the desk, leaned back in his chair, and fired them off in rapid succession, nailing Cruz twice in each eye.

"Impressive," I said.

"It's like everything else. You get better with practice."

"Not like everything," I said. "Some things, like losing your virginity or dying in a plane crash, you have to get right the first time. So, tell me. Did you count the dead guy's money yet?"

"Close the door and sit down."

So I did.

"Are we off the record?" he asked.

"For now."

"The briefcase contained exactly two hundred grand, all in hundreds."

"Good bills?"

"Yeah. No funny money. At the prevailing rate, it could buy you two hundred liquor licenses, forty building permits, or twenty contract killings."

"I gather you've done your homework on Lucan Alfano," I said.

"Of course I have. I don't sit here fixing traffic tickets for the mayor's kids *all* day, you know."

"Wow. Who would have thought?"

"Alfano was a fixer," Hernandez said.

"For the Atlantic City casinos," I said, "although I doubt he would have stooped to anything as mundane as traffic tickets."

"Jesus, Mulligan. You mean to tell me you have sources in *Jersey*?"

"I'm very resourceful, Oscar. It's my best quality."

"So what did your sources have to say about why Alfano was coming to Rhode Island?"

"They were clueless," I said. "Yours?"

"The same."

"Can you trace the money?" I asked. "That could lead us to whoever he was working for."

"Can't be done. They're all circulated bills. No consecutive serial numbers."

"I only caught a glimpse," I said, "but to me they looked like freshly packed bundles with bank bands on them."

"Doesn't help us any," Hernandez said. "Anybody can buy bank bands, manufactured and color-coded to Federal Reserve standards, for less than seven dollars per thousand. And for three hundred bucks, you can buy a counting machine that will spit out counterfeits and bundle the good bills for you."

I slid a Partagás out of my shirt pocket and clipped the end. Hernandez got up and threw open the window behind his desk. Then he sat back down again and said, "Got another one of those?"

I handed him a cigar and leaned across the desk to set fire to it with my Colibri. He puffed, plucked it from his lips, and studied the band.

"Kind of pricy for a scribe who lives in a dump on America Street."

"Not the way I come by them. If you want, I can get you a box."

"How much?"

"No charge. I get 'em for free."

He raised an eyebrow at that.

"Sorry," I said, "but a reporter never reveals his source."

We smoked in silence for a few minutes.

"Alfano owns some pawnshops and a payday loan outfit in Jersey," he said. "The payday loan company deals mainly in checks, but pawnshops are a cash business."

"Which makes them a great way to launder money," I said.

"Yeah. Chances are we're never going to figure out what the hell this was about."

"Anything on the cause of the crash yet?"

"Investigators from the FAA and the NTSB started combing through the wreckage this morning. It'll be at least a couple of weeks before they tell me anything."

"And six months before they release their final report," I said.

"Sounds about right."

"Okay to print the names of the crash victims?"

"Yeah. The notifications were made this morning."

I thanked him, rose to leave, and then turned back when I got to the door.

"I don't suppose you've got a photo of Alfano you could let me have," I said.

"What for?"

"I'm thinking I might show it around. See if it gets a rise out of anybody."

"I'll e-mail you a copy."

I was halfway home when my cell stared playing the theme from *The Godfather,* my ringtone for Zerilli.

"Hi, Whoosh. What's up?"

"I need to see you. We got trouble."

6

The little market on Hope Street was the destination of choice for stocking up on Yoohoo, Ding Dongs, Red Bull, Cheetos, malt liquor, *Juggs* magazines, and illegal tax-stamp-free cigarettes. It was also the place to go in Providence to lay down an illegal sports bet.

The old brass bell over the front door clanked as I pushed through it and wound my way down the cramped grocery aisles to a short flight of stairs in back. At the top, I knocked on a locked, steel-reinforced door. An electric lock buzzed to admit me. I stepped in and found Zerilli hunched over his keyhole desk. He was clothed in a light gray suit jacket, a white dress shirt, a green-and-yellow tie with red parrots on it, and clashing sky-blue boxer shorts. As always, he'd draped his suit pants over a hanger on the office clothes rack to preserve the crease.

Shortstop, who looked like a cross between

a bull mastiff and a Tyrannosaurus, was half in and half out of the office's only visitor's chair, his rump planted on the seat and his front paws braced on the floor. That was as close as he could get to wedging his bulk into the solid oak Windsor. Whoosh tossed a Beggin' Strip into the corner by his black floor safe to coax the beast down. Shortstop slid off the chair, lumbered over, and snatched the treat in his jaws. Then he locked eyes with me and growled like a muscle car. The hair he'd shed on the chair was enough to make another dog. I brushed it off and sat.

"So what's up?"

"Hold on a sec," Whoosh said. He reached up with his left hand, the one without the tremor, and closed the blinds on the long, narrow window that looked out over the grocery shelves. "Anita? The new cashier? I think she reads lips."

"This must be serious."

"Hell, yeah, it's fuckin' serious. You know what your favorite nun's up to, right? You coulda warned me, asshole."

"You mean the governor?"

"Like you ain't already heard."

"Sorry, Whoosh, but I'm clueless."

"What the fuck, Mulligan. I thought you was always on top of things."

"Except nuns," I said. "Besides, my new boss doesn't let me out much."

"Well, from what I hear, the bitch is gonna introduce legislation to legalize sports betting."

"You're shitting me."

"I am absolutely goddamned fuckin' not. You really ain't heard about this?"

"No. Where did you get it from?"

"Coupla statehouse lackeys on Arena's pad."

"Can she do this? I mean, isn't there some federal law prohibiting sports betting?"

"Yeah," he said. "The Professional and Amateur Sports Protection Act. Been the law since 1992. Four states including Nevada, where sports betting was already legal, were grandfathered in, but it's against federal law everywhere else."

Zerilli couldn't have named the chief justice of the U.S. Supreme Court, but he knew more about gambling laws than the Harvard Law School faculty.

"The NCAA, the pro leagues, and the Vegas casinos all lobbied to get it passed. Between you and me, a few heavies from my side of the tracks lent a hand by twisting arms and spreading goodies around on Capitol Hill."

"Like who?"

"Between us?"

"Sure."

"The Outfit in Chicago and the Gambino family in New York did the grunt work, but Kansas City, New Orleans, St. Louis, Detroit, Philly, and the rest of the New York families all chipped in. Once it passed, we figured that was the end of it. Now it's comin' up again all over the fuckin' country."

"Because so many states are in financial trouble?"

"Yeah. That fat fuck Chris Christie got the ball rolling down in Jersey. In 2012, he signed a bill giving Atlantic City casinos the green light to take sports bets so he can tax the action. Ever since, he's been bullying the New Jersey congressional delegation into tryin' to get the federal law repealed so the money can start flowing. The NCAA, the NBA, the NHL, the NFL, and Major League Baseball are all working to head him off. The NCAA is fuckin' pissed. The Prudential Center in Newark will never get another March Madness regional if the cocksucker don't back down."

Zerilli slipped a soft pack from his shirt pocket and shook out an unfiltered Lucky. I reached over to give him a light.

"This is bad for us, Mulligan. Guys like

me ain't got much turf left as it is. Payday loan companies have put most of the loan sharks out of business. The Indian casinos in Connecticut have wiped out our poker rooms. State lotteries control the numbers game, which was our biggest cash cow back in my day. Colorado just legalized marijuana, for fuck sake. The way things are goin', every vice you can think up is gonna be legal. You got a stake in this, too, Mulligan. My offer stands, but if Attila the Nun gets her way, there ain't gonna be shit left for you to run."

I didn't say anything to that.

"Look, I know she's a friend of yours. Can't you talk some fuckin' sense into her?"

"I doubt it."

"Then appeal to her self-interest."

"Meaning what?" I asked.

"Tell her some friends of yours got a six-figure campaign contribution for her if she backs off. If she don't, we're gonna bankroll her Republican opponent, whatever gun-worshipin', union-hatin' dickhead that turns out to be. And that's just my crowd. She's declaring war on the NCAA, the major sports leagues, and the Vegas casinos, and they've got way deeper pockets than we got, believe you fuckin' me. Make sure she understands that."

"I'm sure she already does."

Whoosh stubbed out his Lucky and stuck a fresh one in his mouth. I lit it for him and got a cigar going.

"So," he said. "Got any personal business to conduct before you go?"

"What are the odds on the Celtics stumbling into the playoffs?"

"Even."

"Put me down for fifty on them washing out."

"You got it," he said. "Oh, and I almost forgot."

He rose, shambled to his storeroom door, rummaged around inside, and came back out with a box of illegal Cuban cigars — his gift to me every time I paid him a visit.

"Could I maybe have two boxes this time?"

"Jesus, Mulligan. How many sticks a day are you suckin' down now?"

"It's not for me," I said. "I got a palm that needs greasing."

7

First thing Tuesday morning, Chuckie-boy strutted over to my cubicle and said, "Good of you to finally join us."

"Good for you, maybe."

"I need you to cover a ten A.M. press conference off the TV," he said. "Some preacher is going to announce his candidacy for the Republican nomination for governor."

"Got a name?"

He checked his notes and said, "Lucas Crenson."

"You've got to be kidding."

"You know this guy?"

"Aren't many people in our little state that I don't know, Chuck."

"*Mister* Twisdale to you."

"We gonna go another round on that?"

"So who is he?" he asked.

"He's the founder of the Sword of God Church in Foster."

"Where the hell is Foster?"

"It's a little town in the rural, northwest corner of the state. Rhode Island's only got thirty-nine cities and towns, Chuck. Maybe it's time you learned their names."

"Sword of God? What kind of church is that?"

"A congregation of fundamentalist whack-jobs."

"Mulligan, you eastern media-elite snobs are all alike. You think anybody who believes in God is a lunatic."

"Last time I joined Reverend Crenson and his flock for a Sunday service," I said, "all the members of the congregation, even the kids, brought firearms to church for the annual blessing of the guns. And Crenson offered a prayer for the death of President Obama."

"Okay, but keep your personal opinion out of the copy."

"No problem. If I wanted to be a blow-hard, I'd be writing editorials."

"So does this Crenson guy have a shot at the nomination?"

"Nah," I said. "Rhode Island Republicans aren't like the ones you were used to in Oklahoma. Here, they're mostly moderates. Besides, I hear the party brass is getting in line behind Devereaux."

"Devereaux? He's the mayor of Woon-socket, right?"

"*She* is the mayor of Cranston," I said. "You might want to bone up on mayors, too."

Chuckie-boy tried out his glower again. It still needed work.

"After you cover the press conference," he said, "I need you to get cracking on these press releases."

With that, he dropped a four-inch stack of mail on my desk.

"No can do, Chuck. I'll handle the press conference, but you'll have to find some-body else for the rest of this crap."

"And why is that?"

"I've got a one o'clock sit-down with the governor."

"You do? What for?"

"Background about some big announce-ment she's making next week."

"What about?"

"Don't know yet," I lied.

"Well, okay, but try to bring back some-thing we can print tomorrow. I got a daily paper to put out."

Attila the Nun kept me stewing in a state-house waiting room for twenty minutes before her administrative assistant ushered me into the inner sanctum. I found her sitting primly behind an antique mahogany desk flanked by American and Rhode Island state flags. She rose, waved me toward a plush velvet couch, and joined me there.

"I'm disappointed," she said. "I was hoping you were going to stroll in wearing those black-and-yellow Bruins boxers."

"I could drop my pants if you want to have a look at them."

"I better lock the door first," she said. "It wouldn't do to have anyone walk in on us."

"Do it," I said. "I've always wanted to fool around in the governor's office, but until now, the opportunity never came up."

"How come?"

"Because we never had a girl governor before."

"Keep teasing me," she said, "I might not be able to keep my hands to myself."

"Liar."

"Hey, I'm a politician now. What did you expect?"

"Considering what you're up to, I was expecting to find you in a slinky, low-cut party dress. The sort of thing the croupiers at Foxwoods wear to distract the players."

"Oh, hell. You already know."

"Rhode Island is a small state, Fiona. Makes it hard to keep a secret."

"Who leaked it?"

"I don't know. I heard it from a member of our criminal class who got it from his boss who got it from a mole at the statehouse."

"Muthafucka!"

"Such language from a nun."

"Former nun. I can curse all I want now, and His Holiness can't lay a finger on me."

"So what's your thinking on this?"

"Whatever I tell you is embargoed until after my announcement," she said.

"I understand that."

"I'm thinking that if I don't do something drastic, my legacy is going to be a bankrupt state pension system, more aid cuts to our failing public schools, tuition hikes at the state colleges, thousands of people thrown off Medicaid and Head Start, and the biggest budget deficit in Rhode Island history. We need revenue, Mulligan, and there's no way I could get another tax hike through the General Assembly if I wanted to. Which I don't."

"And the answer is to legalize sports betting?"

"Do you know how much money Americans piss away on that every year, Mulligan?"

"No idea."

"Las Vegas casinos rake in three billion annually on March Madness and the Super Bowl alone. Which is pennies compared to the three hundred and eighty billion that's bet illegally every year. Double that figure and you could fund the Pentagon for twelve months with enough left over to start another small war. That kind of money makes a governor salivate."

"I'll bet."

"At least eighty-five percent of us gamble on sports at least once in a while," she said. "That's darned near everybody. You should know that better than anyone. Why shouldn't the state get a piece of the action?"

"How do you see this working?" I asked.

"In New Jersey, Christie wants the casinos to take sports bets so he can tax the profits," she said. "But we don't have any big casinos — just that little one in Lincoln and the slots-only operation in Newport. I can't see handing anything this big over to them. Besides, why just *tax* the profits when we can have all of it?"

"You want the state Lottery Commission to take sports bets?"

"I do."

"And turn the state into a bookmaker?"

"Hell's bells, Mulligan. It already is.

Wouldn't you rather see people have a little fun betting on their favorite teams than stand in lines to buy lottery tickets?"

"You know those desperate people who blow their paychecks on fistfuls of scratch tickets?" I asked. "The ones you see furiously scraping Jokers Wild and Lucky Diamonds stubs with nickels in convenience store parking lots?"

"Yeah. It's so sad."

"Well, those people will do both."

"My plan addresses that," she said. "We're going to direct lottery outlets to limit scratch-ticket sales to ten per customer."

"Won't work," I said. "Compulsive gamblers will buy the limit and then mosey on down to the next 7-Eleven for more."

"I know, but it's the best I can do."

I reached out and took my friend's hand.

"I'm worried about you, Fiona. You're going to make a lot of enemies with this."

"I'm prepared for that."

"People with something to lose are already gearing up," I said. "I was asked to let you know that there's a six-figure campaign contribution in it for you if you back off — and that it will go to your next opponent if you don't."

"Doesn't surprise me any," she said. "You're not going to tell me where the offer came from, are you?"

"No."

"But I can guess," she said.

"And you'd be right."

"Zerilli and Arena aren't the ones I'm worried about," she said. "Compared to the NCAA, they're a bunch of pussies."

"Sorry," I told Chuckie-boy. "Everything the governor told me is embargoed at least until next week."

"You've been gone for ninety minutes, and you don't have anything I can *print*?"

"Not today, no."

"That is unacceptable."

I shrugged and dropped into one of the leather visitor's chairs across from his desk.

"So what's this big announcement going to be about?" he asked.

"Governor McNerney thinks she can fix the state budget mess by legalizing sports gambling."

"A former *nun* wants to legalize sports gambling?"

"Ever been to a casino-night fund-raiser at a Roman Catholic church?"

"No."

"Too bad. If you had, you wouldn't look so mystified."

"How much revenue does she think this

will raise?"

"She estimates two hundred million a year for starters. Maybe more with an advertising campaign to suck in gamblers from Massachusetts and Connecticut."

"Sounds inflated."

"I doubt it. Lottery-ticket sales generated three hundred and seventy-seven million for the general fund last year. The governor figures sports gambling could eventually top that, and she's probably right."

"Who's going to take the bets?"

"The Lottery Commission."

"The state? Is she serious? Government can't do anything right. She ought to solicit bids from experienced casino operators, turn this thing over to private enterprise. God, I hate these damned big-government Democrats."

"Keep your personal opinion to yourself when you edit the story next week," I said.

Chuckie-boy smirked, rolled his massive shoulders, and fussed with some papers on his desk.

"I can't see waiting for the governor's announcement," he said. "This is a huge story. I don't want to risk getting scooped on it."

"Okay. I'll make some calls this afternoon, see what I can do."

"Why don't we just pretend you did that?"

he said. "Write up what you got from the governor, attribute it to an anonymous statehouse source, and I'll lead tomorrow's paper with it."

"You want me to betray my source?"

"Jesus, Mulligan. You're such a dinosaur. Ethics are overrated. Journalism isn't a calling anymore. It's a business. Or haven't you heard?"

"Oh, I've heard, all right."

"So get cracking."

"No."

"*No?* Are you refusing this assignment?"

"I guess I am."

"That's a firing offense."

"So fire me."

He didn't have anything to say to that.

"Before I go," I said, "can I get a hit from your Purell bottle? I feel an urgent need for disinfectant."

I stomped back to my cubicle and made a round of calls. Nobody was talking. My best statehouse sources pleaded ignorance. Michael DeSimone, the Lottery Commission director, hung up on me, then called back on his personal cell phone.

"Attila's on a rampage," he said. "She's gonna crucify anyone who spills to the press about this."

I gave it up as a lost cause and turned to

the day's stack of press releases. The Vipers, Providence's new entry in the D-League, was inviting local playground legends and former college hoopsters to open tryouts at the Dunkin' Donuts Center, the city's 12,993-seat sports arena, a week from Saturday. To me, it sounded like a gimmick to stir up fan interest. The rosters of the D-League, developmental teams for ball-players not yet ready for prime time, were filled with prospects already signed by NBA teams after being scouted to death during their high school and college careers. A walk-on had as much chance of making the Vipers as I'd have if I walked into the Kennedy Space Center smoking crack and volunteered to become an astronaut.

After I wrote it up, I made a few more calls.

"State Medical Examiner's Office. Ferguson speaking."

"Hi, Glenna. It's Mulligan. Got a cause of death on the Blackstone River floater yet?"

"Like I figured, he bled out from the bullet wound."

"Determine the caliber?"

"Most likely a forty-four or forty-five."

"Find anything else worth mentioning?"

"The body took a battering, most of it

after he went into the water. But some of it was premortem. Somebody gave this poor bastard a hell of a beating."

"With what?"

"I'm guessing a blackjack."

"ID him yet?"

"No."

I'd figured that because Dude hadn't called.

"What's the holdup?"

"I couldn't pull any prints. Too much scavenger damage."

"Dental?"

"I took x-rays, but until someone reports this guy missing, I've got nothing to compare them with."

I thanked her, clicked off, checked my e-mail, and discovered that Chief Hernandez had delivered on his promise. I opened the attachment and stared at the gray, frowning visage of Lucan Alfano. His hooded eyes, broad nose, dimpled chin, thin upper lip, and receding hairline reminded me of Tony Sirico, the Brooklyn tough-turned-actor who'd played the role of Paulie Walnuts on *The Sopranos.*

I forwarded the image to my personal e-mail address so I'd have it handy on my cell phone. That's when a stray thought popped into my head. I hadn't gotten a

single new threat from Mario since the night
he came at me with a gun.

8

"Oscar? It's Mulligan."

"Got something for me?" he asked.

"I don't. I just wanted to thank you for the photo."

"You're working late."

"So are you," I said. "Actually, I'm on my own time. I rewrite press releases for a living now. Real journalism is my fucking hobby."

"Well, I'm glad you called. I've got something new to share."

"So give."

"Better if we do this in person."

So, twenty minutes later, I walked into the chief's office in Warwick with a box of Cohibas under my arm.

"As promised," I said, and placed it on his desk.

He picked it up and studied the printing on the Spanish cedar.

"Cuban?" he said.

"So it would appear."

"*Jesucristo!* These are more illegal than marijuana."

"But neither should be."

"You know I could arrest you for this."

"But you're not going to."

"Guess not, but I can't accept them."

"Of course you can't."

"So why did you bring them?"

"So you could confiscate them in the name of the law."

"I see."

"Perhaps you should investigate to determine whether they are genuine," I said. "There are a lot of counterfeit Cubans on the black market, you know."

"And I would do that how?"

"By smoking a few. Maybe twenty-four of them, just to be sure."

"There are twenty-five in the box, Mulligan."

"Yes, but you are going to ask me to smoke one, too, so that you can avail yourself of my expert opinion."

He laughed at that.

"I won't tell," I said. "I promise."

The chief grinned, pried open the box, and removed two sticks. I tossed him my cutter. He clipped the ends, stuck one in his jaw, and handed me the other. I bent to give him a light and then set fire to mine.

"Now this," he said, "is a damn fine smoke."

"The best," I said. "So what have you got?"

"When we cut Alfano's body out of the wreckage, we discovered something interesting in the pocket of his suit jacket."

"Oh?"

"Have a look," he said, and slid an unsealed letter-size envelope across the desk. "Don't worry about handling it. It's already been examined for prints."

"And?"

"Just one partial that belonged to Alfano."

I picked it up and checked it over. Except for a couple of dried blood streaks, both sides were blank. Inside was a single sheet of paper. On it was a typewritten list of five names. Nothing more.

"Recognize them?" he asked.

"Of course I do. Anyone else seen this?"

"Just the state police. I figured they should know."

"Who did you talk to there?"

"Captain Parisi."

"Good man," I said. "What do the two of you think it means?"

"What do *you* think it means?"

"It's a Christmas list," I said.

"That's our guess. These five upstanding public servants were about to come into some dirty money."

9

"Let's just be friends" used to be my least-favorite sentence in the English language, but it was no longer a match for "The managing editor would like a word." Not even close. As I punched the clock on Wednesday morning, the receptionist said it again.

I strode into the aquarium and found Twisdale hunched over his computer. His scowl, his furrowed brow, and the coffee stain on his yellow silk tie told me his day had not gotten off to a smashing start.

"Top o' the mornin', Chuckie-boy."

The muscles in his jaw clenched, but he decided to let it pass.

"Have you perused *The Ocean State Rag* this morning?" he asked.

"Not yet."

"Have a look," he said, swiveling the computer screen toward me.

I bent down, looked at the story on the

screen, and said, "Aw, shit."

"I told you not to let us get beat on this. You and your goddamned ethics."

"They aren't all bad," I said. "That's why they're called ethics. You should get some for yourself one of these days."

"I ought to suspend you for this."

"Why don't you?"

"I would if I could spare you."

"I wonder how Mason got hold of this," I said.

"I've been wondering the same thing. Did you tip him off to make me look bad?"

"I can't believe you asked me that."

"Well, did you?"

"I don't need to make you look bad, Chuckie. You manage that all by yourself."

"Fuck you. We gotta have something on this in tomorrow's paper, so get cracking."

I turned my back on him and stalked out.

"*Ocean State Rag,* Mason speaking."

"Great story this morning, buddy. How the hell did you dig it up?"

"Come on, Mulligan. You know better than to ask that."

"How about a hint?"

"You got assigned to chase it, didn't you?" he said.

"I did, and I'm nowhere. All my statehouse

80

sources have clammed up."

"Even Fiona?"

"Even her."

"Don't take this wrong, but tough shit."

"One more nail in the coffin, huh?"

"I'm counting on it," he said. "When the paper goes belly-up, I'll be the only game in town."

"Good plan."

"Know what people are calling *The Dispatch* these days?"

"What?"

"The Dispatched."

"As in dead," I said.

"You got it. Most mornings, there's not a damned thing in it worth reading. Finally ready to leave the dark side and come work for me?"

"You still paying slave wages?"

"For now," he said, "but in a year or two that's gonna change. You should get in on the ground floor."

"I'm still thinking about it."

"Well, the offer is always open."

"Thanks," I said. "How's your dad doing?"

"Better. He was on Zoloft for a while, and it helped. He and my mother took the *Albacore* out of Newport last week, and they're cruising somewhere off Bimini right now.

Father still thinks *The Dispatch* was his life. Mother is showing him that it isn't."

"Good for her," I said.

I clicked off just as Chuckie stepped out of his office and strutted to the cubicle where Kate Frieden, the kid city hall reporter, was tapping on her keyboard. He puffed out his chest and loomed over her. I couldn't make out what he was saying, but from the pained look on her face it was obvious he was thrashing her publicly. Lomax had never done anything like that. I thought about butting in, but that would have done her more harm than good. Instead, I tugged on my jean jacket and headed for the elevator.

"Mulligan?" Chuckie shouted. "Where the hell do you think you're going?"

"To find some news," I shouted back. "There isn't any in the office. I've looked."

The state flag that flies atop the Rhode Island statehouse sports a golden anchor on a field of white. The symbol is surrounded by thirteen stars representing the original thirteen colonies. Below them is the state's motto, "Hope." There is no evidence that the flag's designer intended to be ironic.

Inside, the state Senate's Health, Education, and Welfare Committee was debating a bill to make fried calamari the official state appetizer. Its sponsor, the honorable senator from Johnston, was getting a grilling.

"The whole idea is absurd," the senator from Newport snapped. "How could anything but oysters Rockefeller be considered seriously?" His colleague from Cranston shouted him down, extolling the undeniable virtues of fried mozzarella.

I leaned against the back wall, marveling at our tax dollars at work but stunned that nobody had the political courage to stand up for chicken wings.

At eleven A.M., the committee took a ten-minute break, and I followed the majority leader, Ray Tomasso, into the men's room. I waited until he zipped up and washed his hands, then held my cell phone up to his face. He ignored it and brushed past me.

"How well do you know this guy?" I asked his Armani-draped back.

"Never seen him before."

"Maybe so," I said, "but how can you be sure without looking at the picture?"

He hesitated, then turned back and took the cell from my hand. I studied his face as he examined the photo, but it didn't betray anything.

"Nope. Don't recognize him. Who is he?"

"A guy who died with a briefcase full of

cash in his lap and a piece of paper with your name on it in his pocket."

"What are you implying, Mulligan?"

"I'm not implying anything. I'm just giving you the facts."

He leaned against the sink and looked at the photo again.

"What was his name?"

"Lucan Alfano. Mean anything to you?"

"No. I know some Alfanos, but no Lucan. What do you know about him?"

"Just that he was a bad guy from out of town."

"How bad?"

"Bad as it gets."

"How did he die?"

"He was in that plane, the one that hit a house in Warwick last week," I said. "It was in the paper."

"I don't read the paper."

"You don't?"

"Not anymore."

"How do you keep up with the news?"

"I get Google alerts on the things that matter to me — legislative news, business stories, sports scores, anything with my name attached to it."

He handed the phone back, and I put it in my pocket.

"So what's this about, Mulligan?"

84

"I don't know yet," I said, "but I intend to find out."

I braced Peter Slater, the Senate minority leader, and Daniel Crowley, the Speaker of the House, in their offices. They were no help either. They both claimed they'd never heard of anyone named Lucan Alfano. From their puzzled looks when they examined his photo, I was inclined to believe them — and for Crowley, that was a first.

I caught up with Lisa Pichardo, the House minority leader, as she was dashing down a statehouse hallway.

"Got no time for you now, Mulligan. The GOP caucus is meeting on the budget in five minutes."

"So you've got five minutes," I said.

"We have to do this now?"

"We do."

"Then make it quick."

"Take a look at this," I said, and flashed the photo at her.

She glanced at it and blanched under her makeup.

"What am I looking at?" she asked.

"I think you know."

"I've never seen this guy in my life."

"Really? Because your poker face needs work."

She scowled and turned away. I fell into

step with her.

"That pile of cash you were expecting?" I said. "I hope you haven't already spent it, because it's sitting in a Warwick Police Department evidence locker."

"I have no idea what you are talking about."

I watched her scurry away down a corridor and duck into a meeting room. She'd never even asked the guy's name. I figured it was because she already knew.

That left one last name from Alfano's list — the only one I'd been shocked to see on it.

10

That afternoon, I made a round of calls to the NCAA, the NBA, the NHL, the NFL, and Major League Baseball. Their press officers, tipped off by an Associated Press rewrite of the *Ocean State Rag* story, had their talking points ready. They were nearly identical, full of the same sputtering outrage they had dished in response to Chris Christie's plan. They'd been peddling the same hypocritical, self-serving bullshit for decades:

- Legalizing sports betting would irreparably harm the integrity of their games, creating a climate of suspicion about controversial plays, officiating calls, and players' performances.
- It would expand the amount of money wagered on games, increasing the temptation to fix results.
- It would infringe on the leagues' intel-

lectual property by encouraging gambling operations to use proprietary information including statistics, injury reports, and team logos.

- Gambling on sports is an addiction that ruins lives, a scourge that should not be condoned by a benevolent state.

I wrote it up and filed it to the city desk. We were playing catch-up, but at least Chuckie-boy would have something to advance the story Mason had broken.

A half hour after I turned it in, I was summoned to Twisdale's office.

"These guys are *so* full of shit," he said.

"I agree."

"Billions of dollars are already being wagered on sports," he said. "Professional gamblers don't need any more incentive to fix games."

"Of course they don't."

"In fact, legalized gambling would more likely deter game-fixing than encourage it, because the amount being wagered would be public knowledge," he said. "The Arizona State point-fixing scandal was exposed because somebody bet an obscene amount of money against them legally in Las Vegas, and alarm bells went off."

"That's right. You're on a roll, Chuckie."

He didn't even stop to growl at me.

"Gambling is one of the reasons so many people follow sports," he said. "The NCAA and the pro leagues know that, and they profit handsomely from it. That's why they don't object when sports writers cite point spreads. These jerk-offs blackmail cities into spending millions on stadiums by threatening to move their teams out of town, yet they object to state governments sharing the wealth. And by keeping sports betting illegal, they help the Mob stay in business. They and the bookmakers are practically co-conspirators, for godsakes."

"You seem to know a lot about this," I said.

"I've been reading up." He snatched a printout of my story from his desktop and tossed it at me. "Your copy tells only one side of the story. Scare up some quotes from people who can call these assholes on their bullshit."

"Already on it," I said. "I should have more for you in an hour or so."

"Make it a separate," he said. "We'll run the two pieces side by side under a 'Pros and Cons' headline."

"Sounds good."

"Before you go, there's something else we need to discuss."

"Oh?"

"What are you, about six-three?"

"Six-four, last time I checked," I said.

"I hear you were a basketball star at Providence College, is that right?"

"A star? No way. Mostly I rode the bench."

"Do you still play?"

"Once or twice a week. Pickup games at PC's Begley Arena or the outdoor courts at Hope High School."

"Good. I've got an idea I think you're going to like."

"I'm listening."

"I want you to try out for the Vipers and write a series of first-person human interest stories about the experience."

"Oh, hell no."

"Why not?"

"Because I'm forty-four years old, Chuckie."

"Oh, come on now. It's not like I'm asking you to make the team. You just have to show up."

"Why don't *you* do it?" I said. "You're nearly my height, and you're twelve years younger."

"Because I've got a newspaper to run. Besides, basketball was never my sport. I played middle linebacker at Valdosta State."

"There are easier ways to get rid of me,

90

Chuckie. You don't have to try to get me killed."

"This is an order, Mulligan. You already refused one assignment last week. It would not be in your best interest to pull that again."

"He wants you to do *what*?" Attila the Nun asked.

"You heard me right the first time."

We were drinking beer at a table in Hopes while the governor's limo, a state trooper at the wheel, lurked just outside the door.

"Can't you talk him out of it?"

"I tried, but he's got a whim of iron."

"This is crazy, Mulligan. You could kill yourself trying to keep up with twenty-year-olds."

"Who says I'm going to try to keep up?"

"Are you in shape?"

"Do I look in shape?"

She thunked her bottle of Bud on the cracked Formica table and looked me up and down, then glanced at the TV over the scarred mahogany bar, where the Celtics were getting run over by the Clippers.

"Not compared to those guys."

"It's not like I'll be going up against Blake Griffin," I said. "My wind is pretty good, and I can still fill it up from the three-point line."

"You'll have to kick the cigars for a while."

"Aw, fuck."

"What about your knee?" she asked.

"Hasn't bothered me much since the surgery."

"Sounds like you're warming to the idea."

"I hate it," I said. "It's a stupid prank to gin up circulation, but at least it will get me out of the office for a while."

I flagged down Annie, the leggy Rhode Island School of Design teaching assistant who moonlighted as a barmaid, and ordered another round.

"Is this why you wanted to get together tonight?" Fiona asked. "To see if I could talk you out of a heart attack?"

"No. There's something else."

I slid the cell out of my pocket and called up the photo.

"Ever seen this guy?"

"Isn't that Paulie Walnuts?" she said. "I loved that show."

"It does look like him, but no."

"So who is it?"

"A guy named Lucan Alfano."

"That sounds familiar, but —" She stared up at the pressed-tin ceiling, searching her memory. "Oh, wait. Isn't that the Jersey guy who got killed in the plane crash?"

"Yeah. That the only thing you know about him?"

"Uh-huh. What's this about, Mulligan?"

So I ran down what I knew about Alfano, his briefcase full of cash, and the list found in his pocket.

"*My* name was on the list?"

"It was."

"You think the cash was intended for me?"

"Some of it, anyway. At least that's how it looks."

We sipped our beers in silence and thought about it.

"Who was he was working for?" she asked. "And what was he supposed to buy with all that money?"

"I was hoping you could tell me."

"This could be about any one of a number of things," she said. "We're putting some big road-construction contracts out to bid this month. The medical association and the hospitals are having fits about our proposed Medicaid cuts. My bill to tighten wetlands protections is going to the floor in a couple of weeks, and the construction industry is livid about it."

"Or maybe it was a bribe from the fried calamari lobby," I said. "I hear there's a lot riding on the official state appetizer crown."

"But Alfano was mobbed up," she said.

"He was."

"And a fixer for the casino industry."

"Yeah, but not exclusively. From what I hear, he wasn't picky about who he worked for."

"So most likely this was about the gambling bill," she said.

"That would be my guess."

"Which side of the issue do you think he was on?"

"Depends on who hired him," I said. "Personally, he probably didn't give a shit."

I took a pull from my longneck and mulled it over.

"The other four names on the list," I said. "Did they know about the gambling bill before *The Ocean State Rag* broke the story?"

"Of course. I've been working quietly for a couple of months to get the legislative leadership on board."

"Who else knew?"

"Just three members of my staff, a couple of legislative committee chairmen, and the two top guys at the Lottery Commission."

"And where do they stand?"

"They're all for the idea in principle, but the Republicans, Slater and Pichardo, are holding things up. They don't want the Lottery Commission involved. They think we should bring in a private company to run things."

"And one of these people leaked it," I said.

"Either that or somebody one of them confided in."

"Then here's how I see it," I said. "If Alfano was working for the Mob, his job was to get the bill killed. But if he was working for the casinos, he was supposed to grease the skids for privatization so some big shot from Atlantic City can waltz in here and become our official state bookmaker."

"I'm guessing it's the casinos — or maybe somebody who's got a stake in one of them," Fiona said. "When New Jersey legalized casino gambling back in 1976, Atlantic City had the only legal slots, craps tables, and roulette wheels east of Las Vegas. By 2006, they were raking in more than five billion in annual profits. Since then, casinos have opened in more than a dozen states east of the Mississippi including New York, Pennsylvania, and Connecticut. The competition has cut Atlantic City gambling revenue by fifty percent, and half of its casinos have been forced to close. It makes sense that big money people there would want to muscle in on our action."

She paused, then said, "Now that Alfano's

dead, whoever sent him is probably going to send somebody else."

"Yeah," I said. "In fact, he might already be here."

There wasn't much more to say about that, so we turned to small talk. Her younger brother's particle-physics research at MIT. The baby boy my sister and her wife had adopted. But after a few minutes, I turned the conversation back to the gambling bill.

"What's your next step?" I asked.

"Next week's announcement is off," she said. "I have to postpone until I can work out a deal with the leadership. We've got a lot of anti-gambling moralists on both sides of the aisle. No way I can get this thing through without some Republican support."

"Is that on background, or can I run with it?"

She took her time thinking it over.

"Go ahead and print it," she said. "A lot of misinformation is floating around now. I need to get out ahead of it."

I pulled out a pad and was jotting some notes when Whoosh came through the door. He spotted me and hobbled toward my table. Then he saw who I was sitting with and peeled off to grab a stool at the bar.

Fiona glanced his way and said, "Think your bookmaker pal has a line on what's going on?"

"No idea."

"If he does, will he tell you?"

"Probably not," I said.

With that, we turned to the TV for the last five minutes of the Celtics-Clippers debacle. When the horn signaled the end of the game, the conversation turned light.

"So, Mulligan. Are you wearing those hot Bruins boxers again?"

"No. I'm sporting my Red Sox briefs tonight. I've got two pair of each, and I rotate them once a week whether they need changing or not."

"I love a man who's a stickler for hygiene."

Then a worried look crossed her face.

"What if we've got this wrong? You said Alfano also arranged contract killings, right? Maybe that's what all the cash was for. The five names could be a hit list."

As I reached across the table for Fiona's hand, a camera flash lit us up. I turned in time to see a blond stranger at the bar snap a second shot of us with her cell phone. I didn't think anything of it. People were always sneaking photos of Fiona and posting them on Facebook to make it look as if they were drinking buddies with the governor.

"Don't get paranoid about hired killers,

Fiona," I said. "I mean, do you really think Alfano would commit a hit list to paper?"

"I don't know," she said. "I have no idea what someone like him would do."

Later that night, I drove up Olney Street and pulled into the deserted lot at Hope High School. I parked beside the basketball courts and fetched my Spalding from the back. Somebody had shot out the lights that hung over the courts, so I worked on my crossover dribble, my left-handed runner, and my jump shot in the glare from Secretariat's lone working headlight.

For years, basketball had been my life. From the age of seven, my buddy Felix and I spent hour after hour shooting baskets in his driveway and playing horse on these same outdoor courts. Our boyhood hero was Ernie DiGregorio, a local legend who had led Providence College to the Final Four. Ernie D., as he was affectionately known, went on to win the NBA Rookie of the Year Award and, despite a gimpy knee, played eight seasons as a pro, the last as a member of our beloved Boston Celtics. Felix and I had read about how, as a child, Ernie dribbled a basketball everywhere he went. So we did, too, bouncing our worn Spaldings and Wilsons even when we walked to school.

Together, we made the Hope High freshman team; and by then, I had big dreams. I was going to lead our varsity in scoring for three years, star for the PC Friars, and then get drafted by the Celtics. But by our junior year of high school, Felix had grown taller, stronger, and faster than I. It was he who led the team in scoring and rebounding, dominating the paint while I planted myself at the three-point line to discourage the defense from collapsing on him. My jump shot was deadly from thirty feet. When he kicked the ball out to me, I rarely missed.

I pictured the two of us doing the same for PC; but during our senior year, Felix tanked his SATs, and I wasn't good enough to get scholarship offers. I ended up making the PC team as a walk-on. Felix matriculated in the fast food industry until he decided to pursue a career as a pimp and drug dealer.

The Friars' starters and most of the bench players were also faster and stronger than I, so I didn't get much playing time. But my jump shot? A thing of beauty.

I had no delusions about impressing the Vipers' coaches, but I didn't relish the thought of embarrassing myself. As I practiced, I ran through what I knew about Alfano and his briefcase full of cash. It wasn't much. I still didn't think the names were a hit list, but the more I thought about it, the more I wondered who he was working for and what they were after.

If I'd been right about Pichardo recognizing Alfano's picture, the fatal crash wasn't his first trip to Rhode Island. It was merely his last.

11

First thing next morning, I was refilling Tuukka's water dish when I heard footsteps pound up the stairs to the second floor. Then a heavy fist rattled my apartment door.

"Providence PD. Open up."

So I did.

In stepped the homicide twins: Jay Wargart, a big lug with a five o'clock shadow and fists like hams, and Sandra Freitas, a bottle blonde with a predatory Cameron Diaz smile.

"I don't recall poisoning, bludgeoning, garroting, stabbing, or shooting anybody this week," I said, "so this must be a social visit."

"Mind if we sit?" Freitas asked.

I waved them toward the kitchen table, where Tuukka was curled up in his aquarium, blissfully digesting his breakfast.

"Jesus!" Freitas said. "What the hell is that?"

"Exactly what it looks like."

"You have a *snake*?"

"Why are you surprised, Sandy?" Wargart said. "You know the old saying. Birds of a feather."

"Feathers?" I said. "Snakes don't have feathers. Their ancestors shed both their feathers and their legs millions of years ago. *I* don't have any feathers either, although there's a feather boa around here some-where. One of my overnight guests left it under my bed."

I went to the kitchen counter and dumped what was left of the morning's coffee into three chipped mugs. Then I carried them to the table and sat down with my guests.

"Seen Mario Zerilli around lately?" Wargart asked.

"Not for a couple of weeks."

"His girlfriend has reported him missing."

"That so?"

"Yeah."

"Did this girlfriend have a black eye or a split lip?"

"Both."

"That must be her, all right."

"We're thinking the corpse the Pawtucket PD fished out of the Blackstone might be

102

Mario," Wargart said. "Same height and weight. Same shoe size. Same Bruins sweatshirt he had on when the girlfriend last saw him."

"Wouldn't surprise me."

"Why's that?" Freitas asked.

"The guy was a punk," I said. "He was bound to come to a bad end."

"Didn't you have a run-in with him outside Hopes a while back?" Wargart asked.

"Where'd you get that from?"

He smirked, then said, "The way we heard it, he pulled a gun on you."

"Sounds like the sort of thing he'd do," I said.

"What was the altercation about?" Freitas asked. Altercation? I grinned at her. The detective had been working on her vocabulary.

"You aren't going to tell us about it, are you?" she said.

"No."

"Why didn't you report it?" Wargart asked.

"If I bothered you every time somebody threatened me," I said, "the mayor would have to double the size of the police department."

"I'll bet," he said.

"We're thinking you might be the last person to have seen him alive," Freitas said.

"Except for the good Samaritan who iced him," I said. "Assuming he's dead, of course."

"The victim was shot with a large caliber pistol," Freitas said. "Don't you own a Colt forty-five?"

I didn't say anything.

"You've got a nine mil, too," Wargart said. "They're both registered in your name. Where are the weapons now?"

"In a safe place."

"Go get them."

"No."

"No?"

"Not unless you have a warrant."

Wargart hadn't touched his coffee. He picked up the mug now and slammed it down. Tuukka startled and fled to a corner of the aquarium as coffee sloshed over the tabletop.

"Look," I said. "You don't even know for sure if Mario's dead."

"Somebody is," Wargart said.

"We'll know if it's Mario soon enough," Freitas said. "We can't find a record of him ever getting dental x-rays, but we collected a comb and toothbrush from his bathroom, and the crime lab is running the DNA as we speak."

"Bullshit," I said. "There's a huge backlog

for DNA tests. If that's what you're waiting on, it'll be a year before you know dick."

With that, the homicide twins pushed back from the table and clambered to their feet. Wargart loomed over me, trying to intimidate with his bulk. I rose and crowded him, a subtle reminder that I had him by two inches.

"We've got our eye on you, Mulligan," Wargart said. "Don't leave town."

After they left, I called Ferguson at the M.E.'s office and Lebowski at the Pawtucket PD and asked if there was anything new on the floater. There wasn't. Then I rang the receptionist at *The Dispatch* to call in sick.

It was eight on the dot when I climbed into Secretariat, tuned the radio to WTOP, and rumbled down Broadway toward downtown Providence under a slate-colored sky.

"Good morning, Row Dyelin!"

The mellifluous voice of Iggy Rock, the state's most popular morning drive-time radio host, oozed from my tinny speakers. Iggy's shtick was a toxic mix of Laura Ingraham–style moralizing, Rush Limbaugh–style liberal bashing, and Glenn Beck–style lunacy.

"Our topic this morning is Governor Mc-

Nerney's shameful plan to legalize sports betting. It's bad enough that the state squanders the millions of dollars it rakes in from the sale of lottery tickets. Now Attila the Nun wants to be your bookmaker so she can get her claws on millions more. Make no mistake, my fellow patriots. Her scheme is nothing more than a disguised tax increase to fuel our bloated state government.

"Our guest this morning is the Reverend Lucas Crenson, pastor of the Sword of God Church in Foster and announced Republican candidate for governor. Welcome to the show, Reverend."

"Thank you, Iggy. And you are so right. State-sponsored gambling isn't just a tax. It's a regressive one that steals money from the pockets of people who can least afford it. The answer to our budget crisis isn't more taxes. It's cutting waste and eliminating the endemic corruption that is bleeding our state dry. I pledge to you that when I am elected, I will do everything in my power to set Rhode Island on an honest and godly path."

I backed Secretariat into a metered space next to Burnside Park and let the engine idle.

"But this isn't just about taxes," Iggy said.

"Gambling is also a moral issue. Isn't that right, Reverend?"

"It certainly is. Gambling is a sin. One that ruins lives and destroys families. Government-sponsored gambling is even worse. It poisons our democracy, making all of us complicit in this unholy vice. And the money it generates fills the coffers of a nanny state that squanders our hard-earned dollars on free abortions and handouts to people who refuse to work for a living and are not deserving of our largess."

"The phone is lit up," Iggy said, "so let's take some calls. June from Barrington, you are on the air."

"Good morning, Iggy."

"Good morning, June. What's on your mind?"

"I can't believe the governor wants to allow the Lottery Commission to take sports bets," she said. "If we're going to go down this road, we should turn it over to private enterprise."

"Right you are, June. That's the only sensible way to go about this," Iggy said, blissfully oblivious that he was contradicting everything he and his guest had just said.

"Governor McNerney will never do that because she's a socialist," Reverend Crenson chimed in. "When she renounced her role in the church of Rome, she chose to forsake God, and as governor she has renounced freedom. She's as evil as the Kenyan-born Muslim tyrant who illegally occupies the White House."

Swell. I killed the engine, fed the parking meter, crossed the park, and slipped into the diner near city hall. As I grabbed a stool at the counter, Charlie, the fry cook who owns the place, cracked three eggs on the grill without taking my order and slapped five strips of bacon down beside them.

"So whaddaya think about the governor's plan to legalize bookmaking?" he asked.

"I don't have an opinion. You?"

"My three brothers all work for the state. If this'll bring in enough dough to save their pensions, I'm all for it."

We kicked that around for a while as I ate, then chatted about how the Red Sox were shaping up. We finished critiquing the starting lineup and had just started in on the bullpen when Frieden, the kid city hall reporter, pushed through the door.

"Mulligan? I thought you were supposed to be sick."

"I'm feeling a wee bit peaked," I said. "Not sure I'll be able to keep Charlie's bacon and eggs down."

"Liar."

"Okay, you caught me," I said. "But maybe this can be our little secret."

"No worries. I won't tell."

"So, how are you doing?"

"Fine, I guess."

"Why was Chuckie-boy on your case the other day?"

"He gave me three times more work than I could finish and then yelled at me because I didn't finish it."

"Don't let him get you down, Kate. The man's a bully."

She plopped down on the stool next to me. Without meeting my eyes, she said, "Working for a newspaper isn't what I thought it would be."

I was pretty sure she didn't expect a reply, and I was in no mood to nurture. I drained my coffee and wiped the grease from my mouth with a paper napkin. Then I dropped a ten on the counter, turned up the collar of my jean jacket, put on my Red Sox cap, and stepped out into a light morning rain.

The Turk's Head Building was located in a modest cluster of office towers that Mayor Carozza called the Providence financial district. He actually said this with a straight face. The sixteen-story, V-shaped structure, loosely modeled after New York City's

Flatiron Building, was the tallest in Rhode Island when it was erected in 1913. A century later it was a dwarf, but it remained one of the state's most fashionable business addresses.

I sloshed down Westminster Street toward a snarling concrete figurehead suspended three floors above the main entrance. Adorned with a turban and a Fu Manchu mustache, it was supposed to represent a Turkish sultan. I thought it was a dead ringer for Flash Gordon's arch-enemy, Ming the Merciless.

I ducked through the revolving door, shook the rain from my cap, and scanned the tenant directory: TD Ameritrade, Janney Montgomery Scott, the BankRI Art Gallery, Café la France, a pride of life insurance companies, a bloat of boutique law firms . . . Then I rode the elevator to the fourteenth floor and strode to the end of a spit-shined hallway. There I found a frosted-glass door discreetly labeled in gold paint:

McCracken & Associates
CONFIDENTIAL INVESTIGATIVE SERVICES

Inside, a secretary who resembled Rihanna stabbed at a keyboard with glitter-polished nails. Putting my own investigative skills to the test, I deduced from the nameplate on her desk that this was not the actual pop star but rather a pretender known to her friends and colleagues as Sharise Campbell. Behind her were three oaken doors. A golden metal plate on one of them said "Mr. McCracken." The other two doors were blank.

"Good morning, sir," she said. "Do you have an appointment?"

"I don't, but I was hoping your boss might be able to squeeze me in."

"That would be quite irregular, sir, but it would be my pleasure to ask if you can tell me your name and what this is regarding."

"They call me Mulligan, and I'm here to see if the resident gumshoe can weasel me out of a murder rap."

She didn't even raise an eyebrow. She just lifted the receiver of her desk phone and murmured into it. Then she beamed at me and said, "You're in luck, sir. Mr. Mc-Cracken is able to see you now." She rose on Rihanna's legs, opened the door to her right, and ushered me inside.

"May I bring a refreshment for you and your guest, Mr. McCracken?"

"Yes, Sharise," he said as he got up to greet me. "Two cups of your excellent coffee, please. Mr. Mulligan takes it with cream

111

and one sugar."

"Right away, sir."

As McCracken crushed my fingers in his grip, I took inventory. Gone was my friend's dated Sears blazer. Now his five-foot-eight-inch weight-lifter's body was draped in a chalk-striped navy-blue suit that hung like it had been made for him. A Glock automatic and a gun-cleaning kit rested on the glare of his desk, a modernistic slab of glass and steel big enough to accommodate off-street parking. To the left was a small cherrywood bar stocked with Johnnie Walker Black, Chivas Regal, Knob Creek, Rémy Martin, and Grey Goose in three vile fruit flavors. Behind the desk, high windows looked down on a neighborhood of restored colonial homes nestled just across the shit-brown ribbon of the Providence River. The red-and-green rug in the center of the white marble floor looked like real Persian.

The office's bone-white walls were adorned with framed autographed photos of Ernie DiGregorio, John Thompson, Marvin Barnes, Johnny Egan, Lenny Wilkins, and a dozen more basketball legends from Providence College, where McCracken and I were undergrads together a lifetime ago. The last time I saw those photos, they were hanging in a shabby, one-man storefront office shoehorned between a bucket-of-blood bar and the police station in the sorry waterfront town of Warren, Rhode Island. My friend's fortune had taken a turn for the better.

"Nice," I said.

"The office or Sharise? She's engaged, so do your ogling from a respectful distance."

"I'll try to behave."

The woman in question returned with a silver tray that held two china cups, matching creamer and sugar bowl, two silver spoons, and a pair of monogrammed cloth napkins. She placed the tray on a cherry coffee table in front of a cognac-colored sofa that smelled like real leather. McCracken and I sank into it and picked up our cups as she left and silently shut the door.

McCracken leaned back and plunked his shiny black Bruno Maglis on the tabletop.

"I gather business is booming," I said.

"It's getting there. I'm on retainer with five law firms and two insurance companies now, and the wayward-spouse racket is outta sight."

"That's enough to support all this?"

"Not quite yet. The rent here is steep. But you gotta look the part if you want to attract a deep-pocket clientele."

"So who are these associates I read about

on the door?"

"There aren't any."

"The other two offices are empty?"

"Yeah, but I got plans to expand," he said. "Hold on a sec."

He pulled himself to his feet, padded across the rug to his desk, and rummaged in a drawer. Then he came back and handed me an engraved brass nameplate. The name on it was Shamus Mulligan.

"I know you don't like your first name," he said, "so Liam was out. I was gonna make it L. S. A. Mulligan, like your byline, but then I realized one of those Gaelic middle names of yours worked better."

"Because Shamus is slang for private detective?"

"Bingo."

"On my birth certificate, it's spelled S-E-A-M-U-S."

"So what? The sign goes on the door as soon as you're ready to start."

"I'm still thinking on it."

"Don't take too long, okay? I could use some help around here."

"I hear you."

"So tell me, now," he said. "Who did you kill this time?"

"Whaddaya mean, this time? The creep I shot last year made a full recovery."

"I know. Thanks to you, the taxpayers have to provide him with free food and shelter for life. I hope your aim is better now."

"It is the way the homicide twins tell it."

"The corpse have a name?"

"Mario Zerilli."

"Mario's dead?"

"Maybe," I said, and gave him the rest of it.

"Well, I can't say I'm surprised," he said. "That asshole was into some nasty shit."

"I know. It would be fine by me if *all* the women-beaters and gay-bashers end up facedown in the Blackstone."

"If that *was* his body in the river," Mc-Cracken said, "a lot of people had reason to put it there. So what can I do to help?"

"Nothing. I'm not losing any sleep over this one."

"You're here about something else?"

"I am," I said. "What do you know about the video surveillance system at Green Airport?"

"Not much, but I can make a call. A buddy of mine runs the crew that installed it."

"Can you find out how long they keep the video, if they have face-recognition software, and if they do, whether we can get somebody to check, say, the last three months for me?"

"You're joking, right?" he said.

"What do you mean?"

"Face-recognition software? You've been watching too much junk TV."

"But I thought —"

"You thought wrong," he said. "The technology's in development, but unless the NSA or the CIA has come up with something they aren't sharing, it works less than half the time. It's pretty good if the camera catches the face straight on, but the more it veers toward profile, the less reliable it gets. And it's easily fooled by facial expressions, too. Even a grin or a frown can throw it off. And sunglasses? Fugettaboutit. Most times, it can't tell the difference between Osama and Obama."

"Just like Fox News," I said.

"Exactly."

"So if I wanted to find a face in the crowd," I said, "I'd have to go through all the video myself?"

"If you could get you access to it, yeah. Who is it you'd be looking for?"

"This guy," I said, and handed him my cell phone.

McCracken's jaw dropped.

"What is your interest in Lucan Alfano?" he said.

Then it was my jaw that dropped.

"What's yours?" I asked.

12

"The sign on the door says *confidential* investigative services," McCracken said.

"So you're not going to tell me?"

"Not unless you have something to trade. Even then, it would have to be off the record."

"Alfano died with a briefcase on his lap," I said. "Inside it was two hundred grand in hundred-dollar bills."

"You know this how?" he asked, so I told him.

"What else have you got?"

So I spilled about the list of names.

"Did you already know about this?" I asked.

"No."

McCracken rubbed his jaw and took a moment to decide what he was willing to share.

"About a month ago," he said, "a public official came in here with a story. He

claimed a stranger who looked like Paulie
Walnuts had walked into his statehouse office unannounced on March third and offered him a large sum of cash in return for
a favor. The offer came with a warning not
to call the police."

"You took his case?"

"I did."

"Did this favor have something to do with
the governor's gambling bill?"

He nodded.

"The man wanted the bill killed?"

"He wanted it modified."

"To turn the bookmaking over to private
enterprise?"

"That's right."

"It was Alfano who made the offer?"

Another nod.

"Your client knows this how? Did Alfano
give his name?"

"He didn't."

"So?"

"So my client trailed him outside and
watched him walk down the hill toward
downtown. The guy crossed the street and
entered the Omni Hotel."

"Then what?"

"After I took the case, I dropped by the
hotel and asked the desk clerk if he'd
recently had a guest who looked like Paulie

Walnuts. He remembered the guy, all right. Said he'd registered under the name Michael O'Toole and paid with an unusual credit card."

"Unusual how?"

"It didn't have his name on it. Just a company name, Bucks and Pesos Inc."

"I thought all credit cards are supposed to have the holder's name on them."

"So did I," he said. "Turns out there's at least one so-called bank that issues credit cards with just business names."

"Sounds fishy."

"You think? Far as I can tell, the bank exists only on the Internet. According to its website, it will also register your company name in Central America and set you up with an offshore bank account."

"Alfano and this Bucks and Pesos are one and the same?"

"They are."

"How did you find that out?"

"I gave the desk clerk a hundred bucks for the credit card information, and then I traced it. Had to call in a lot of favors before I was able to link it to Alfano. Once I had his name, I called a P.I. I know in Atlantic City and got the lowdown on him. The P.I. also sent me Alfano's picture."

"Then what did you do?"

"I phoned the client and gave him my report. I told him I couldn't do anything more for him and urged him to call the state police."

"Did he?"

"I don't know. I haven't heard from him since. Hasn't paid his bill yet either."

"What's the client's name?"

"You're butting up against that confidentiality thing again."

"Was it on the list found in Alfano's pocket?"

"No."

"I still want a look at the airport surveillance video," I said, "but I think we can limit it to the first week of March."

"What do you expect to learn from that? I already told you Alfano was in town then."

"I won't know until I see it," I said.

After dinner that evening, I popped open a bottle of Killian's and flopped down in front of the television to watch *Revolution*. The show was one of those sagas of a dystopian future that were more popular than ever this year. You couldn't snap on the TV or wander into a movie theater without being menaced by marauding militias, brain-eating zombie armies, homicidal super-villains, or aliens hell-bent on exterminating the human race.

We were already doing a bang-up job of that without their help according to the so-called news spewed by cable TV pundits, talk radio demagogues, and lunatic-fringe websites. I'd come to dread their daily blizzard of paranoia, misinformation, and outright lies about climate change, Sharia law, secret government concentration camps, and phony wars on everything from guns to Christmas. Conspiracy nuts were in ascendance, hallucinating about communists in the White House, spreading fear about jihadists in the State Department, praying for the Apocalypse, buying gold as a hedge against impending social disorder, stockpiling assault weapons to defend themselves from their freely elected leaders, and ranting about the New World Order, black helicopters, autism-causing vaccines, immigrants who don't learn English fast enough, and imaginary assaults on a Constitution most of them had never read.

I tried to be hopeful about the future, but sometimes, like now, I believed that I was living in an insane asylum. Tens of millions of Americans, so buried in bullshit that they were no longer able to distinguish fact from fiction, had lost the capacity for rational debate. They shrieked insults across a widening chasm, treated political opponents as mortal enemies, and thought compromise was synonymous with treason. I couldn't see a way out of the mess. Newspapers were dying, and nothing was on the horizon to replace them as honest brokers of information.

I clicked the TV off and opened a mystery novel by the late Robert B. Parker, eager to immerse myself in an imaginary world in which problems had solutions and the good guys always won.

Five chapters in, Jesse Stone, the police chief in the mythical coastal town of Paradise, Massachusetts, learned that the body he'd found on the first page belonged to a fear-mongering radio talk-show host who reminded me of Iggy Rock. Jesse didn't think the guy would be missed.

13

By Monday, I'd recovered enough from my fake illness to return to work. Several days' worth of mail had piled up on my desk, and it was mostly the usual crap. The lone bright spot was an offering from Lieutenant Governor Pasquale Mancuso, the undisputed winner of my daily stupid press release challenge.

The Lieutenant Governor wishes to offer his sincere apologies to anyone who may have been embarrassed by his faux pas at the Blue Grotto Restaurant on Federal Hill Thursday night. The unfortunate incident occurred when he felt a case of the sniffles coming on. He reached into the inside pocket of his suit jacket and pulled out what he thought was a handkerchief. Unfortunately, he found himself wiping his nose with a pair of women's panties. The Lieutenant Governor doesn't know how this piece of apparel found its way into his pocket, but he wants to make it perfectly clear that it belongs to his wife.

This would have been witnessed by no more than a couple of dozen people. Why Mancuso wanted to spread the news to everyone who still took *The Dispatch* was a mystery until I did a Google search for "Mancuso + panties" and found three separate videos of the incident on YouTube and another on The *Ocean State Rag* website. Between them, they already had more than sixty thousand hits.

I wrote it up word for word with one minor alteration. The garment the lieutenant governor had wiped his honker with was actually a pink thong with a grinning black pussycat on the front.

At noon, I slipped out to wolf down a burger and fries at my favorite diner. When I was done, I figured I had forty minutes or so to do some real reporting before Chuckie-boy released the hounds. I jogged up the hill to the statehouse and found Pichardo, the House minority leader, eating Chinese takeout from the carton in her cluttered office.

"I already told you I don't know anything about this," she said.

125

"Yeah, but now I'd like the truth."

She narrowed her eyes and bared her teeth.

"Look," I said. "Alfano was a dangerous guy. Whoever he was working for is probably going to send somebody else. In fact, his replacement might already be here."

She folded her hands, the nails painted blood red, and stared at her desktop.

"Off the record?" she said.

"Sure."

"Okay, you're right. I recognized the picture."

"You met with Alfano?"

"I did."

"What were the circumstances?"

"I already reported this to the state police. Why should I tell you?"

"Because I'm trying to figure out what's going on," I said, "and some of the people who talk to me would never spill to the cops."

She took a few seconds to think it over, then said, "He came to my office unannounced and offered me a bribe."

"When was this?"

"A couple of weeks before he was killed."

"Remember the date?"

"Give me a sec to check my calendar," she said, and turned to her computer screen.

"It was the day we voted on the redistricting bill, so that would have made it March 3."

"Four weeks ago."

"Uh-huh."

"And he asked you to hold up the gambling bill until the governor agrees to privatize the bookmaking?"

"He did."

"That's exactly what you are doing, isn't it?" I said.

"I resent the implication. I told him that was already my position and that he should keep his dirty money."

"Did he warn you not to call the police?"

"He said things would go badly for me if I did."

"Go badly for you? Were those his exact words?"

"Yes."

"But you called the police anyway?" I said.

"I figured things might go worse for me if I didn't."

I ducked back into the newsroom before I was missed, sat down in my cubicle, and made a call.

"State Police Headquarters, Parisi speaking."

"Afternoon, Captain."

"Mulligan? What is it this time? I'm pretty busy here."

"Lucan Alfano," I said.

He fell silent, then said, "Aw, shit."

"We need to have a chat about him."

"The usual place in twenty minutes," he said, and hung up.

I tugged on my jean jacket and meandered toward the elevator, hoping Chuckie-boy wouldn't notice.

Johnston City Hall was halfway between *The Dispatch* and state police headquarters in Scituate. When I arrived, Parisi's unmarked car was already in the parking lot. I pulled in beside it, nose to tail, and we lowered our driver's-side windows.

Parisi, always impeccably groomed, with a gray military brush cut and knife-scarred knuckles, was well past fifty now and bearing down on retirement age. Over the years, he'd put a dozen murderers away, solved scores of other violent crimes, and broken the back of New England's largest drug ring. The scalps of three corrupt mayors, fifteen crooked state legislators, and at least twenty members of the Patriarca crime family hung from his gun belt. He was the best cop I'd ever known.

Parisi tended to be tight-lipped with the press, usually taking at least five seconds, and often more, to frame cautious responses to my questions. I'd learned to wait him out.

"Jesus," he said. "You're still driving that piece of crap?"

"Stop it," I said. "You're eroding Secretariat's self-esteem."

"Only women and assholes name their cars."

"You left out vigilant watchdogs of the fourth estate."

"Like I said. Assholes."

"So how's the Alfano investigation going?" I asked.

Five seconds, and then, "What Alfano investigation?"

"The one about him offering bribes to public officials."

Another pause. "Bribes? Where'd you hear that?"

"Some of the people who talked to you have been talking to me."

Five seconds again, and then, "Alfano's dead."

"I know that. It was in the paper."

"So any investigation, and I'm not confirming there was one, would be dead now, too."

"You're not curious about who he was working for?"

Ten seconds this time. "Do you know?"

"I'm working on it."

"If you find out, be sure to let me know," he said, and started to roll up his window.

"Hold on," I said.

"What?"

"Besides the five names on Alfano's list, did he offer bribes to anyone else?"

Five seconds. "What list?"

"The one Oscar Hernandez showed you."

Ten seconds. "Off the record?"

"Sure."

"If such a list exists, and I'm not confirming that it does, there could be reason to suspect it is not complete."

"How incomplete is it?"

Five seconds. "Hard to say."

"Come on, Captain. Give me something to go on."

Twelve seconds this time. "I don't know what I don't know. Could be a lot of others. Could be just one or two."

"Meaning there's at least one more for sure?"

Five seconds. "If I were in your position, that would be my assumption."

Parisi wasn't giving me much to go on, but I was betting this meant McCracken's client, whose name was not on the list, had taken the P.I.'s advice and called the state police.

"Can you lighten up and give me the damned names?"

There was no delay this time.

"Get that broken headlight fixed," he said, "or next time I'm going to give you a ticket. Oh, and when you see Hernandez, tell him I said he's got a big fucking mouth."

With that, he cranked the ignition and peeled out of the lot.

Not bad for Parisi, I thought. He'd tossed me a morsel and suggested there might be a next time.

I was on my way back to Providence when the cell phone played my ringtone for Chuckie-boy. I ignored it. He kept calling. Finally, I pulled over in a KFC parking lot and picked up.

"Mulligan."

"Where the hell are you?"

"At the doctor. I've had a relapse. Looks like I came back to work too soon."

"Bullshit. Get your butt back here right now."

"I don't think so, Chuckie. The doc says I need to go home and lie down. You don't want me too weak to try out for the Vipers on Saturday, do you?"

"I'm going to need a doctor's note."

"No problem," I said.

Doc Israel was a fan. A few months back, he'd given me a short stack of his stationery for just such eventualities.

14

The men in mismatched T-shirts and basketball shorts lined up single file along the sideline so Coach Derrick Martin and his two assistants could look us over. By my headcount, there were sixty-two of us, and we were mostly a sorry lot.

There was Ruben Mendoza, a twenty-five-year-old Providence playground legend with what looked like needle tracks on his arms. And Butch Bowditch, a slow-footed center who'd packed on twenty pounds of fat since his graduation from Brown University two years ago. And Chris Sears, an All–Big East shooting guard who'd been cut from the PC squad last December after getting caught stealing laptops from dorm rooms for the third time. And the unfortunately named Freddie Krueger, a former URI power forward who might have been drafted in the second round two years ago if he hadn't torn his ACL to shreds in a snowboarding accident. And Marvin Benton, a dazzling former PC point guard who'd been ignored in last year's draft because he was only five foot eight. And twenty-year-old Keenan Jefferson, so dominating at Hope High that he was being compared to Kevin Durant until he dropped out two years ago to marry his pregnant girlfriend and take a job slinging burgers.

Earlier, as I laced my Nike All Stars, I watched Krueger strap a brace on his surgically repaired knee while Sears prowled the overcrowded locker room and talked trash.

"You ain't nothin' but a bunch of has-beens and never-weres. I'm gonna burn the lot of ya." Then he spotted me and snarled, "And what the fuck are *you* doin' here, grandpa?"

I grinned, peeled off my white T-shirt, and printed "GRANDPA" on the back with a Sharpie. I still figured the tryout was a sham, but I wished all of them but Sears good luck. Jefferson, the kid who'd tried to do the right thing by his girl, was the one I'd be rooting for the hardest.

As we stood on the sidelines, I stared up at 12,993 empty seats and remembered how, on those rare occasions when I got off the bench for PC, every one of them had been filled.

Coach Martin and his two assistants were strutting down the line like drill sergeants now, giving each of us the once-over. When they reached me, Martin smirked and said, "I hear they're calling you grandpa."

"Yeah," I said. "I kinda like it."

"You sure you don't want to go on home, old-timer? Maybe fix yourself some warm milk and take a nap?"

The others laughed. I joined in. Then I broke the line, ambled over to the two carts that held the basketballs, picked one up, squared myself to the basket, and swished a thirty-foot jump shot.

"Beginner's luck," Sears growled.

I smiled and kept shooting until I emptied both carts. Sixteen of twenty hit nothing but net.

"Great form," Martin said. "Any of you other wannabes think you can match that? No? Okay then. Break off into groups of five for suicides. Six times down and back."

A basketball court is ninety-four feet long. Six times down and back meant a sprint of more than eleven hundred feet. I finished next to last in my group, well ahead of Bowditch, who jogged the last two laps. I was winded and drenched in sweat, but not bending over and gasping for breath like some of the others.

135

When we were done, the coaches lined us up again, asked Bowditch, Mendoza, and sixteen others to take one step forward, and told them to go home.

We spent the rest of the morning and early afternoon on standard basketball drills: the four-spot fast break shooting drill, the elbow shooting drill, the post feed/spot up drill, and the wing screen. The guys who'd played college ball mostly did okay. The unschooled playground legends struggled.

Shortly after one P.M., they lined us up on the sidelines again, told another twenty-four that they were done, and asked the remaining twenty of us, including Sears, Krueger, Benton, and Jefferson, to come back the following Saturday.

As the exhausted winners and losers trudged to the locker room, I pulled Martin aside.

"Why me?" I asked.

"Because the fix is in. The ownership is desperate for publicity, so you were gonna stick no matter what. Now that I've seen what you can do, I might have kept you around anyway. You're slow, you can't jump, and you couldn't guard Danny DeVito if he played in a wheelchair. But your shooting form reminds me of Ray Allen. Think you can teach the rest of these clowns the proper way to stick a jump shot?"

15

"Fiona? It's Mulligan."

"Huh? What time is it?"

"Did I wake you?"

"Yeah."

"It's eleven o'clock Sunday morning. Why aren't you in church?"

"I attended midnight mass."

"Are you alert enough to answer a question, or should I call back?"

"Give me a sec."

I heard her drop the phone and rustle around for half a minute. Then she was back.

"Okay, shoot."

"Remember telling me that a couple of committee chairmen knew about the gambling bill before the news leaked?"

"Uh-huh."

"Guys who weren't on Alfano's list?"

"Yeah."

"Who are they?"

"Phil Templeton and Joseph Longo." Templeton, I knew, was the chairman of the House Corporations Committee, and Longo headed the Senate Finance Committee. "They're my point men on this," Fiona was saying. "I'm counting on them to line up support, make the necessary horse trades, and count the votes so we can drive the bill through the legislature."

"I need to talk to them."

"About what?"

"Alfano."

"Why?"

"I think he might have tried to bribe them, too."

"But you're not sure?"

"No."

"The legislature is in recess now," she said, "but you can find Longo at home in Bristol or in his office at Bayside Construction."

"What about Templeton?"

"I don't know. I've got something I need to run by him; but his cell goes straight to voice mail, and he's not answering his home phone either."

"He's a bachelor, isn't he?"

"He's gay."

"I hadn't heard that," I said.

"He's not exactly in the closet," Fiona

said, "but he's private about his personal life. Far as I know, he lives alone."

"Any idea at all where he might be?"

"No."

Forty minutes later, I parked Secretariat at the curb outside McCracken's condo and punched his number into my cell phone.

"Hey, Mulligan. What's up?"

"It's a glorious spring afternoon. How about taking a drive with me?"

"Where are we going?"

"To visit your client — the one you advised to go to the state police about Alfano."

"You figured out who it is?"

"I've got it narrowed down to two, and I'm right outside."

"Aw, hell. Sit tight. I'll be right out."

Five minutes later, he lumbered through his front door in a Red Sox T-shirt and cap that matched my own and climbed into the passenger seat.

"It's Longo or Templeton," I said. "You could save us both time by telling me which one."

"Sorry," he said, "but I'm a still stickler for client confidentiality."

I smirked and cranked the ignition. Secretariat sputtered to life and galloped south on Route 114.

"Any news about the airport surveillance video yet?" I asked.

"No, but I might have something for you later this week."

Longo lived in a McMansion in Bristol Highlands, a fashionable neighborhood that abuts Colt State Park. He answered the door in a sky-blue Nike sweatsuit, looked me up and down, and growled, "Oh my God, it's the press!" Then he laughed heartily, ushered us in, and said, "And who might this be? Your photographer?"

I made the introductions. From the looks on their faces as they shook hands, I was pretty sure Longo and McCracken hadn't met before.

"So, what brings you two out here on a Sunday afternoon?" Longo asked.

"The gambling bill," I said.

"Sorry. Can't help you with that. I don't mean to be uncooperative, but anything I might say on that subject would be premature. The governor hasn't even sent it to the legislature yet."

"I understand that," I said, "but perhaps you can tell me if you recognize this man."

I showed him the photo on my cell phone. He studied it for a moment, frowned, and said, "Please come this way."

He led us down a gleaming, porcelain-

141

tiled hallway that emptied into a sunny family room with a view of a tulip bed and a kidney-shaped swimming pool. He waved us into a black leather sofa, turned the sound down on a seventy-two-inch flatscreen tuned to the Red Sox–Orioles game, and seated himself across from us in a matching recliner.

"I take it you already know something about this, or you wouldn't be here," he said.

"That's right," I said.

"The scuttlebutt around town is that you've got a high-ranking source at state police headquarters. Is that where you're getting your information?"

Parisi hadn't told me much, but I figured it was best to let Longo think otherwise.

"You told the state cops about Lucan Alfano's bribe offer," I bluffed. "Isn't that right?"

"Lucan Alfano?" he said.

"The man in the photo."

"The greasy bastard didn't give me his name."

"But you recognized the picture?"

Longo hesitated. "Can we go off the record?" he asked.

"If you insist."

"I do."

142

"All right," I said.

"In that case, yeah."

"He offered you a bribe to hold up the gambling bill until the governor agrees to turn sports betting over to private enterprise. Is that right?"

"He did."

"Did he specify who he had in mind to run things?" McCracken asked.

"He did not. He said he'd let me know who to throw my weight behind when the time came."

"Can you confirm the amount of the bribe offer?" I asked.

"Twenty-five thousand dollars. But if the people he represented got the contract, he'd slip me another twenty-five on the back end."

"How did he approach you?" McCracken asked.

"He walked into my company unannounced and placed several bundles of bills on my desk."

"Then what?" I asked.

"He told me what the money was for and threatened me when I declined to accept it."

"How did he word the threat, exactly?" McCracken asked.

"He said things would go badly for me if I

didn't agree to his proposition."

"Clever," the P.I. said. "It could be explained away as a warning that things could go badly politically."

"Yes, but I'm sure that's not how he meant it," Longo said. "From his tone of voice and the look on his face, I took it as a threat to do bodily harm."

"What happened next?" I asked.

"I told him to leave, and I called the state police. I spoke to someone in the detective division. I forget the name. But a couple of hours later, Captain Parisi arrived to take my statement."

"Are you aware of anyone else getting similar bribe offers?" I asked.

"No, but I have my suspicions."

"Tell me about that."

"A few weeks after I met with — what was that name again? Albano?"

"Alfano."

"A few weeks later — it was after that website broke the news about the bill — a couple of legislators who initially voiced support for the governor changed their positions. Suddenly they were insisting that sports gambling should be privatized."

"Can you tell me their names?" I asked.

"I'd rather not. They could have had legitimate reasons for changing their minds.

I'm not one to publicly cast aspersions that I can't prove."

"Did you tell Parisi about your suspicions?" I asked.

"Somewhat hesitantly, but yes. It seemed to me it was something he should look into."

With that, we thanked him, and he led us to the door.

"He was helpful," McCracken said as we settled into the Bronco.

"He was."

"So I guess we're going to go see my client now, huh?" he said.

"Yup."

"Fine," he said, "but can we grab an early dinner first?"

We drove back north on 114 and stopped at Jack's on Child Street in Warren for clam chowder, littlenecks, and beverages. As one Killian's led to another, and then to several more, the conversation turned to my possible future as a McCracken & Associates operative. By the time McCracken ponied up for the tab, the sun was setting, and a steady rain had begun to fall.

Phil Templeton lived in a raised ranch on Pace Court in Lincoln, just a few miles from the North Central State Airport. I parked the Bronco in a turnaround at the end of the cul-de-sac and took a moment to study the dark house. Then I fetched my flashlight from the glove box, and together Mc-Cracken and I splashed up the flagstone walk.

McCracken rang the bell, then spotted jimmy marks on the front door. He nudged it open with his shoe, and we stepped into the foyer.

"Mr. Templeton?" he called out. "Hello? Is anybody home?"

We crept down a short hallway, and I swept the flashlight beam over the living room. The coffee table had been knocked over. Shards from a broken carafe and a shattered wineglass or two sparkled against a red stain on the hardwood floor.

"Blood?" I asked.

McCracken dropped to one knee, slid a cheap ballpoint from his pocket, and scraped the end of it against the stain. Then he raised the pen to his nose and sniffed.

"Wine, I think."

He rose and slid the Glock from his shoulder holster. I tugged the Kel-Tec from my waistband. Together, we prowled the house.

The other six rooms were dark and empty. Upstairs, we found Templeton's home office, a computer humming on his keyhole

146

desk. McCracken pulled on a pair of latex gloves and tapped a key. The screen came to life. He took several minutes to search the legislator's e-mail but found nothing of interest.

We backed out without touching anything else, skipped down the stairs, and left the way we had come. I waited until we were half a mile down the road before I flicked on the headlights.

"So what do you think?" I asked.

"Could be anything," McCracken said. "A simple break-in. A fight. Maybe he just threw a tantrum when his latest pickup wouldn't sleep with him."

"Doesn't feel like a housebreak," I said. "The place wasn't tossed."

"And you say he hasn't been answering his phone?"

"Yeah. For a couple of weeks." My mind flashed on the still-unidentified floater. If it wasn't Mario, then maybe — "I've got a bad feeling about this."

"I don't suppose you have a burner phone," McCracken said.

"In the glove box."

"Smart," he said. "It's always good to have a cheap prepaid handy in case you need to make a call that can't be traced back to you."

He popped open the box, grabbed the phone, and called the Lincoln PD.

"I'd like to report a housebreak at number six Pace Court. . . . No, the intruder is no longer present. . . . No, you can't have my name."

With that, he clicked off.

I dropped McCracken off at home and drove back to Providence in the rain. By the time I parked in front of my place, it was nearly ten P.M. I tromped up the stairs, walked down the short second-floor hallway, and stopped dead in front of my apartment.

The door yawned wide open. I stole a quick glance and saw that the wood around the deadbolt was splintered.

I slipped the pistol from my waistband, raised it, and stood six inches to the left of the doorframe for a minute, maybe two. I heard nothing but the hum from the refrigerator.

Leading with the gun, I stepped inside and hit the switch for the overhead kitchen light. The refrigerator gaped open. The bottles of beer and jars of pickles and tomato sauce that had been inside were now a swamp of shards and goop on the linoleum floor. A heap of metal and plastic that used to be my microwave had been hurled into a

148

corner. The kitchen chairs and table had been tipped over, shattering Tuukka's aquarium.

I stepped into the bedroom and snapped on the light. The bureau drawers had been dumped, the chest tipped over on top of them. The mattress was ripped to shreds, a butcher knife from my kitchen tossed onto the stuffing.

In the sitting room, my battered sofa and stuffed chair had been given the same treatment. The TV lay in pieces between them. My books had been yanked from their shelves and thrown around the room. My turntable lay twisted and broken on the floor, and my treasured collection of vintage blues vinyl, which I'd been picking up at flea markets for years, had been stomped to pieces.

I tucked my pistol back in my waistband and returned to the kitchen. My first thought was of Tuukka. I'd grown fond of the little guy, and now he was on the loose. I rushed to close the apartment door, just in case he was still inside.

And there he was, hanging from the back of the door, his body still twitching. A steak knife from my kitchen drawer had been driven straight through his skull.

Tuukka was just a snake. A cold-blooded

reptile. He didn't bark or purr. He didn't greet me with a thumping tail when I came home. He didn't even want to be petted. But I liked him. After years of living alone, I'd taken comfort in his company. He hadn't deserved to be stabbed through the head — but whoever murdered him did. I yanked the knife out and gently laid his body on the counter.

Suddenly I realized I was forgetting something. I sprinted back to the bedroom and threw open the footlocker. It was empty. My grandfather's gun was gone.

16

Next morning, I curled Tuukka into a shoebox and buried him in the dirt in the narrow, grassless yard behind my building. A half hour later I was bent over my desk in the newsroom, sorting through the day's press releases, when the security guard called from the lobby.

"Mulligan?"

"Yeah?"

"A couple of Providence police detectives just came in looking for you. I asked them to wait till I called up, but they brushed past me and got on the elevator."

"It's okay, Johnny. Thanks for the heads-up."

The homicide twins, Wargart and Freitas, were stepping off the elevator now. They scanned the newsroom, spotted me, and swaggered to my cubicle.

"You need to come with us," Wargart said.

"Am I under arrest?"

"Not just yet."

"Then you're shit out of luck."

"You've got some questions to answer, ass-hole," Freitas said.

"Come with me," I said.

I led the detectives to a small, vacant meeting room where we sat at a round butcher-block table with a computer on it.

"You reported a break-in at your apartment last night," Freitas said.

"I did."

"And you claimed that your forty-five was stolen," she said.

"It was."

"The same gun we asked you about the last time we paid you a visit," Wargart said.

"Uh-huh."

"How convenient," he said.

"Not for me. You must have read the incident report, so you know my place was completely trashed. The bastard even killed Tuukka."

"Who the hell is that?" Wargart said.

"My snake. You must remember Tuukka. The one without the feathers."

"Nice cover story," Freitas said.

"You think I did all that to myself?"

"Sure you did," she said. "And then you lied to the responding officers and said you think Mario Zerilli did it. That would make

152

him pretty lively for a corpse, don'tcha think?"

"Maybe he's a zombie," I said. "From what I see on TV, lots of dead people are turning into zombies nowadays. It's a goddamned pandemic."

Wargart reached across the table and grabbed the neck of my T-shirt with his left fist.

"What did you do with the forty-five, dickhead?"

"If you want to keep that hand," I said, "you better remove it right now."

"Are you threatening a police officer?"

"Bet your ass."

Wargart gave me his best hard look, then let go of me.

"He probably threw the gun in the river," Freitas said.

"Or down a storm drain, maybe," Wargart said.

"I didn't," I said, "but if I had, I sure as hell wouldn't tell you two hard cases about it."

"You know, Mulligan," Freitas said, her voice softer now, "Mario was a women-beating, gay-bashing punk who will not be missed. He threatened your life, for godsakes. I bet you shot him in self-defense. Nobody could blame you for that. Why don't you calm down and tell us what happened so we can all wrap this up and go home early."

"Really?" I said. "Does anybody ever fall for that?"

"You'd be surprised," Wargart said.

"Where's that other gun you own?" Freitas asked.

"None of your business."

With that, they pulled themselves to their feet and stomped out.

Once they were gone, I returned to my desk and rushed through the rest of the press releases. I needed to clear the decks, because this was going to be a big news day. The circus was coming to town.

The NCAA and the four major sports leagues had scheduled a joint press conference for three in the afternoon, giving local TV plenty of time to chop the speechifying down to a half minute of out-of-context sound bites for the five o'clock news. But just before one o'clock, Chuckie-boy shoved some empty Chinese food cartons aside, perched on the corner of my desk, and announced that he had something more pressing for me to do first.

"Wait till you hear this," he said. "The police just busted some mall cop they found living in an unused utility shed inside the Providence Place Mall parking structure. He'd actually set up housekeeping in there. Had a sectional sofa, a dinette set, lamps, a microwave, a space heater, a TV. They say he was even stealing electricity and cable from the mall."

"Okay, I'm on it."

"Try to wrap this one up before the press conference starts, okay? It should make a hilarious page-one bright."

I didn't think it was funny.

According to the police report, thirty-one-year-old Joseph DeLucca had been arrested and charged with trespassing and theft of services, namely an estimated fifteen hundred bucks' worth of the mall's electricity. He'd already been arraigned and was being held in lockup in lieu of three hundred dollars bail.

After scribbling the details in my notepad, I went to the bank, got a cash advance on my Visa, and got him sprung. Fifteen minutes later we were sitting in a booth at the diner near city hall waiting for Charlie to finish scorching our burgers.

"Well," Joseph said, "the fuckers finally caught me."

He'd moved into the shed eighteen months ago because he couldn't afford both beer and rent on the pittance the mall paid him to strut around in a uniform and discourage theft. Given the thousands of bucks in cosmetics, running shoes, and small electronics he liberated from the loose-fitting clothes and oversize handbags the shoplifters favored, Joseph figured he was entitled. I thought he had a point.

I'd first met Joseph about five years ago when the cottage he was living in with his elderly mother got burned down in the Mount Hope arson spree. Back then, he'd been nearly as wide as he was tall, but he'd dropped a hundred pounds the year he took a job as a bouncer at the Tongue & Groove. There, he got into a dispute over employee benefits. The manager accused him of abusing the strip club's free-beer-and-blowjobs perk. Joseph insisted he'd been practicing admirable self-restraint. So they agreed to part ways, Joseph moving on to the mall cop job and the club manager to months of painful physical therapy. The manager made a sensible decision not to whine about it to the authorities.

I'd visited Joseph occasionally in his illicit mall digs to guzzle Narragansett, eat pizza, and watch the Patriots and the Red Sox on TV.

"So what are you going to do now, Joseph?"

"Go to jail, I guess."

"This is your first offense, right?"

"Second. Got busted with a quarter-ounce of weed a coupla years ago."

"You'll get off with a lecture and fine. Probably less than a grand. But you'll have to make restitution for the stolen electricity."

"And if I can't pay?"

"That could be a problem," I said.

"Shit."

"Maybe I can find a way to help you with that by the time your court date comes around. But first things first. Do you have a place to crash?"

"If I did, you think I woulda been squattin' in a fuckin' shed?"

"Tell you what. Why don't you bunk down at my apartment for now?"

"You'd do that for me?"

"When we're done eating, I'll drop you there."

"Thanks, Mulligan. I owe you big time."

"I'll get a key made for you tomorrow. Meanwhile, the place is wide open. Somebody broke in and trashed it last night. I'm afraid it's an awful mess right now."

"Aw, hell. Did they catch the guy who

done it?"

"No, but I've got a pretty good idea who it was. If I find him, maybe you can hold him down for me while I break all his fingers and toes."

"You bet. Meanwhile, the least I can do is help you clean up."

"That would be great, Joseph. There's some cleaning supplies under the sink. I'll let the landlord know I've got a guest so he won't be surprised when he comes by to fix the door."

"Okay."

"Are you still driving that piece-of-crap pickup truck?"

"Yeah."

"It's trash day on the East Side, and wealthy people there tend to throw out a lot of good stuff. Think you could cruise around and see if you can salvage a few things we need?"

"Like what?"

"Anything but a refrigerator, bookshelves, and a kitchen table. Everything else in the place is wrecked."

No bigwigs stood behind the microphone-spiked lectern that had been placed on the statehouse steps. No Roger Goodell, Adam Silver, Gary Bettman, Rob Manfred, or

Mark Emmert. Instead, the commissioners of the four major sports leagues and the president of the NCAA had dispatched their press flunkies, all of them schooled in the art of manipulating the media.

As the local TV affiliates, a half-dozen radio reporters, an AP reporter, and stringers for *The Boston Globe* and ESPN recorded the action, I roamed through the sparse crowd. Three members of the governor's staff, the assistant director of the state Lottery Commission, and more than a dozen Rhode Island legislators had shown up to hear the speakers spout the same crap they'd spoon-fed me on the phone last week. I didn't take many notes.

I was chatting with Mason, who was covering the proceedings for his *Ocean State Rag,* when I spotted a middle-aged woman in a gray business suit working the crowd. She flitted from one legislator to another, shaking their hands and whispering furtively into their ears. The woman looked familiar, but I couldn't place her at first. Then it came to me. I raised my Nikon and snapped a few shots of her before I made my approach.

"Excuse me. My name is Mulligan. I'm a reporter for *The Providence Dispatch.*"

"I have nothing to say to you, Mr. Mul-ligan."

"Can you tell me your name and who you represent?"

"Fuck off."

"Look, lady. I already took your picture. I can always show it around until I find someone who knows who you are. Why not save me the time?"

"You photographed me?"

"I did."

"Who authorized you to do that?"

"The same person who authorized you to take pictures of me and the governor at Hopes the other night."

"Oh. You noticed that, huh?"

"I did."

She narrowed her eyes and tried to stare me down. It didn't work.

"Why not be civil and introduce yourself?" I said.

"Fine. My name is Cheryl Grandison. I'm the vice president of Stop Sports Gambling Now."

"What's that?"

"A super PAC."

"Never heard of it."

"We formed last year to oppose Governor Christie's plan to legalize sports betting in New Jersey."

"Where's your funding come from?"

"Good luck figuring that out," she said. Then she turned her back on me and stalked off.

Federal law allowed super PACs to raise unlimited amounts of money. It also permitted them to spend it on lobbying, political advertising, or just about anything else as long as they didn't contribute directly to political candidates. They were supposed to publicly disclose the names of their contributors, but they could accept donations from other organizations that didn't have to say where *their* money came from. Regulators called it the Russian doll loophole. As a result, big donors could remain anonymous, and usually did.

I took out my phone, punched in the number for the Campaign Finance Division of the State Board of Elections, and asked for Bud Henry.

"I've got a question about a super PAC that just showed up in town to influence the pending sports gambling legislation," I said.

"Sorry, but I don't think I can give you much help on that," he said. "Super PACs aren't required to register with the state."

"You don't regulate them at all?"

"We haven't dealt with them much," he said. "Most of them are only active in

161

federal elections. Sometimes they get involved in big-state gubernatorial races, but until now they haven't bothered with Little Rhody."

"Are there any state rules they have to follow?"

"Well, yeah. Whenever they spend at least a thousand dollars advocating for a political candidate, they have to report that to us within seven days."

"What about money spent to advocate on a public issue?"

"If we're talking about a ballot initiative, they would have to comply with the same reporting requirement," he said. "But if they just launch a media campaign to advocate on an issue like sports gambling, they don't have to disclose their spending."

"Aw, crap," I said. "That's what I thought, but I wanted to make sure."

"Hey, Mulligan?"

"Yeah?"

"Off the record, I don't like it any more than you do."

Back in the newsroom, I wrote up the mall-guy story and then banged out a column of copy about the press conference, mentioning the super PAC high up and hinting that big out-of-state money would soon be flooding in to influence the legislative process.

An hour after I turned the copy in, Chuckie-boy called me into his office.

"Did you get the woman's phone number?" he asked.

"What woman?"

"The super PAC woman. What was it, again? Grandison?"

"No, I didn't."

"You should have."

"I don't see why," I said. "She wasn't that hot."

"Well, we need it. Our ad director wants to give her a call. The super PAC's probably got a huge advertising budget. Most of it will be spent on TV spots, but we want to get a piece."

"Oh."

"You should be alert to opportunities like this, Mulligan. Where do you think your paycheck comes from?"

"The tooth fairy?"

"Can the jokes and track her down for us."

"Can't advertising do that?"

"Just call the area hotels and find out where she's staying, okay?"

"What about the Chinese wall between news and advertising?" I said.

"Didn't you hear? We tore that sucker down."

17

After informing Chuckie-boy that Grandison was staying at the Omni, I needed beer to wash the bile from my throat. I figured it was going to take more than one.

Ten minutes later, I pushed through the door to Hopes and was greeted by heartbreak on the jukebox and dark the way alcoholics crave it. I waited by the entrance until my eyes adjusted, took one step forward, and froze.

Yolanda Mosley-Jones was sitting alone at the battered mahogany bar, her long legs curled around a rickety stool. She looked at once professional and sultry in gold hoop earrings, matching bangles on her right wrist, and a pearl-gray silk business suit that fit like it had been cut and stitched just for her. The shoulder-length, raven hair I remembered was gone now. In its place was a close-cropped Afro that looked great on her. I'd never seen Yolanda in Hopes before.

She looked as out of place as Mario Andretti in a Volkswagen Beetle.

Behind her, five off-duty firemen were drinking Budweiser and playing Texas Hold 'Em at the table by the pinball machine. One of them tossed his cards down, wet his index fingers with his tongue, and used them to smooth his unruly eyebrows. Then he slapped a grin on his face, strutted to the bar, and whispered something in Yolanda's ear. Never raising her eyes from her drink, she murmured two words, three at the most. His grin vanished, his shoulders slumped, and he slinked back to his buddies. I knew exactly how he felt.

I started to back out, but she spotted my reflection in the mirror behind the bar. She spun, lit me up with her high-beam smile, and beckoned me with red talons. I hesitated, then went to her on unsteady legs and claimed the adjoining bar stool. Without a word, I took the glass from her right hand, held it up to the light, and then took a small sip.

"This is a shot-and-a-beer kind of joint," I said. "Did you bring the martini in with you?"

"The barkeep had the fixins'," she said, "but I had to instruct him on how to mix it."

"Any good?"

"You tasted it."

"Yeah, but I wouldn't know the difference."

"It's not bad enough to toss out."

"So how have you been, Yolanda?"

"Good. You?"

"I'm doin' okay."

"I've missed you," she said.

"I've missed you, too."

"So why haven't you called?"

"You haven't called me either," I said, and
immediately wished I could retract it. I
sounded like a pouting high-schooler.

A couple of years ago, Yolanda and I had
spent time together, going on long walks
around the city, sharing drinks in a better
class of joint, taking in a couple of ball
games at Fenway, and once even grooving
to Buddy Guy in a Boston blues club. But
she'd insisted that going places together
didn't mean we were "goin' together." She'd
succumbed to my clumsy attempts at seduc-
tion by letting me hold her hand, but that
was as far as I got. I'd fallen hard for her
anyway.

The night she told me she was getting
serious about a Brown University chemistry
professor, she made me promise that we'd
always be friends. I assured her that we

would, but I knew we wouldn't. I was no good at not wanting more. I'd gone on a few dates since then, but after Yolanda, nobody else measured up.

Her martini glass was empty now, so she asked the barkeep for another. I still wanted the beer I'd come in for, but it wasn't going to be enough. I needed a shot of morphine, but Hopes didn't carry it, so I settled for a double shot of Bushmills and a Killian's back.

"I didn't mean for this to be awkward," she said.

"Sounds like you came in here looking for me."

"I thought I might find you here after work. You always were a creature of habit."

"Something on your mind?"

"A couple of things."

"Why don't you start with the easy one?"

"Okay. I know you've been covering the gambling bill, so thought you ought to know what I've been working on."

"You're still a partner at McDougall, Young, and Limone?"

"I am."

"Go on."

"We've been retained to prepare a federal lawsuit that will be filed if the governor's bill, or some version of it, gets passed. The

167

suit will seek to enjoin the state from permitting any form of sports gambling."

"Retained by whom?"

"A super PAC called Stop Sports Gambling Now. I understand you met its vice president, Cheryl Grandison, this afternoon."

"I had that pleasure."

"Miss Grandison instructed me to inform you that her organization is prepared to spend upwards of twenty million dollars on legal fees, lobbying, and media buys to defeat the governor's plan."

"Why didn't she tell me that herself?"

"For one thing, she prefers to remain in the background and has asked me to be the group's local media contact. For another thing, she took an immediate dislike to you."

"Imagine that," I said.

"She said you were rude."

"I prefer to think of it as persistent."

"She was quite upset that you took her photograph."

"Tough shit."

"So from now on," Yolanda said, "any questions you have for her should be directed to my office."

"I've got a few now."

"Okay."

"Twenty million is an astounding amount

of money for Rhode Island," I said. "It's more than double what all our candidates for governor, the U.S. Senate, and the U.S. House of Representatives spent in our last statewide election."

"I know."

"Why did Grandison want to telegraph this?"

"She didn't say, but I could speculate."

"Please do."

"I believe she hopes the figure will intimidate the bill's supporters."

"Do you know who's funding the super PAC?"

"I can't say," she said.

"Can't, or won't?"

"Won't."

"I'm betting it's the NCAA and the four major sports leagues," I said.

"Off the record?" she asked.

"How about not for attribution?"

Yolanda picked up her martini and drank, taking a moment to think it over.

"How would you phrase the attribution?" she asked.

"How would you like me to phrase it?"

"To a source familiar with the organization."

"Works for me," I said.

"In that case," she said, "your assumption

169

is correct except for one detail."

"What?"

"It's not four major sports leagues. It's five."

"Five? What am missing?"

"The MSL," she said.

"Huh?"

"Pro soccer."

I nodded and picked up my glass. Seeing her had unnerved me. I wanted to chug the whiskey down. Instead, I took half a minute to sip a third of it, hoping she'd feel compelled to fill the silence and reveal more of what she knew. Sometimes, like this time, that reporters' trick doesn't work.

"You know, Mulligan," she finally said, "things are going to get crazy around here."

"How do you mean?"

"If the anti-gambling side is going to spend this much, imagine what the pro-gambling side is going to spend."

"Sounds like our struggling economy is about to get an unhealthy injection of out-of-state funds," I said.

"*Un*healthy? You don't think this will be good for us?"

"It won't," I said. "Rich people who treat the state legislature as their private super-market are never a good thing. Besides, they won't spend all of their war chests on lawyers, lobbyists, and media buys. They'll tuck some of it into our lawmakers' pockets."

"You shouldn't be so cynical," she said.

"Yolanda, I know for a fact that it's already happening."

She didn't have anything to say to that.

"Of course, there are worse things than bribery," I said.

"Such as?"

"Soccer."

I picked up my glass and drained it.

"You said there were a couple of things on your mind," I said. "What's the other one?"

She circled a finger around the rim of her glass. "I thought maybe we could talk about us."

18

"Us?" I asked.

"Us."

"There's an *us*?"

She sighed. "I should have known you were going to make this difficult."

"I'm sorry, Yolanda. I'm just surprised by your choice of words."

She sipped from her glass and set it down on a cocktail napkin. Then she spun on her stool and looked into my eyes.

"Are you seeing anyone?" she asked.

"I was living with a slinky creature named Tuukka for a while, but that's over now. She died."

"Oh, my God! I'm so sorry."

"But last night, somebody new moved into my place."

"Oh. . . . Is she nice?"

"*He* drinks a six-pack a day and farts a lot, but he's good company. Oh, and did I mention that Tuukka was a garter snake?

Could have been a girl snake, but I'm not sure. Our relationship never got that far."

She lowered her head and closed her eyes. "You done with the jokes now?"

"I've been trying to cut down." My sense of humor wasn't helping matters, but it was the only shield I had.

"You've been on my mind a lot lately," she said, her voice almost a whisper.

"I have?"

"Yes."

"What about that Brown professor you shacked up with?"

"We never shacked up, Mulligan. Besides, that's history now."

"What happened?"

"He took up with one of his grad students."

"Oh. I'm sorry."

"No you're not."

"You're right. I'm not. I never liked him."

"You never met him."

"I didn't have to."

"You know what the worst part is?"

"What?"

"She's white."

"Damn. That must have pissed you off."

"Let's just say they better cross the street next time they see me coming."

"So is that why you're here now? To get

173

back at him by breaking your I-don't-fuck-white-guys rule?"

She turned her head away, snatched up her purse, and stood.

"Don't go, Yolanda. I'm sorry. I should never have said that."

"No, you shouldn't have."

And then she was gone.

19

"Jesus!" Joseph said. "Even for you, that was fuckin' stupid."

"It was."

"Couldn't of gone any worse if you hauled off and slugged her."

A former strip club bouncer wasn't the best source for relationship advice, but Joseph was the only one handy.

We were sitting on opposite ends of a blue-and-green striped sofa he'd found on the street, a six-pack of cold Narragansett and a Caserta Pizzeria pie between us on a wine-stained seat cushion. He'd furnished the place with a few other trash-day treasures — a battered maple rocker, a couple of wobbly mahogany end tables, and an old microwave that still worked. He'd also bought me a mattress for a few dollars at the Salvation Army and dragged it up the stairs. He'd hauled all the slashed and broken furniture out to the curb, mopped the kitchen floor, scrubbed the counters, and swept all three rooms. He'd placed my books back on the shelves, arranging them alphabetically by author. He'd even cleaned and restocked the refrigerator, although the only thing he'd stocked it *with* was cheap beer.

"By the way, thanks for doing all this, Joseph," I said. "You're going to make someone a fine wife someday."

"Fuck you, Mulligan," he said, but he was laughing when he said it. "So whaddaya gonna do about this broad?"

It took a second to realize who he was talking about. Yolanda was no broad.

"No idea."

"What's she look like?"

"Remember Marical?" I asked.

"The Haitian chick?"

"Uh-huh."

"Fuck, yeah," he said. "Great ass on her. Legs up to here. Skin so black it was almost blue. Always wore a pink thong with sequins. Never bothered with pasties."

"Like that," I said, "but taller. And with class."

"Damn! You want her back?"

"I think so."

"You're not sure?"

"I guess maybe I do, but —"

"But she ripped your heart out the last time, and you're afraid she's gonna do it again."

"Yeah," I said.

"She probably will, but I still think you gotta go for it."

"Why?"

"Ain't she worth it?"

"She is, but after tonight, I wouldn't know where to start."

Joseph rubbed his brow with a big paw, popped open a can of beer, and guzzled half of it.

"Maybe you could buy her somethin' romantic and send it to her," he said.

"Like what?"

"Shit, I dunno. Chocolates? Flowers? A box of ribbed condoms?"

I laughed at that, but Joseph didn't. I had to entertain the possibility that he wasn't kidding.

After two more beers, I decided I needed advice from a more genteel source. So fifteen minutes later, I was sitting in the wet grass at Swan Point Cemetery, running my fingers over an inscription cut into a marble slab. It was too dark to read, but I knew the words by heart.

ROSELLA ISABELLE MORELLI.
FIRST WOMAN BATTALION CHIEF OF THE
PROVIDENCE FIRE DEPARTMENT.
BELOVED DAUGHTER. FAITHFUL FRIEND.
TRUE HERO.
FEBRUARY 12, 1968–AUGUST 27, 2008.

I unfolded an autographed Manny Ramirez jersey and draped it over the shoulders of her gravestone, just as I did every time I visited. Manny had been Rosie's favorite Red Sox player, not because he could hit but because she thought he was, as she'd often put it, "smokin' hot."

Rosie and I had been best friends since we were six years old, and we'd always told each another almost everything. She'd died in a car crash before Ramirez got caught up in the steroids scandal, but I figured she didn't need to hear about that.

"I've spent two years trying to forget her, Rosie. And now she shows up out of the blue. . . . What does she want? I'm not sure. . . . No, I didn't ask.

"What do I want? Jesus, I don't know. . . . Okay, you're right. I do know. But she scares the hell out of me. I couldn't stand losing her a second time."

I don't how long I sat there with my arms wrapped around the headstone. When I finally headed home, it was with the same advice Rosie had given me the last time I thought I was in love: Buy her something pretty that she can wear against her skin.

At midnight, I sat at my kitchen table and scanned jewelry sites on the Internet while Joseph snored on the couch in the next room. Yolanda usually wore gold, but that was out of my price range. A sterling scales-of-justice pendant on a delicate silver chain seemed fitting for a lawyer. I arranged for it to be shipped to her with a terse message.

Forgive me.

20

"Mulligan?"

"Yeah?"

"I've got that airport surveillance video you wanted."

"Fantastic. I'm on my way."

"No need," McCracken said. "I'll walk over and drop it at your office."

Ten minutes later he stepped off the elevator, strode to my cubicle, and handed me a high-capacity portable hard drive.

"We've got video from the three cameras that cover the passenger pickup area," he said. "All seven days for the first week of March. My source wouldn't part with anything from inside the terminal. Something about not wanting to reveal internal security procedures."

"Jesus," I said. "It's going to take seven days just to scan through all this."

"No, it won't."

"How do you mean?"

"I checked the arrival times for flights originating in Atlantic City," he said, and handed me a slip of paper. "This should narrow it down."

"Good thinking," I said. "I should have thought of that."

"Yes, you should have."

"Have you looked at it?" I asked.

"No."

"Got time now?"

"I can spare an hour or two," he said, so we slipped into a vacant meeting room off the newsroom and attached the drive to a desktop computer.

The second March 3 flight from Atlantic City had touched down at quarter past eleven in the morning. Fifteen minutes later, one of the video cameras caught Lucan Alfano strolling out of the terminal doors dragging a small rolling suitcase with his left hand and clutching a black briefcase in his right. A wiry man in a Bruins sweatshirt got out of a waiting car, stepped behind it, and popped the trunk. Alfano tossed the bags inside. Then they got into the car and drove away.

"Bet there's a shitload of cash in that briefcase," McCracken said.

"No doubt."

I rewound the video, slowly rolled it

forward, and froze it just as the driver slammed the trunk lid down.

"Isn't that Mario Zerilli?" McCracken asked.

"Either him or his twin."

"I don't think he has a twin."

"He doesn't."

A theory was taking shape inside my head. Alfano had tried to bribe Phil Templeton and been turned down. Templeton subsequently had gone missing. Mario was violent, and he worked for Alfano. So maybe Mario had beaten Templeton, shot him, and dumped his body in the Blackstone. True, the little pistol Mario had threatened me with was a .22, and Templeton had been killed with a large-caliber handgun. But a thug like Mario probably had more than one firearm. Chances are, the murder weapon was lying in muck somewhere along the bottom of the river.

"I'll be damned," McCracken said. "What do you think this means?"

"Can't say for sure," I said. "But nothing good."

21

At eight o'clock sharp on Saturday morning, Coach Martin split the twenty remaining Vipers hopefuls into four five-man teams. Benton, the flashy but undersized point guard, and Krueger, the leaper with the brace on his knee, were on my team for the first thirty-minute scrimmage. Benton penetrated and dished often enough for me to nail four three-pointers with only one miss. But on defense, I had to guard Sears, the former All–Big East shooting guard. It was no contest. He blew by me for sixteen easy points, and we lost by twelve.

As we walked to the bench after time expired, Krueger bumped me so hard that he almost knocked me down.

"What the hell?"

"Play some fuckin' defense, grandpa," he said. "Keep up this shit and Sears is gonna get the spot that's s'posed to go to me."

"Yeah?" I said. "Maybe you could grab a

rebound once in a while, asshole."

During the second game, we sat on the bench and watched Keenan Jefferson, the kid who'd quit high school to marry his girlfriend, out-shoot, out-pass, and out-defend everyone on the court.

"Hey, Krueger," I said.

He looked down the bench and glared.

"If Martin keeps anybody, it won't be you," I said. "It'll be Jefferson."

"You think? Wait till I go up against him. I'll eat his lunch."

Late that morning, when the coaches pitted us against Jefferson's squad, that's not how it worked out. Fifteen minutes in, Krueger was visibly frustrated. When Jefferson flashed to the basket and dunked over him, the jerk fouled the kid hard, knocking him to the floor.

Jefferson sprang up, went nose to nose with Krueger, and snarled, "Do that again and you'll need a brace on your *other* damned knee."

Good for him.

First thing Monday morning, Chuckie-boy summoned me to his office.

"How you holding up, grandpa?" he asked.

"My knees are aching, and I've got a slight

strain in my left calf. Other than that, I guess I'm doin' okay."

"Good. The copy's great. It's generating a lot of chatter on our website."

"I saw."

"Readers are rooting for you and Jefferson to make the team, and they've got a big hate on for Sears and Krueger. Sears because he's a thief and Krueger because he's an asshole. Heroes and villains always make good copy."

"So I've heard."

"Vipers' management is loving it, too. Now that they've seen your first two stories, they've made good on their promise to buy a weekly quarter-page ad in the sports section once the season starts."

"You're telling me it's a quid pro quo?"

"Damn straight."

"I'm not comfortable with that," I said.

"Like I give a shit."

I was limping back to my desk when my cell phone rang.

"Mulligan?"

"Yeah?"

"It's Lebowski."

"Hey, Dude. What's up?"

"The M.E. finally ID'd the floater, and this one's a doozy."

"Don't keep me in suspense."

"It's a state legislator."

"Let me guess," I said.

"Shoot."

"Phil Templeton."

"How in hell did you know?"

"He's been missing for a few weeks," I said. "Who's running the investigation now, you or the Lincoln PD?"

"Neither. The staties are big-footing us."

"Captain Parisi?"

"You got that one right, too."

"State Police. Parisi speaking."

"Good afternoon, Captain. It's Mulligan."

"I know who you are. What is it this time?"

"Phil Templeton."

Five seconds of silence, and then, "Usual place in thirty minutes."

In less than that, we were parked nose-to-tail behind the Johnston City Hall, our driver's-side windows rolled down.

"What about Templeton?" he asked, not bothering with a hello.

"Turns out it was his corpse that got fished out of the Blackstone."

A five-second delay, and then, "The Providence cops think it was Mario Zerilli."

"But we both know it wasn't," I said. "You've got a high-profile murder case on

186

your hands again, Captain."

"Worst kind," he said.

"How do you mean?"

He glanced at me and blew out a long sigh. "Why should I tell you?"

"Hey, I'm just trying to make conversation."

Ten seconds. "Can we talk off the record?"

"Sure."

"Dunkin' Donuts on Killingly Street in five minutes." He cranked the ignition and took off.

A state police captain doesn't concern himself with speed limits, so he was already sitting in a corner booth when I walked in, his knife-scarred hands cradling an extra large. I picked up a medium regular at the counter and joined him. For a minute or two, neither of us spoke.

Parisi and I had worked different sides of the street on a lot of the same cases over the years, and I'd developed a profound respect for him. If the feeling was mutual, he'd never let on. But a few years ago, when we were both investigating a child pornography ring, we'd nearly had a moment.

The case was so ugly that it tore at our souls. One evening, after we'd both stumbled on a cache of online snuff films, we sat across a table from each other at

Hopes. Taking turns buying each other shots of whiskey, we made a feeble stab at talking things out; but neither of us could find the words. That night, I thought there was a chance we might become friends, but Parisi wasn't the type to let anyone get close.

As I looked at him now, I sensed another moment coming on.

"Jesus, Mulligan. I hate cases like this."

"Why's that?"

"You know how it goes. The governor's office calling the state police superintendent for updates every day. Him all over my ass for results. Assholes with TV cameras trailing me around. Reporters shouting their dumb-ass questions."

"Some cops love the spotlight."

"I'm sure as hell not one of them. I was hoping I could avoid another freak show before I put in for retirement, but I guess I should have known better."

"When are you planning on leaving?"

He gave me a hard stare.

"Sorry. None of my business," I said, and he softened a little.

"Some days, I'm just so tired of it all. I got another year left in me, I think. Two at the most."

"What will you do?"

"June and I have been talking about selling the house in Coventry and buying a cottage on the Maine coast. Get ourselves a couple of Labrador retrievers, some fishing gear, maybe a little sailboat."

"Sounds nice."

"What about you?"

"Me? I'm only forty-four."

"Yeah, but there's no future in what you're doing. I hear your buddy McCracken wants to take you on. You've got the stuff to be a decent P.I., Mulligan. You ought to jump at it."

"I'm thinking it over."

"As P.I.'s go, McCracken's okay," Parisi said. "He's the one who sent Templeton to me."

"I heard."

"What else have you heard?"

"Hold on. I'm the reporter here. This is supposed to work the other way around."

"Humor me."

This time, I was the one who needed the ten-second delay.

"A few days ago," I said, "the Lincoln cops responded to a tip that Templeton's house had been broken into. They found the front door jimmied and signs of a struggle. Sometime today, the ME identified his body. He'd been beaten and then shot through the neck with a large-caliber slug."

"That all you got?"

"I know Lucan Alfano tried to bribe Templeton. I know Templeton refused the money. And I know Alfano warned him that things would go badly for him if he didn't cooperate."

Five seconds, and then, "Alfano couldn't have done it. He got dead before Templeton went into the river."

"Somebody working with Alfano could have done it," I said.

"Hell, Mulligan. *Anybody* could have done it." Five seconds. "But it's a plausible theory."

"Do you have a suspect?" I asked.

"If I do, I'm sure as shit not telling you."

"I bet you don't."

"Are we done?"

"One more thing," I said.

"Yeah?"

"Have you looked at the Green Airport surveillance video for March 3?"

Ten seconds this time. "Why would I want to do that?"

"To see who picked Alfano up at the airport that day when he arrived on a late-morning flight from Atlantic City."

Five seconds. "You've seen this video?"

"I have."

"How the hell did you manage that?"

"By asking nicely."

"Gonna tell me who's on it?"

"No," I said. "It's something you should see for yourself."

22

"That new profession you've been nudging Mario into? It's strong-arm work, isn't it?"

"What?" Whoosh said. "Where'd you get that idea?"

"I can't say."

It was early Tuesday evening, and we were sitting in Whoosh's office at the back of the convenience store, him in his swivel chair and me on a corner of his keyhole desk. This time, not even a Beggin' Strip could lure Shortstop's rump out of the visitor's chair.

"This ain't something I can talk about, Mulligan."

"No?" I said. "Then let's try it this way. You know this guy?"

He took the cell phone from my hand and studied the photo.

"No," he said. "Who is he?"

"Lucan Alfano."

He looked at the photo again.

"*That's* Alfano? He looks sorta like Paulie

192

Walnuts."

"So you've heard of him, then," I said.

"Fuck, yeah. Everybody in my line of business had *heard* of him."

"Talk to him lately?"

"Of course not. He's dead."

"But you talked to him sometime in late winter, didn't you?"

Whoosh slipped a deck out of his shirt pocket, shook out a Lucky, and set fire to it with a cheap disposable lighter.

"That bet you made against the Celtics?" he said. "It's startin' to look like it's gonna pay off."

"Here's what I think happened," I said. "Alfano needed muscle for a job in Rhode Island. He called up here looking for a name, and somebody suggested Mario. If Alfano had reached out to Arena or Grasso, they would have steered him to someone more reliable. Dickie Theresa, maybe, or one of the Sirica brothers."

"So?"

"So the way I see it, Alfano must have reached out to you."

Whoosh chose to ignore that.

"The Bruins are one-to-four to make it to the Stanley Cup round," he said, "and you ain't laid down a bet yet."

"I like their chances," I said. "Put me

down for a nickel."

"You got it."

"Here's what I don't get," I said. "You're against legalizing sports betting, but Alfano was for it."

"Where'd you hear that?"

"From a bunch of state legislators he tried to bribe."

"Huh."

"Why would you and Mario want to help somebody who was working against you?"

"If he was, it's news to me," Whoosh said. "What was his angle?"

"Apparently, he was working for Atlantic City gambling interests who want to swoop in after legalization and run the show."

"The governor wants the Lottery Commission to take the bets."

"Yeah," I said, "but Alfano was trying to get the bill held up until she agreed to privatization."

"No shit?"

"No shit."

"Okay, I'll take your word for it. But what's this got to do with Mario?"

"Alfano's bribe offers came with a warning," I said. "He told the legislators things would go badly for them if they didn't play ball. I think the badly part was Mario."

Whoosh stubbed out his cigarette and

started another, taking the time to consider how much he was willing to tell me.

"Can we talk hyper— What's that fuckin' word?"

"Hypothetically?" I said.

"Yeah."

"Go on."

"Let's say Alfano did call me. He woulda been careful not to let on what he wanted muscle for, and I woulda been smart enough not to fuckin' ask. And if he decided somebody needed to be tuned up, he never woulda told Mario why. He woulda just given him a name."

"Okay," I said. "I get that."

"We done?"

"Not yet. Whoever sent Alfano must have sent somebody else by now. Any idea who?"

"Uh-uh."

"Haven't gotten any more calls from Jersey?"

"No."

"You heard Phil Templeton got shot, right?" I asked.

"Yeah."

"He's one of the guys Alfano tried to bribe," I said, "but he didn't take the money. He called the state police instead."

"So?"

"I think that's why Mario shot him."

"Aw, Christ. You sure it was Mario?"

"I can't prove it," I said, "but it's more than a hunch."

"The cops are looking at him for this?"

"I'm not sure if they're on to him yet," I said, "but they will be. There's surveillance video of him picking Alfano up at the airport."

"Shit. Is there anything solid connecting the kid to the shooting?"

"I don't think so," I said. "They don't know where Templeton was killed, and they don't have the murder weapon. The shot was a through-and-through, so they don't have the slug either. Looks like Templeton was grabbed at his house, but according to the Lincoln cops, none of the neighbors saw anything."

"No prints?"

"None that point to the killer. At least that's what my sources are telling me."

"Okay then," he said. "Thanks for the heads-up."

With that, he pulled himself to his feet, shuffled into his storeroom, and returned with a box of Cubans for me.

"Think you could give me a hand with somethin'?" he asked.

"And what would that be?"

"I got no clue what odds to offer on the

Vipers' tryouts."

"People want to bet on *that*?"

"Hell, Mulligan. People bet on every fuckin' thing. You know that. Besides, them stories you been writin' have stirred up a lot of interest."

"Huh."

"Thing is, I don't know whether any of the former college players have stayed in shape. And I got no feel at all for the playground guys."

"You want *me* to figure the odds?"

"Be good practice for you."

"In case I end up taking over."

"Yeah."

"Okay. Give me a second."

"Take your time, and get it right."

"At first, I figured the tryouts were just a publicity stunt."

"But now you think they ain't?"

"Coach Martin seems to be taking it seriously," I said. "And a few of the players look pretty good. Do you know if the Vipers actually have a roster vacancy?"

"When the tryouts started, they had one open spot," Whoosh said. "But from what I hear, Cartwright, the kid from Kent State who's under contract with the Pistons, needs shoulder surgery and is gonna miss at least half the season."

"Two spots, then?"

"Yeah."

"Okay," I said. "I'd make it even money that none of these guys make it."

"With two spots open?"

"Right. There are still a lot of unsigned free agents out there, Whoosh."

"Okay."

"Of the ten players still left in the tryouts, I'd make Jefferson the favorite at two to one. I'd put Benton at four to one, Sears at six to one, and Krueger at ten to one. The rest of the guys have no shot, but I'd put them down at fifteen to one to generate some action."

"What about you?"

"Me?"

"Yeah. I got a bunch of people wanting to lay down a few bucks on you making the team."

"You've got to be shitting me."

"Most of them are broads, Mulligan. You know the type. Gals who decide what horse to bet on based on how pretty they look. I'll put you down at twenty to one. Since you got no shot, that'll make me some easy money."

"Okay."

"Want a piece of the action?"

"Probably shouldn't."

"Why the hell not?"

"I'd hate to have anybody think I was doing something shady to influence the outcome."

"Like playing matador defense against a guy you bet on?"

"That or breaking somebody's arm."

"Nobody but me will know you placed a bet."

"Okay. Give me a nickel each on Benton and Jefferson."

"Done."

"About you taking over?" he said.

"Yeah?"

"Best we wait to see how this legalization thing shakes out."

"Understood."

"And Mulligan?"

"Um?"

"I want you to know I didn't see none of this shit about Mario comin'."

"No?"

"If Alfano reached out to me, and I still ain't sayin' he did, he never mentioned anything about killin'. No way I woulda involved the kid in anything that heavy."

"Maybe Alfano lied to you," I said.

"Coulda, I guess."

"Or maybe Mario was just supposed to rough Templeton up but couldn't control his rage."

"*Rage?* It was just a job."

"Templeton was gay," I said.

"A homo? You fuckin' sure?"

"I am."

"Aw, fuck."

On the drive home, I figured I should tell Joseph to put a few bucks on Jefferson. Then I remembered that he didn't have any money.

23

It wasn't quite nine P.M. when I parked Secretariat on Washington Street outside Hopes, shoved through the door, and found Yolanda perched on that same bar stool.

She was dressed in a mint-green business suit with no blouse visible beneath the jacket, and black high heels she didn't need to make those legs look great. She wasn't wearing any gold tonight. Instead, a sterling pendant dangled from a silver chain and fell between the swell of her breasts. Two empty stemmed glasses rested on the bar in front of her. Yolanda was a sipper. She must have been waiting for a long time.

As I took the stool next to her, she caressed the pendant with the fingers of her left hand and fixed her eyes on me.

"This was sweet," she said.

"But did it work?"

"Let's not get ahead of ourselves."

"It was Rosie's idea," I said.

"You still talk to her?"

"All the time."

"Does it ever worry you that she talks back?"

Oh-oh. How could I make the woman I wanted a relationship with understand my relationship with a dead woman? Buying time to find the words, I waved the bartender over and ordered another martini for Yolanda and a Killian's for me.

"Better make mine a club soda," Yolanda said. "Martinis are like breasts. One is too few, but three is too many."

"I disagree."

"Oh, yeah?"

"There can never be too many breasts — as long as they come in even numbers."

"Mulligan, you're such a boy."

"Um."

"So can we get back to Rosie?"

"Sure. The way it works is, I talk and Rosie listens."

"What do you talk about?"

"I tell her what's going on in my life. I ask for her advice."

"And she gives it?"

"We knew each other so well, Yolanda. I can always sense her answer."

"But do you actually hear her voice?"

"Not the way the Son of Sam killer heard

a demon whisper orders in his ear. I mean, it's not like I'm psychotic. But whenever I need her, she's there. In fact, she's with me now."

Yolanda leaned back to look at the empty stool on the other side of me. "She's keeping a pretty low profile. What's she saying?"

"She's warning me not to say anything stupid."

"Too bad she didn't tell you that the last time."

"Maybe she did. Koko Taylor's wailing from the jukebox probably drowned her out. That's another woman who speaks to me from the grave."

"You really remember what was playing on the jukebox? Or did you just make that up?"

"Yolanda, I remember everything that happens when we're together."

"Smooth line, white boy. Ever use that one before?"

"Never. I swear. You're the only Yolanda I know." My nerves were bringing Mulligan the smartass to the surface again.

She sipped, smiled slightly, and stared at me over the rim of her glass.

"You look hungry," she said.

I was sure I did.

She laughed then. "For food, I mean. Eat yet?"

"Not since breakfast."

"Me either. I'm famished."

I tossed some bills on the bar, and we strolled to the Trinity Brewhouse, our hands tangling. We took a table by the mullioned windows that look out on the Providence Public Library.

Over drinks, hers another club soda and mine a Pickman's Pale Ale, we talked about work until the food arrived. The calamari appetizer and a Cobb salad wrapped in a tortilla for her. The nachos appetizer and cowboy burger for me. Yolanda reached across the table, plucked a gooey nacho with her fingers, and popped it between those lips I longed to kiss. She'd always helped herself to my plate whenever we dined together.

"Mulligan?"

"Um?"

"Did I ever tell you about my parents?"

"No, you never did."

"They met in a Chicago candy factory where they both worked the line. Mama always smelled like sugar. Daddy smelled like sugar and cigarettes."

"How sweet," I said.

"Please. No more jokes tonight."

"I'll try."

"They'd moved up north in the early sixties, Mama from Mississippi and Daddy from East Texas. They must have had it rough down there because I could never get them to talk about it. Daddy's gone now, and my mama still won't talk."

"Probably didn't have it all that easy up north either," I said.

"They found steady work, but we never did have much. Clothes somebody else wore first, furniture handed down by church folk, and an apartment on the second floor of a walk-up on the West Side. Every damned day, we had to fight the roaches for it."

That sounded like the way I was living now, but I knew enough to keep my mouth shut.

"The city was split into black and white back then. Still pretty much is, I guess. The only white folks I knew growing up were the teachers at the for-shit public schools I attended. White cops were on patrol, but they never got out of their cars unless they were looking to shoot somebody. To get to my elementary school, I had to cross West Madison, which hadn't been rebuilt since a twenty-eight-block stretch was looted and burned ten years before I was born."

"On the night of the King assassination," I said.

"That's right. My folks never talked much about that either."

She paused to nibble at her Cobb salad and perhaps to consider how much more of her past to share with me.

"For my first eighteen years, white folks were a mystery to me," she said. "I'd decided not to trust them. I didn't have any white friends at all till I got to Illinois State."

"Your parents must have given up a lot to pay for that."

"They did what they could, but I still had to take out twenty-five grand in college loans."

She stopped talking again and toyed with her food.

"I'd like to hear more," I said. "I want to know it all. But I can't help wondering why you're telling me this now."

"I'm getting to that," she said. "At college, the black kids mostly kept to themselves. Hardly anyone dated outside of that circle. The few white boys who did ask black girls out mostly treated them like whores."

"Did that happen to you?"

"No. But to a couple of my friends."

"That's why you vowed not to date white guys?"

"It was more than that. Interracial dating wasn't just rare back then. A black guy risked his life just being *seen* with a white girl. In some places that's still a sin. But black girls were expected to stick to their own kind, too. Sisters who dared to date white boys were either pitied or scorned. Older black folks, especially, thought they were letting themselves be used and saw them as traitors to their race."

"Times have changed, Yolanda."

"Maybe that's true," she said. "But time changes slower for some folks. A lot of older black people, like my mama, still think stirring the pot is a mistake."

She paused for a moment to sip from her drink.

"These days, some black women seek out white men out of desperation," she said. "With so many brothers behind bars, it's a numbers game. But mostly, most young people don't think about race as a barrier anymore. Somebody looks good, they go for it."

"But not you," I said.

"No," she said. "I'm not *that* young. It's taken me a long time to even *think* about letting my guard down."

"And now?"

"Like I said, I've been thinking a lot about

207

you lately."

"Why me? You're a goddess, Yolanda. You can have anybody you want."

"Baby," she said, "didn't Rosie tell you not to say anything stupid?"

Our entrees had barely been touched, and they were getting cold. I picked up my burger and took a few bites. She nibbled again at her Cobb salad. When the waitress returned, we declined coffee and dessert. I reached for the check. Yolanda beat me to it and fished an AmEx card out of her purse.

"Don't let male pride get in the way," she said. "I make way more money than you."

We finished our drinks. Then I took her by the hand and led her outside. Empire Street was nearly deserted. She turned to face me, and I wrapped my arms around her. She draped her arms around my neck and pulled me closer. Then she tilted her head the way women do when they want to be kissed.

"So then what happened?" Joseph asked.

"I said, 'Your place or mine?' "

"You were gonna bring her *here*?"

I looked around at the salvaged furniture, the ravaged pizza boxes, the crushed beer cans, and Joseph sprawled on the couch where he'd been sleeping in his boxer shorts for a week. The couch had started to smell like Joseph.

"I guess her place would have been better."

"And what did she say?"

"She said, 'Let's not rush things, baby.' "

"Aw, fuck. Well, at least she called you baby."

"She calls the mailman baby."

"So when you gonna see her again?"

"Lunch tomorrow."

"Lunch? Sheee-it. Not much bangin' goes on at noon. But I guess it's better than nothin'."

But that's not the way it worked out.

24

"We found the Colt forty-five you reported stolen," Wargart said.

"Where?"

"We think you know where," Freitas said.

"I don't."

"Oh, no?" she said. "Get up. You're coming with us."

"Sorry, I said, but I have a prior engagement."

"Get out of that chair, or I'll drag you up," Wargart said. "You're under arrest."

He ordered me to empty my pockets and toss everything on my desk. Then he pulled my arms back, snapped the handcuffs on tight, patted me down, and read me my rights. Chuckie-boy came out of his office and watched openmouthed as they led me out. He didn't ask what was going on. He didn't ask if he should call a lawyer. He didn't say a word.

At the station, they shoved me into an

interrogation room, removed the cuffs, and forced me into a metal chair that was bolted to the floor. Then they cuffed my hands in front, left the room, and let me stew for more than an hour.

The acoustic ceiling tiles looked to be twelve inches square. There were eight of them running along the wall to my left and twelve along the wall in front of me. If my math was correct, that meant the room was ninety-six square feet in size. It also meant that ceiling was covered with exactly ninety-six tiles. I counted them anyway. Yup. Ninety-six. Then I counted them again. The distance from floor to ceiling looked to be the standard eight feet, which meant the room had a volume of seven hundred and sixty-eight cubic feet. The scuffed and gritty floor tiles were the same size as the ceiling tiles. That meant there had to be ninety-six of those, too, but I still counted them. Three times. Then I counted the coffee cup rings on the heavy oak interrogation-room table. There were sixteen. It was something to do.

When Wargart and Freitas returned, they brought a video camera on a tripod and three paper cups filled with black coffee. They pulled up chairs across from me, sat down, pried the lids off the coffees, and plunked one of them down in front of my face.

"Be easier to drink this if you take the cuffs off," I said.

"Not gonna happen," Wargart said.

"Wow. I'm considered an escape risk? That's quite the honor."

I grasped the cup with both hands and drank. The coffee wasn't bad, but it wasn't the lunch, or the lunch company, I'd been planning on. I pictured Yolanda waiting, wondering why I'd stood her up.

Freitas recited Miranda again for the benefit of the video camera. I waived my right to a lawyer. I wanted to hear their questions. I figured it was the best way to find out what the hell was going on.

"How well do you know Frances Mirabelli?" Freitas asked.

"Never heard of him."

"It's a she," Wargart said. "But of course, you knew that."

"No, I didn't."

"She knows you," Freitas said.

"Oh, yeah?"

"She says you've been sniffing around her place for a couple of weeks. Claims you've been trying to pork her."

I couldn't help laughing. "Pork? Nobody says pork any more unless they're ordering barbecue."

"Let me rephrase," Freitas said. "She says you've been coming around trying to *bang* her."

"Is she hot?" I asked.

"If you like 'em doe-eyed and stacked," Wargart said.

"Then it does sound like the sort of thing I might do."

"So you admit it," Freitas said.

"Admit what? Did our state legislature outlaw the horizontal bop when I wasn't looking?"

"God, I hope not," Freitas said, "but the law does take a dim view of this."

She slid a photograph out of a manila file folder and placed it on the table.

"Jesus! Is she saying I did this to her?"

"Signed a sworn statement to that effect," Wargart said.

"It's not true," I said. "I've never seen this woman before. Besides, I have a strict policy against sleeping with anyone named Frances. Got the same issue with Leslie, Dana, Casey, Jackie, Hilary, and Leigh. Too much potential for gender confusion."

"You're a liar," Freitas said.

"Okay," I said. "Now I understand why I got dragged in here. But why you two? Why are the homicide twins wasting time on a

213

routine assault case?"

"Homicide twins?" Freitas said.

"S'what people are calling us," Wargart said.

"Really?" she said. "I hadn't heard that."

"Yeah," Wargart said. "I kinda like it."

"You haven't answered my question," I said.

"This is part of an ongoing murder investigation," Wargart said.

I looked at the photo on the table again.

"Murder? The girl took an awful beating, but she doesn't look dead."

"She's not," Wargart said.

"So who is?"

"Her boyfriend," Freitas said. "Is that why you killed him? So you could get in his girlfriend's pants?"

"Who's her boyfriend?"

"Mario Zerilli," Wargart said.

"Mario? I'd never put my dick anyplace his has been. Wouldn't even want to use the same urinal, for chrissake. Besides, in case it's slipped your mind, he's not dead either."

"Oh, no?" Wargart said.

"The corpse they pulled out of the Blackstone was somebody else," I said.

"True," Wargart said. "But that doesn't mean Mario's still sucking air. Nobody's seen him in weeks."

I looked up at the ceiling for a moment and thought things over.

"I gather all this has something to do with my gun," I said.

"It does," Wargart said.

"Where'd you recover it?"

"In Frances Mirabelli's apartment," he said.

"Huh," I said. "Mario must have left it there after he trashed my place."

"That's not how she tells it," Freitas said. "She says you had it with you when you kicked down her door. It fell out of your waistband when you were knocking her around, and she managed to grab it. She pointed it at you, and you bolted out the door."

"And you want to hear the best part?" Wargart said.

"You mean it gets better?" I said.

"We ran the ballistics," he said. "Turns out it's the same gun you used to shoot Phil Templeton."

I couldn't help myself. I laughed out loud.

"I'm confused," I said. "Who is it I killed again? Phil Templeton or Mario Zerilli?"

"We're thinking both," Freitas said.

"I already told you," I said. "The gun was stolen."

"You reported it stolen after Templeton

was killed," Wargart said.

"True," I said.

"So even if we believed your bullshit story, which we don't," Freitas said, "you could have used it on him."

"Why would I kill Templeton? Did I want to bang his girlfriend, too? Oh, wait. That can't be it. Templeton was gay."

"You shot him because he was a key supporter of the governor's gambling bill," Wargart said.

"Why would I care about that?" I asked.

"Because you're scheming to take over Dominic Zerilli's bookmaking business," Freitas said.

"*What?* Where the hell did you get that?"

I figured they weren't going to tell me, and they didn't. It must have been something else they got from Mario's girlfriend.

"We hear Mario was mad as hell about it," Freitas said. "We think that's why you killed him, too."

"Wait a minute," I said. "You're losing me again. I thought I killed Mario because I wanted to hump his girlfriend."

"Two motives are better than one," Wargart said.

I tried to come up with a snappy riposte, but nothing came to me, so I picked up the

216

paper cup and swallowed the last of my coffee.

"Where were you when Templeton was shot?" Freitas asked.

"No idea."

"And why is that?" she asked.

"Because I don't know when he was shot," I said. "Nobody does. Nobody knows what he was shot *with* either. No way you linked my gun to it. That's bullshit."

"What makes you say that?" Wargart asked.

"Because the slug was never found."

"Where'd you hear that?"

"I'm a reporter," I said. "I hear all kinds of stuff."

I picked up the photo with my cuffed hands and took a closer look at Frances Mirabelli's split lip and blackened eyes.

"Poor thing," I said. "You know Mario's been abusing her for years, right? He even did six months in the state pen for it. This time, he must have told her to blame it on me."

"Why would he do that?" Wargart said.

"You'd have to ask him."

"Dead men don't talk," Freitas said.

I placed the photo back on the table.

"Look, when does she say this happened?" I asked.

"Last night," Wargart said.

"What time?"

"You got to her apartment at nine thirty and left about ten minutes later."

I rattled off a ten-digit number.

"What's that supposed to be?" Freitas asked.

"My alibi," I said. "And when you call it, please tell attorney Yolanda Mosley-Jones I'm very sorry I had to miss our lunch date today. I was unavoidably detained."

25

"Lunch would have been nice," I said, "but dinner is better."

"Why is that?" Yolonda asked.

"Because we've got the whole night ahead of us."

She didn't respond to that. Instead, she picked up her fork and went to work on her lobster and crab cakes. I shoveled in a forkful of the wagyu beef with wasabi arugula. The Capital Grille, located in the city's renovated old Union Station, was Yolanda's kind of place. She'd chosen a bottle of La Crema Pinot Noir from the wine list. They didn't carry Killian's, so I settled for Samuel Adams Summer Ale that was served in a tall glass instead of the bottle I preferred.

When she finally spoke, she changed the subject.

"You should have called me, baby. It's not smart to talk to homicide without a lawyer present."

"I don't like lawyers, present company excepted," I said. "Besides, if I asked for one, the interrogation would have ended, and I wouldn't have learned anything."

"And you learned what?"

"That Mario Zerilli tried to frame me. He stole my gun, planted it in his girlfriend's apartment to place me there, beat her up, and got her to lie to the cops."

"What's he got against you?" she asked.

I took out my wallet, removed a five-dollar bill, and slid it across the table.

"What's this?" she asked.

"A retainer. We are now covered by attorney-client privilege."

"It's like that?" she said.

"It is," I said, and then told her about Whoosh's offer.

"Don't tell me you're seriously considering this," she said.

"Not exactly."

"What does that mean?"

"When I get it worked out, I'll let you know."

"It sounds like Mario isn't the only one out to get you," she said. "Wargart and Freitas seem to have it in for you, too."

"They do. They've been eager to pin something on me for a couple of years now."

"Why?"

"I've written a lot of unflattering stuff about the Providence PD over the years. The homicide twins always seem to take it personally."

"Let me help," she said.

"How?"

"I can get a restraining order against Mario. Might be able to get one against the Providence PD, too."

"Thanks," I said, "but no thanks."

"Why not?"

"I don't want them to go away," I said. "Every time they show up, there's a chance I might learn something."

Later, as we sipped our coffee and shared a slice of coconut cream pie, Yolanda turned the conversation back to us.

"Ever dated a black woman before?"

"Uh-huh."

"Tell me."

"A few years ago, I was seeing a devastatingly beautiful black lawyer, but she dumped me for a Brown chemistry professor. Oh, and I had a few dates with a Jamaican girl when I was in college."

"Did you sleep with her?"

"The Jamaican girl? Yeah. The lawyer? Not yet, but I haven't given up hope."

"You're not one of those white guys who's obsessed with the sisters, are you?"

"Just with one of them."

"Serious question."

"I gave you a serious answer."

"Maybe," she said, "but I think it requires elaboration."

I leaned forward, right into those big, dark eyes.

"You love baseball. You know your way around the blues. When you're not reading, you're talking about something you've read. You're smart and tough and one of the best there is at what you do. You always do the right thing, even when it's difficult. When we talk, there's an intimacy I don't feel with anyone else. And I love the bluesy sound of your voice. It's got smoke in it."

"That's sweet," she said, "but I wonder if there's more to it."

"A lot more," I said. "You're fuckin' gorgeous. Those incredible legs. The curve of your neck. The way your skin shimmers even in this low light. Yes, I love it that you're black, if that's what you're getting at."

"It is," she said.

"And you want to know why."

"I do."

This was treacherous territory. Taking my cue from Captain Parisi, I took five seconds to frame my response.

"Having things in common is important," I said. "Most guys think that, and good looks, are the only things that matter. They want a woman who likes the same kind of music, roots for the same team, eats the same kind of food, worships in the same church. Not me. I prefer women who are different from me in at least a few important ways."

"Why?"

"The differences are what make life interesting," I said. "When I'm with you, I see the world through fresh eyes. I can't tell you how much I treasure that. I could learn something new from you every day of my life."

She smiled, reached across the table, and took my hand. "Baby, you're getting way ahead of yourself."

Yolanda picked up the check again, and we strolled to her car. I opened the door for her and walked around to the other side. She hesitated, then unlocked the passenger door and let me in. I pulled her close for a kiss. And then another. It was ten minutes before we came up for air.

"My place is a mess," I said, "and I've still got that roommate."

"Go home," she said, "and tell him you didn't score tonight. Or lie to him if you want. I don't mind."

"Aw, hell."

"But, baby?"

"Um?"

"You've given me a lot more to think about."

26

When I got home, the first thing I noticed was that Joseph had scrounged an old oak bookcase from somewhere. In it, he'd shelved the set of leather-bound Dickens novels he'd inherited from his mother. They were charred around the edges and still smelled faintly of smoke from the arson that had taken her house.

When I first got to know Joseph, I was astonished that a lug who had trouble piecing words together to make grammatical sentences was reading his way through the master's works. Tonight, he was stretched out on the couch, drinking from a can of Narragansett and reading the new Woodrow Wilson biography I'd picked up free at *The Dispatch*. The paper didn't run book reviews anymore, but publishers who hadn't figured that out yet were still shipping us copies.

"Any good?" I asked.

"Ain't sure yet," he said. "I'm only on

page five. I plowed through a coupla your Elmore Leonard novels this afternoon. There's another guy what can fuckin' write."

"Good as Dickens?" I asked.

"Oh, yeah," he said, "but different. Never uses two words when he can get by with one. And the best dialogue ever. That fuckin' guy knows how real people talk."

"I thought you were going to look for a job today."

"I was out lookin' all mornin'."

"No luck?"

"You know how it is."

"Don't give up, Joseph," I said.

"I won't. So how'd it go with the babe?"

"Good, I think."

"Then why you home so fuckin' early?"

"Not that good," I said.

"Gonna see her again?"

"I think so, yeah."

"Well, at least that's somethin'."

"It is."

"So listen. There was some trouble here when you was gone."

"What kind of trouble?"

"Had a problem with a guy," he said.

"The landlord?"

"Nah. Some other guy."

"Tell me."

"I heard someone messin' around outside

the door, so I yanked it open, and there was this tall, skinny dude with a crowbar in his hand."

"What did you do?"

"Took it away from him."

"And then?"

"I asked him what the hell he was doin', and the dumb fuck took a swing at me."

"Did it land?"

"Not so you'd notice. He hits like a fuckin' girl."

"Then what?"

"I picked him up and threw him down the stairs."

"Hurt him bad?"

"Not so bad he couldn't pull himself up and limp away. Bounced all the way down on his ass, though, so he's gonna be sore for a few days."

"Why didn't you tell me this when I first came in?"

"You started talkin' about books and I got dis— . . ."

"Distracted?"

"Yeah."

"Did you recognize him?"

"Uh-huh. He was a regular at the Tongue and Groove back when I was workin' there. Looked kinda young, so I always carded him. First name began with an *M,* I think.

Marco, maybe. Or Mario. Yeah, I think that was it. Mario somethin'. Pretty sure the last name was Italian."

"Mario Zerilli?"

"Sounds right," he said. "He the same asshole who trashed the apartment?"

"I think so. He's dangerous, Joseph. You're lucky he didn't pull a piece on you. If he comes back, you should call the cops."

"Nah. I've taken guns away from way tougher guys than him. If the fucker comes back for another beatin', which I doubt he's gonna, I can handle it."

"I'm sure you can," I said, "but don't take any foolish chances."

27

"What the hell was that about yesterday?"
Twisdale asked.

"A misunderstanding," I said.

"That was the second time police came in
here looking for you."

"The second you know of."

"You mean there were more?"

"Not lately, but yeah."

"I don't like cops barging into my newsroom, Mulligan."

"So why didn't you do something about
it, Chuckie?"

"Like what?"

"Call a lawyer for me."

"Why would I do that?"

I hadn't wanted a lawyer, but that wasn't
the point.

"When a reporter is arrested," I said, "his
editor is supposed to call the company
lawyers in to represent him."

"Our attorneys have more important

things to do than bail you out of trouble, Mulligan. Get yourself arrested, and you're on your own."

"Good to know," I said. I snatched the Purell bottle from his desk, squirted some into my palm, and stomped out.

"Hey!" he shouted. "We're not done."

I turned back and slouched against his doorframe.

"What?"

"That anti-gambling super PAC, Stop Sports Gambling Now, placed a full-page ad in the sports section today."

"I saw."

"They're planning to run it daily for at least a couple of weeks."

"Great," I said. "Maybe now you can afford to give me a raise."

"Not happening."

"Of course not. What was I thinking?"

"Did you watch any TV last night?" he asked.

"No."

"You should have."

"Why? Did I miss you on *Dancing with the Stars*?"

"Several organizations, some for and some opposed, started running ads about the gambling bill on the local broadcast stations," he said. "Cable and satellite TV, too."

"I don't have cable or satellite."

"Why not?"

"You don't pay me enough."

"I got Time Warner," he said, "but I asked around. Turns out they were on Xfinity, Dish, and Cox, too."

"So?"

"So they're running all day long. Pretty slick, too. Celebrities, high production values, the whole ball of wax."

"Can I go now?"

"I need you to monitor the TV for a few hours this morning. Jot down the names of the groups paying for commercials and see if you can find phone numbers the ad department can call."

"That's not my job."

"Your job is whatever I say it is."

It was ten A.M. when I stepped into Hopes and watched the day bartender lug a crate of Budweiser out of the storage room. He clanked it on the bar, tore it open, and shoved the longnecks into an ice chest. Besides me, he was the only one in the place.

"A little early for you, isn't it?" he asked.

"It is."

"We're not really open yet."

"That's okay. I'm not here to drink. Just

231

need a place to hang out for a while."

"Oh. I've got a pot of coffee going. Can I get you a cup?"

"Thanks, Craig. That would be great. And if you don't mind, could you turn on the TV and let me have the remote?"

I started with the local broadcast affiliates, then ran through ESPN, CNN, MSNBC, Fox News, MTV, Comedy Central, Lifetime, Animal Planet, the Food Channel. Even the Cartoon Network. Cable channels set aside only two or three minutes per hour for local commercials; but in less than two hours, I caught the same three sports gambling commercials a dozen times — even though I lingered over *SportsCenter* for twenty minutes.

One spot featured apocalyptic warnings about the evils of sports gambling, the sort of mournful music you hear on commercials about abused animals, and New England sports heroes representing the major pro leagues, including soccer. The players mouthed the tag line in unison: "Stand up for integrity. Save our games."

Another anti-gambling spot, this one paid for by a different group, included soft-focus photographs of kids shooting baskets in driveways and playing baseball and soccer in the sunshine. The soothing radio voice of the Boston Red Sox delivered the message: "Sports. They should be about fun — not money." Funny. I didn't remember him complaining when the Sox's payroll ballooned to a hundred and eighty million dollars.

In the third spot, Kenny Rogers touted the virtues of privately operated sports betting. As he spoke, the jaunty melody from his best-known stinker — the one with the lyric *You gotta know when to hold 'em, know when to fold 'em"* — played softly in the background. Kenny delivered the tag line in his down-home drawl — "Stop big government's takeover of sports gambling. Support free enterprise."

By quarter of twelve, the serious midday drinkers had gathered at the bar, their arms curled around their boilermakers as if they were afraid somebody might confiscate them. When they started grumbling about my channel surfing, I tossed one of them the remote, carried my fourth cup of coffee to a table in back, and made a call.

"Campaign Finance Division, Bud Henry speaking."

"Hi, Bud. It's Mulligan."

"I had a feeling I'd be hearing from you this morning."

"So you must know what I'm calling

233

about," I said.

"The super PACs that are running all those gambling ads."

"Yeah. What do you know about them?"

"Officially, nothing at all."

"What about unofficially?"

"It's looks like we've got four big-money players in the game."

"Can you run them down for me?"

"The NCAA and the pro sports leagues are behind Stop Sports Gambling Now," he said, "but I think you already knew that. The scuttlebutt is that at least one Atlantic City casino, maybe more, is funding Americans for the Preservation of Free Enterprise, the super PAC advocating privatized sports gambling. And don't ask me which casino, 'cause I don't know."

"Okay," I said.

"And Don't Gamble with Our Kids' Futures, the super PAC running the ad with the soft-focus photos of little kids? I think their money's coming out of Vegas."

"How'd you find that out?"

"Last Thursday," he said, "I got a call from an attorney claiming to represent them."

"A local lawyer?"

"He was calling from Nevada. Had some questions about the fine points of Rhode

Island campaign finance law. After we hung up, I did a little checking. Turns out his firm also represents a trade association that lobbies on behalf of Las Vegas casinos."

"Interesting."

"But odd, don't you think?" he said.

"How do you mean?"

"That the Atlantic City Casinos are *for* sports gambling in Rhode Island and the Las Vegas casinos are against it."

"Not really," I said.

"How do you mean?"

"The Vegas casinos want to protect their monopoly on legal sports betting," I said. "The Atlantic City casinos want to muscle in on it."

"Aren't they pretty much owned by the same people?"

"Not all of them," I said. "You said there were four players. What's the last one?"

"Have you driven down I-95 today?"

"Not yet."

"The AFL-CIO put up a bunch of new billboards overnight."

"What's on them?"

"Photos of a working man in a hard hat and a student hovering over a textbook. The message in big red letters urges everybody to 'Save Our Pensions and Support Our

Schools' by supporting the governor's plan for state-operated sports gambling."

28

State Senator Mark Reynolds had a dandy idea. He wanted to anoint Mr. Potato Head the official mascot of the state of Rhode Island. By happy coincidence, the national headquarters of Hasbro, the toy's maker, happened to be located in Reynolds's district.

The senator was silent on what the duties of the state's mascot might entail. Do a funky dance on the sidelines during legislative debates? Douse visitors with buckets of confetti at Green Airport? Mock Mr. Met? Stand on the state line and blow raspberries at Massachusetts?

I decided to play it straight and was writing it up when the opening riff of Johnny Rivers's "Secret Agent Man," my ringtone for McCracken, started playing in my pocket.

"Got something for me?" I asked.

"My guy at the airport's been keeping an

eye on incoming flights from Atlantic City," he said, "and last night something interesting came up."

"Oh?"

"Mario Zerilli met the last evening flight. I just e-mailed you a couple of frame grabs from one of the security cameras."

"Hold on a sec," I said.

I opened the e-mail on my desktop computer and clicked on the attachments. One grainy photo caught a short, stocky man in a business suit standing behind the trunk of Mario's car. He was clutching a black briefcase in one hand and holding the handle of a small rolling suitcase in the other. In the second photo, which showed his face more clearly, he was sliding into the passenger seat. He had thin lips, slits for eyes, a hawk's beak, and luxurious salt-and-pepper hair arranged in a pompadour.

"Who is he?" I asked.

"I asked my Jersey P.I. pal, but he wasn't sure."

"Okay, thanks."

"There's more," McCracken said.

"Oh?"

"After my guy at the airport came up with this, he went back over the video of incoming flights from South Jersey for the last couple of weeks. Turns out the same man arrived on an afternoon flight a week ago and got into a cab."

"Okay," I said. "I'm on it."

I ended the call, forwarded the photos to Judy Abbruzzi at *The Atlantic City Press,* and dialed her number.

"I wondered when I was going to hear from you," she said. "I thought maybe you were blowing me off."

"Check your e-mail," I said, "and call me right back."

So that's what she did.

"Recognize him?" I asked.

"Oh, yeah."

"So?"

"First tell me what the hell's going on."

I took a moment to think it over and decided to give her most of it — the super PACs competing to influence Rhode Island gambling legislation, the bundles of cash in Lucan Alfano's briefcase, his attempts to bribe state legislators, and the unsolved murder of Phil Templeton.

"Do you know the names of the legislators Alfano tried to bribe?" she asked.

"Some of them."

"Give."

"I don't feel comfortable sharing that."

"Why?"

"I got it off the record."

She paused, taking her time deciding if I'd given her enough for her to reciprocate.

"The guy in the photo is Romeo Alfano," she finally said. "He's Lucan's younger brother."

"They were in business together?"

"In the payday loan company, yeah."

"And as fixers?"

"So the Jersey state cops are telling us."

"The murder-for-hire business, too?"

"Maybe, but they can't say for sure."

"What else have you got?" I asked.

"The three super PACs you mentioned are active down here, too. All three have made big media buys."

"Anybody bribing state legislators down there?"

"All the time," she said.

"Well, sure. But on Christie's sports gambling proposal?"

"I don't have anything solid on that."

We promised again to stay in touch and signed off.

At noon I skipped lunch, walked a couple of blocks to the Omni, and asked the desk clerk if Romeo Alfano was registered. He wasn't.

"What about Michael O'Toole?" I asked. That, I remembered, was the name his late brother had registered under.

"Hold on a moment, sir. . . . Yes, he is a guest. Would you like me to ring his room for you?"

"No thanks, but could you give me his room number?"

"I'm sorry, sir," he said, "but that would be a violation of company policy."

I nodded, took two twenty-dollar bills out of my pocket, and dropped them on the counter.

"Suite 914," he whispered.

I considered going it alone, thought better of it, and rang McCracken. Fifteen minutes later, we rode the elevator to the ninth floor and knocked on the door to 914. I sensed someone peering at me through the peephole. Then the door swung open.

"Good afternoon, Mario," I said.

"What the fuck do you want?"

"A word with your boss."

"Get lost, assholes."

He pushed against the door. McCracken pushed back and shoved Mario deeper into the room.

Romeo Alfano was seated on a beige sectional sofa, a black briefcase by his side. A carafe of white wine and a room-service luncheon of mixed seafood were tastefully arranged on the coffee table in front of him.

I elbowed Mario out of the way and headed for him.

The kid didn't like that. He grabbed my shoulder with his left hand, spun me, and reached for his waistband with his right. That was a mistake.

McCracken popped him in the nose with a stiff left jab, grabbed his left wrist, yanked his arm behind his back, and bulled him against the wall. Mario's head bounced against a framed Rhode Island Tourist Bureau photo of Newport Harbor, cracking the glass. The P.I. calmly lifted Mario's T-shirt and slid the silver revolver from his waistband.

"Piece of junk, Mario," the P.I. said. "Damned thing could have blown up in your hand."

He opened the cylinder, shook out the shells, wiped his prints away with his shirt-tail, and tossed the gun on the carpet. Mario raised the hem of his T-shirt and used it to stanch the blood flowing from his honker.

Alfano looked up at us and smiled. Then he calmly picked up his wineglass and took a sip.

"If this is a robbery," he said, "you two bozos are fuckin' with the wrong people."

"What's in the case?" I said.

He smirked and took another sip.

"Let's have a look," I said.

That's when Mario decided to take a swing at McCracken. The P.I. slipped the punch and shoved him against the wall again, less gentle about it this time.

"No can do," Alfano said.

I pulled my Kel-Tec and pointed it at him.

He gave me a blank stare, then worked the combination lock and raised the lid.

"Still full, huh?" I said. "What's the story? Doesn't anybody want your dirty money?"

"Hey, give me a chance. I only got to town last night."

"You were here last week, too."

"With a different briefcase," he said. "I don't like to lug too much cash in a single trip."

"Afraid you might get ripped off?"

"Nah. I never worry about that. The people I work for? Only a fool would steal from them."

"Why, then?"

"Cash is heavy, pal."

I took the chair across from him, rested the automatic on my lap, picked up the wine bottle, and downed a slug.

"Nice," I said, although I had no idea if it was.

"A 2007 Stonestreet chardonnay. I always go first class."

"Sorry about your brother," I said.

"You know my name?"

"I do."

"You're not here to rob me?"

I shook my head no.

"Who sent you?" he asked.

"The question is, who sent *you.*"

"Are you from Zerilli?" he asked.

"The bookie? No. I work for *The Dispatch.*"

"Ah. The newspaper."

"That's right."

"Piece of shit," he said.

"I agree."

Out of the corner of my eye, I saw Mario lunge for the revolver. What did he think he was going to do with an unloaded gun? Throw it at us?

"Leave it be," McCracken said, "if you want to keep that hand."

"So let me ask you again," I said. "Who sent you?"

Alfano didn't say anything.

"I know it was Atlantic City casino interests," I said. "What I don't know is which ones."

"If you want to live to see your next byline," Alfano said, "you should stop trying to find out."

I slid a Partagás from my shirt pocket and

clipped the end. "Mind if I smoke?"

Alfano didn't say anything.

I dug the lighter out of my pants pocket.

"It's a nonsmoking room," Mario said.

"And you're never one to break a rule?" McCracken said. "I guess shooting a state legislator doesn't count."

I set fire to the cigar, took a long draw, and blew a smoke ring. Alfano's eyes followed it as it drifted toward the ceiling.

"You know," I said, "you and my buddy Mario here are quite the odd couple."

"How do you mean?" Alfano said.

"Mario's got high hopes. He's angling to inherit his uncle's bookmaking business. But if sports gambling is legalized, it would ruin everything for him. You, on the other hand, are bribing legislators to get the gambling bill passed."

I glanced at Mario in time to see his eyebrows shoot up.

"What?" McCracken said. "You didn't know what your boss is doing here?"

Mario looked at the carpet and didn't say anything.

"Well," I said. "I've enjoyed our little chat, but I must be running along. Tomorrow's newspaper won't come out all by itself, you know."

I rose, plucked the cigar from my lips, and

245

doused it in his wineglass. I hated spoiling a good cigar, but I thought the gesture gave our departure the proper cinematic effect.

"You just put a target on our backs," McCracken said as we rode the elevator down.

"I know," I said. "So let's put one on theirs."

From the lobby, McCracken listened in as I called state police headquarters and asked for Parisi.

"If you hurry," I told him, "you can find Mario Zerilli in room 914 of the Omni Providence. The suite is registered to Michael O'Toole of Atlantic City, New Jersey."

"Who the hell is that?"

"It's the fake name Romeo Alfano is registered under. Romeo is Lucan Alfano's brother, and he's holding a suitcase full of cash. He's using the money to bribe state legislators, and he's paying Mario to do strong-arm work for him. And Captain? Be careful when you bust in. Mario's packing."

Then I rang Wargart at the Providence PD and gave him the same tip. That, I figured, would finally get the homicide twins off my back about killing Mario.

29

Late that afternoon, I was sitting in my cubicle bantering with Hardcastle, the metro columnist, about how the other Hasbro toys were taking Mr. Potato Head's pending elevation.

"The way I hear it," I said, "G.I. Joe's so jealous that he wants to stab all the spud's eyes out."

"And the My Little Ponies are planning to stampede," he said. "They want to trample him into mashed potatoes and feed him to Pokémon."

Hardcastle, who'd been looking for an angle to write a satirical column about time-wasting state legislators, thought the idea had potential.

We were still tossing it around when the security guard rang from the lobby to warn me that three plainclothes cops were on their way up.

I met Parisi and the homicide twins at the

elevator. Wargart and Freitas were grinning. Parisi looked grim. I led them to the meeting room, where we seated ourselves around a small table.

"Did you catch Mario?" I asked.

"Course not," Wargart said. "He was never there."

"Sure he was," I said.

"Bullshit," Freitas said. "We aren't buying your lies."

"What about Romeo Alfano?"

"Oh, he was there, all right."

"And the briefcase full of cash?"

Wargart and Freitas didn't answer. I glanced at Parisi. He shook his head no.

"Alfano's in custody?" I asked.

"Not exactly," Wargart said.

"Don't tell me you let him go," I said.

Wargart and Freitas smirked and exchanged glances.

"Romeo Alfano is in the morgue," Parisi said.

"Aw, hell."

"And you," Wargart said, "are the last person to see him alive."

With that, he rose, ordered me to stand, told me to empty my pockets, and pulled my hands behind my back.

"There's no need to cuff him," Parisi said.

Wargart slapped the bracelets on anyway.

Chuckie-boy looked on stone-faced again as the three detectives led me out. This was getting to be a habit.

At Providence police headquarters, Wargart and Freitas sat across the table from me and hurled questions. Parisi, arms folded across his chest, leaned against the wall and silently observed. From the interrogation, I deduced that Alfano was found dead on his hotel room couch, shot twice in the chest and once in the head.

"We found a cigar in a wineglass," Freitas said. "Same brand you tossed on the table when you emptied your pockets. Pretty careless of you to leave it at a murder scene."

"Wasn't a murder scene when I left," I said.

"Bullshit," Wargart said.

"It was Mario," I said, "and now he's on the run with a couple of hundred grand in hundred-dollar bills."

"Blaming the zombie again, huh?" Wargart said. "Where did you stash the money, asshole?"

That rattled me. I nearly blurted out that McCracken could back up my story. But it wouldn't be right to involve him without making sure he was going to be okay with it. For now, I kept my hole card hidden and invoked my right to an attorney.

When Yolanda bustled in, she told the cops to get out and had me fill her in. Then she summoned Wargart and Freitas and demanded that they charge me or release me.

"We can hold him for twenty-four hours," Freitas said.

So they stuck me in a holding cell till late the following afternoon.

When I finally got home, I found Joseph doing housework again.

"The cops?" I asked.

"Yeah. They showed me a search warrant and tossed the place. Threw stuff all over the fuckin' floors. Made a hell of a mess."

"They take anything?"

"Your nine mil."

"Anything else?"

"They took a grocery bag out of the bedroom, but I got no clue what was in it. What's going on, Mulligan?"

I spilled just enough to satisfy him.

Then I spent an hour trying to figure out what could have been in that grocery bag. Far as I could tell, the Kel-Tec was the only thing that was missing.

30

"I've been dreaming about us having breakfast together after a night of unbridled lust," I said, "but fending off a gangbanger hell-bent on a jail-cell blowjob wasn't the lust I had in mind."

"Are you okay?" Yolanda asked.

"Better than the gangbanger. He should see a dentist about those teeth."

"Your meeting with Romeo Alfano didn't go as planned either," she said.

"It didn't."

We were seated in a booth at Charlie's, I with my customary bacon and eggs and Yolanda with a grapefruit half and a cup of coffee.

"One thing I'm not clear on," she said. "Why did you tell Mario what Alfano was up to?"

"I wanted to drive a wedge between them. But I didn't figure on Mario whacking the guy."

"Feeling guilty about that?"

"Not especially."

"You have to promise me something."

"What?"

"If you get picked up again, you'll call me immediately and not answer any more questions."

"Maybe."

"No maybes this time."

"Okay. You win, Yolanda."

"They ran ballistics on your pistol and determined it wasn't used to kill Alfano."

"Good to know. Can you get it back for me?"

"I'm working on it. You know, for a newspaper reporter, you sure get into a lot of trouble."

"Always have."

"Why is that?"

"Trouble is my business."

"I think I heard that line somewhere before."

"It's the title of a Philip Marlowe short story by Raymond Chandler."

"Marlowe was a private detective," she said, "so trouble *was* his business. The business of a journalist is to report the news."

"You really want to get into this?"

"I do. And none of your jokes."

I drained my coffee and waved Charlie

over for a refill.

"You know how most reporters spend their days, Yolanda?"

"Tell me."

"They regurgitate lies spewed by politicians. They interview self-serving celebrities. They write features about the nutty lady who has fifty cats or the coot who's amassed the state's largest ball of string. And they cover public meetings as if they matter, creating the illusion that democracy is going on."

"Isn't it?"

"Of course not. When the political stakes are high or there's big money to be made, deals are cut out of sight over whiskey and cigars. Or sometimes, cocaine. Journalists try to convince themselves that their jobs are noble and exciting, but mostly the work is pointless and boring."

"If that's how you feel, why'd you get into it in the first place?"

"Because it wasn't always this way," I said. "In the good old days, which weren't all that long ago, the job was a license to dig out the truth behind the facade, to expose incompetence and corruption, to explain how the world really works. Now, outside of a few big-city metros like *The Washington Post* and *The New York Times,* news organizations don't have the staff — or the balls — to do much of that anymore. Hell, even the big boys don't do as much of it as they used to."

"So you're a dinosaur," she said.

"That's what my boss keeps telling me."

"But he lets you keep at it?"

"No, he doesn't. He buries me in press releases and assigns me to write weather stories about stuff readers could find out for themselves if they looked out the window. The velociraptor act is on my own time now."

"Does he know what you've been up to?"

"I haven't got around to telling him."

"Why not?"

"Because he'd order me to stop."

"Maybe it's time you confided in him," she said.

"Why would I want to do that?"

She picked up her cup and sipped some coffee before deciding how to answer.

"Usually, I tell murder suspects to keep their mouths shut," she said, "but most of them don't have the big megaphone you've got to get your story out. I think your best move now is to get out ahead of this."

"How do you suggest I do that?"

"By putting what you know about the Alfanos, the bribery, and the Templeton murder in the paper."

"I don't have it nailed down yet."

"Are you close?"

"That depends."

"On what?" she asked.

"On whether I can talk a few reluctant sources into going on the record."

Charlie dropped the check on the table. I beat Yolanda to it and threw down a twenty. The Capital Grille was out of my price range, but I could spring for half a grapefruit without taking out a loan.

"How about dinner later this week?" I said.

"I don't think so."

"Oh. Did I say something stupid again?"

"It's not that."

"What, then?"

"The things you told me last time? That stuff about why you value the differences between us?"

"Yeah?"

"I'm still thinking about it."

31

Next morning, I punched the clock and was promptly summoned to Twisdale's office.

"We need to talk," he said.

"Later, Chuckie. There are some people I've gotta see first."

"No. We have to do this now."

I shrugged and flopped into the chair across from his desk.

"What's on your mind?"

"A couple of little things," he said.

"Like?"

"Like why the cops dragged you out of my newsroom again."

"What do you know about the murder at the Omni," I asked.

"Just this," Chuckie said. He folded *The Dispatch* to the metro front and pointed to a one-column headline. The story beneath it was thin on details, saying only that Romeo Alfano, a businessman from Atlantic City, had been found shot to death in his hotel room and that police were investigating.

"The Providence cops questioned me about it," I said.

"Why?"

"Because I might have been the last person to see him alive."

"Are you a suspect?"

"The homicide twins seem to think so."

"Holy shit!"

"Yeah."

"Who is this Romeo Alfano?"

"A mobster who's been bribing state legislators to change their votes on the sports gambling bill."

"Jesus! And you've been looking into this behind my back?"

"On my own time, yeah."

Chuckie stared at me for a moment. His eyes narrowed and his jaw muscles clenched. When he spoke, his voice was an octave lower.

"Okay, Mulligan. You're going to have to start trusting me. I need you to turn your cards over and tell me everything."

"Not yet. I need a few days to tie up loose ends first."

"We don't have a few days. If corporate gets wind that you're a suspect in a murder case, they'll want me to fire you. I won't be able to protect you unless I know what the hell's going on."

"Protect *me*? You're just trying to cover your ass."

"That too," he said.

The determined look on his face made it clear that I was out of options. Reluctantly, I ran it all down for him: The suitcase full of cash pried from Lucan Alfano's lap. The list of public officials found in his pocket. His attempts to bribe Lisa Pichardo, Joseph Longo, and Phil Templeton. My confrontation with Mario Zerilli and Lucan Alfano's brother Romeo at the Omni. New Jersey state cops' assertion that the Alfanos were fixers for Atlantic City casinos. And my suspicion that Mario had killed both Romeo Alfano and Templeton.

With each revelation, Twisdale's eyes got a little bigger. When I was done, he put his hands on his head, leaned back in his chair, and studied the ceiling.

"That's one hell of a story," he said.

"Yeah."

"How much of it can you prove?"

"With a little more time, most of it. Maybe all of it."

"Why did you keep me in the dark about this?"

"Because you would have called me off."

"You got that right."

"Coward."

He sighed and shook his head. "Do you have any idea how lucky you've been, Mulligan?"

"It's not luck, Chuckie. I'm good at this."

"I know you are. What I mean is that you got to work here back in the days when *The Dispatch* was a *real* newspaper."

"How would you know what it was like?"

"I've been reading through the archives," he said. "Twenty, fifteen, even ten years ago, there was something amazing in the paper almost every day. Great beat reporting. Remarkable explanatory journalism. Superb storytelling. Blockbuster exposés." He sighed. "You have no idea how much I wish I could have been part of that."

At first, I thought he was blowing smoke. Then I caught the way his eyes lit up. I slid two cigars out of my pocket, clipped the ends, and tossed him one. He surprised me by picking it up and sticking it in his jaw. I gave him a light, then got mine going. We smoked in silence for a couple of minutes, blatantly disregarding both company policy and state law. Reporters stationed at nearby desks stared at us openmouthed through the aquarium's glass walls.

"I know you don't respect me," Twisdale

said. "If I were in your shoes, I'd probably feel the same way. But you don't understand the pressure I'm under. Corporate doesn't give a rat's ass about covering the news or serving the public. All they care about is the bottom line."

"You knew that when you took this job," I said. "It's what you signed up for. But maybe it's not too late to grow some balls."

"It is if I want to keep working here."

"A paycheck means more to you than self-respect?"

Twisdale grabbed the picture frame on his desk and turned it around to show me his pretty blond wife and three towheaded little boys. "No," he said, "but they do." He frowned and slowly shook his head. "Besides, I don't have the resources to let you run around chasing long shots."

"Like I said, it was all on my own time."

"Only if we don't count your bullshit sick days," he said.

"Fair enough."

"But this isn't a long shot anymore, is it."

"No."

He leaned back in his chair and studied the ceiling. Maybe trying to decide what to do about me. Maybe searching for some courage up there.

"What's left to do before you can write?"

"I need to get a few key sources to go on the record."

"Then I guess you better get cracking."

This time I didn't feel the urge to crack his head.

"One last thing," he said.

"Yeah?"

"Don't tell anybody else what you're working on. If word gets out around the building, I'll get pressure from the business side to kill the story."

"Why?"

"That super PAC you say is funded by Atlantic City casinos? They've scheduled a series of full-page ads that start on Thursday."

"And if my story pisses them off," I said, "they might pull them."

"Exactly."

"You're prepared to take the heat for that?"

"I'm thinking about it," Twisdale said. "You know the saying — 'Act now, apologize later.'"

As I walked back to my desk, I wondered. Chuckie-boy had shown some guts today, but would he stand up when the heat came down?

Lisa Pichardo sat behind her desk in the

House minority leader's office, arms folded defensively across her chest.

"No way, Mulligan," she said. "You promised everything I gave you would stay off the record."

"That was before," I said. "Things have changed."

"In what way?"

"The bribery story's going to break any day now. If you go on the record, people will know you blew the whistle. Otherwise, they might think you took the money."

"I still don't like it," she said. "I've been threatened. If my name comes out, somebody might come after me."

"Your name's going to come out anyway once the state police make their case," I said. With the Alfanos both dead, Parisi's bribery investigation probably had stalled, but I was hoping Pichardo didn't realize that.

"How can I be sure you'll be fair with me?" she asked.

"Haven't I always?"

She shook her head emphatically.

"You've made a lot of trouble for me over the years," she said. "For one thing, I didn't much like how I came off in that highway contract story last winter."

"The one about you pressuring the DOT

to turn down the low bid and hire a paving company from your district?"

"Yeah, that one."

"I know it caused problems for you, but it *was* fair, wasn't it?"

She sighed and uncrossed her arms.

"Maybe so," she said.

"So what do you say?"

"First show me exactly how you plan to quote me."

The conversation with Joseph Longo, head of the Senate Finance Committee, went pretty much the same way — minus the part about the DOT bill.

"Okay," he said. "Go ahead and use my name. Be good to finally get this dirt out in the open."

At Warwick police headquarters, I found Chief Hernandez in his office, reviewing the results of the latest sergeant's exam and puffing on a Cuban.

"Any chance you can get me more of these?" he asked.

"Sure thing, Oscar, but first I need a favor."

"Name it."

"I need you on the record about Lucan Alfano."

"What about him, exactly?"

"The part about the briefcase full of cash and the list you found in his pocket."

"How are you going to use it?" he asked.

So I told him.

"Your work got this whole thing started," I said. "You ought to get the credit for it."

"I'm not looking for credit."

"Fine. Be humble. But can you help me out here?"

"Okay," he said. "I'm good with this."

On the way out, I glanced at his bulletin board and saw that the photo of Ted Cruz was riddled with fresh holes.

Parisi slid his car window down, listened to my pitch, and shook his head.

"Forget it, Mulligan. The state police do not comment on ongoing investigations."

"Except when it serves your interests," I said.

"Which this time it doesn't."

"It might. The story's going to shake the trees, and something ripe might fall out."

Five seconds, and then, "Do you have enough to run with if I decline to comment?"

"No."

Five seconds again. "Why not?"

"My editor's skittish. No way he's going

264

to press with something this big unless he has official confirmation."

Ten seconds, and then, "If I tell you anything — and I'm not saying I'm going to — you can't use my name. It would have to be attributed to a high-ranking state police official."

"That works."

"So what's the absolute minimum you've got to have from me?"

"I need confirmation that Templeton, Pichardo, and Longo reported bribery attempts and that the state police are conducting an investigation."

"Sorry. I'm not confirming any names."

"Can you at least say that there were three?"

Ten seconds this time, and then, "No. That would not be accurate."

"There were more?"

Five seconds. "There were."

How many?

"Five more so far."

"Who am I missing?"

"You'll have to get that from somebody else. Are we done here?"

"Do you know who the Alfanos were working for?"

"I thought you already had that," he said.

"Atlantic City casinos, yeah," I said. "But

which ones?"

"I'm not going there."

"I'm guessing you don't know."

Ten seconds. "Do you?"

"No."

With that, he turned away and cranked the ignition.

"One last thing," I said.

"I think I've said enough."

"Not quite, Captain. I need you to confirm that Mario Zerilli is your chief suspect in the Templeton and Romeo Alfano murders."

Five seconds. "The Providence PD thinks you shot them."

"But you know better," I said.

He turned away and stared out the windshield.

"Mario Zerilli is being sought for questioning in both killings," he said. "That's as far as I'm willing to go."

"Thanks. And Captain? Take care."

Late that evening, I called McCracken and invited him to meet me for a beer.

"Trinity Brewhouse at eight," he said.

"Too noisy. We need a quiet place to talk."

So a half hour later, we slipped into Hopes and found it nearly deserted. Just one alkie hunched over the bar and a couple of off-duty cops taking turns at the pinball machine. None of them had fed the jukebox. We picked up bottles of Killian's at the bar and claimed a wobbly table by the back door.

"What's up?" McCracken said. So I filled him in.

"When I write the part about our visit to Romeo Alfano's hotel room," I said, "is it okay if I use your name?"

"Can you leave out the part about me roughing up Mario?" he asked. "I don't want to expose myself to an assault charge."

"I can do that."

"Then you're good to go. Ready for another round? I'm buying."

"Thanks," I said, "but I need to keep a clear head tonight."

I swallowed the last of my beer, left him alone at the table, and walked back to the newspaper in the dark.

By one A.M., the newsroom had cleared out. I was the only one in the place.

I wrote mostly from memory, referring to my notes occasionally for dates and verbatim quotes. I got up from the keyboard only to fortify myself with vile vending-machine coffee. Finally, around four A.M., I was finished.

I e-mailed the story to Twisdale, drove home, and poured myself a shot of Bushmills. Then I tore off my clothes, flopped onto my mattress, pulled the pillow over my head to muffle Joseph's snoring, and fell right to sleep.

32

"Kinda late for breakfast, ain't it?" Charlie asked.

I checked my watch — two P.M.

"You still got eggs, right?"

"Yeah."

"Bacon?"

"Sure."

"Okay, then," I said.

Charlie poured me some coffee, then cracked three eggs on the grill and slapped five strips of bacon down beside a dozen sizzling burgers.

Someone had left the day's *Dispatch* behind on the counter. I opened it to the sports page, caught up with last night's Red Sox win over the Blue Jays, then browsed through the rest of the paper. An ad from the super PAC funded by Atlantic City casinos took up all of page five.

So this must be Thursday. That's when the group's ad was scheduled to start.

I shoveled in Charlie's masterpiece without tasting it, swigged my coffee, and walked three blocks to the newspaper. There, I found Twisdale hunched over his computer screen. He was concentrating so hard that he didn't hear me step into his office.

"Boss?"

"What is it now? Oh, hey, Mulligan. Thanks for dropping by."

"I still work here, right? I found my time card next to the punch clock."

"For now, anyway, but you're six hours and forty-five minutes late."

"Gonna dock my pay again?"

"Perhaps I can let it slide this time."

"So what do you think?"

"I think I need another hour or so to finish going over this. There's a stack of press releases on your desk. I'll call for you when I'm ready."

Ninety minutes later, he did.

"I've got some concerns," he said.

"I thought you might."

"I want to make sure we've eliminated any libel risk."

"You're not running it by the company lawyers?"

"If I do, they'll advise me not to run it. They won't care whether the story actually libels anyone. They're paid to forestall any risk that somebody *might* sue. If they catch the slightest whiff that I'm not taking their advice, they'll rat me out to corporate."

"The Alfanos are libel-proof," I said. "Dead men can't sue."

"What about Mario Zerilli?"

"He's on the run from the cops. Hiring a libel lawyer is the last thing on his mind now."

"But he might get around to it later," Twisdale said. "The story *does* implicate him in two murders."

"All I say is that he's wanted for questioning."

"Yeah, but the suggestion of guilt is clearly there. And that's not all. You say flat out that he was doing strong-arm work for two Jersey mobsters who were offering bribes to public officials. You've got to admit that tends to damage his reputation."

"Not really," I said. "Mario is a drunk driver, a domestic abuser, and a gay-basher. The whole town knows he's a violent punk. There's not much we can say that would make people think worse of him."

"I see your point."

"Anything else?" I asked.

"Yeah. I think we need to cut out the part about the Alfanos working for Atlantic City casinos."

"Why? The information's solid."

"Because we don't know which casinos," he said. "As written, the story throws suspicion on all of them."

"Okay, I'll give you that one," I said. "How about changing 'casinos' to 'New Jersey gambling interests'?"

"That does the trick," he said.

"So when will it run?"

"I'm stripping it across the top of page one on Sunday," he said. "With mug shots of the bad guys and photos of Parisi, Hernandez, and Templeton, it'll eat up a full page inside."

"Okay," I said, and got up to leave. Then something else occurred to me. "Who's going to copyedit this?"

"Good question. No way I can send it to the copy center in Wichita. They might squeal to corporate. Guess I better take it home and do it myself."

"Thanks, *Mister* Twisdale."

"Aw, what the hell. Go ahead and call me Chuck."

I owed three people a heads-up.

That afternoon, I batted out the day's weather story — warm and sunny with an 85 percent chance of bribery — and rushed through a stack of press releases. When that was done, I called Judy Abbruzzi at *The Atlantic City Press.*

"Things are moving fast, here," I said. "We're breaking the story about the Alfanos' bribery scheme on Sunday. I'm e-mailing a copy to you now. It's got enough named sources for you to match it if you hurry. Just don't break anything until we do, okay?"

"I promise. Thanks."

"And Judy?"

"Yeah?"

"If you dig up anything I don't have, give me a call, okay?"

"Count on it."

Four o'clock found me sitting in an antique visitor's chair across from the governor's desk. Fiona was in a foul mood.

"You know I have the Capitol Police sweep my office for bugs every month, right?"

"I've heard that, yeah."

"Yesterday they found something."

"What, exactly?"

"Voice-activated listening devices. One in the lamp beside the couch. One stitched into a corner of the state flag. And another concealed inside the desk phone."

"Any idea who put them there?"

"At first I thought the state police might have done it as part of their bribery investigation."

"Because your name was on Lucan Alfano's list," I said.

"Yeah, but Captain Parisi swears it wasn't them."

"Are we talking high-end, super-spy stuff?"

"Parisi came by himself to look them over. According to him, they're devices anybody can buy over the Internet. Says they would have picked up pretty much everything that was said in the office."

"And both sides of every telephone conversation?"

"That's right."

"It was all being broadcast to an outside receiver?"

"With a range of about three thousand feet," she said.

"So whoever was listening in could have been sitting behind any desk in the statehouse or hanging out in the parking lot," I said. "Any idea what they were after?"

"Everything lately seems to have something to do with the gambling bill."

"A bug in the governor's office is big news," I said. "Okay if I write about this?"

"Not just yet. Parisi wants to keep it under wraps for now."

"Too bad. It would have made a nice sidebar to the story I'm breaking Sunday."

"Oh?"

So I laid it out for her.

"Wow," she said. "That's going to shake things up."

"How do you think it will affect the gambling bill?"

"Hard to say."

"It could cost the privatization advocates some votes," I said.

"Because anyone who votes for privatization now will risk being suspected of taking payoffs?"

"That's what I'm thinking."

"But it also might encourage others to walk around with their hands out, hoping to grab a share of the dirty money."

"Probably will," I said.

"Think the anti-gambling side is handing out bribes, too?" she asked.

"I don't have anything solid on that, but it wouldn't surprise me."

"I'd be surprised if they aren't," Fiona said.

"So what are you going to do?"

"I didn't want to submit the bill until I was sure I had the votes," she said, "but I can't get a solid count. A dozen senators and House members keep switching positions, and about a third of them won't get off the fence."

"Probably hoping to milk cash cows from both sides," I said.

"So I don't see the point in waiting any longer," Fiona said. "I'm going to submit the bill next week and let the chips fall where they may."

"Okay if I print that?"

"Yeah. Go ahead."

A half hour later, Zerilli buzzed me into his inner sanctum. I lured Shortstop out of the visitor's chair with a peanut butter–stuffed beef bone I'd picked up at Petco for the occasion. The dog snatched it and retreated to a corner. I brushed the hair off the plank oak seat and sat down.

"The state police are hunting Mario," I said. "They think he's good for the Templeton and Romeo Alfano murders. If he keeps his mouth shut, I doubt they can make the Templeton charge stick. But Alfano? The cops aren't saying much about it, so I'm not so sure about that one."

"Aw, fuck."

"I thought you should hear this from me before it hits the paper."

"Okay. Thanks, Mulligan."

"The cops probably aren't the only ones looking for him, Whoosh," I said. "The Jersey gambling interests must be pissed about Alfano, and you *know* they want their briefcase full of cash back."

"Humpf."

"If you're in touch with him, you ought to tell him to turn himself in."

"He rang me up a couple days ago," Zerilli said. "Asked me if I could float him a loan, and could I put him with a guy who could fix him up with a good phony ID."

"He's got the two hundred grand he took when he shot Alfano," I said. "What the hell does he need a loan for?"

"He swears he doesn't have it."

"What did he say, exactly?"

"The way he tells it, he bolted from the hotel room right after you and McCracken left. He claims Alfano was still breathing."

"Believe that?"

"I don't know what the fuck to believe."

"Did you give him money and help him with the fake ID?"

"He's my late brother's kid, Mulligan."

"Any idea where he is?"

"No."

"If you did, would you tell me?"

"You shittin' me? Fuck, no."

I heard the bone snap in Shortstop's jaws. His eyes, narrow with suspicion, followed me as I rose from the chair and turned toward the door. And then he growled, the sound a low rumble in his throat.

33

Friday night, Joseph asked if he could tag along with me to the Saturday morning basketball tryouts.

"Why would you want to?" I asked.

"Ain't got nothin' better to do."

Judging by the empties heaped next to the couch, I didn't think there was much chance he'd actually get up for it, but the next morning, he surprised me.

As we scrimmaged, he sat behind the bench in dark glasses and sipped from a Thermos. Inside was his homemade hangover remedy, a slurry of green tea, banana, raw eggs, and crushed vitamin B tablets.

Three seats away, a slim woman in tan shorts and a yellow tank top, draped well-muscled legs over a seat back and sipped coffee from a paper cup. Beside her, a little boy, maybe three years old, played a video game on a tablet. His mom reminded me a little of Yolanda. During a break in the action, I couldn't help but stare.

Jefferson, the former Hope High standout, gave me a nudge.

"Don't get your hopes up, grandpa. She's taken."

"You sacrificed a lot for them, Keenan."

"They're worth it, man," he said. "You got no idea how lucky I am."

Which made me like him a little more.

This morning, the coaches had put Jefferson and Benton, the flashy point guard, on the same team. Separately, each had more talent than the rest of us. Together, they were better than all the rest of us combined. Jefferson was in constant motion without the ball. Benton drove and dished. My team, which included Sears and Krueger, never had a chance.

Halfway through the game, we were down by eighteen. Sears, who'd drawn the assignment to cover Benton, started clutching and grabbing, giving the point guard the opportunity to show off his free-throw shooting. Krueger, assigned to guard Jefferson, seemed to have given up, doing little more than watching as the kid drilled long jumpers and blew by him to sky toward the rim. Each time Jefferson threw down a thunderous dunk, his wife let out a lonely cheer.

When the clutching and grabbing didn't

work, Sears got rougher with Benton, shooting elbows into the point guard's ribs. I expected a fistfight as soon as Benton retaliated.

Instead it was Krueger who suddenly lost it, grabbing Jefferson by both shoulders and hurling him to the floor. The kid bounced up and they squared off, Krueger throwing a wild left that whizzed past Jefferson's ear. I jumped in, planted the flat of my hand against Krueger's chest, and shoved him backward. He knocked my hand away, tossed me aside as if I were an annoying child, and charged Jefferson.

Suddenly Joseph materialized between them. Krueger slammed into him and bounced off.

"You're gonna have to go through me," Joseph said.

"Let him come," Jefferson shouted. "I ain't scared of that bitch."

Joseph ignored him and kept his eyes on Krueger.

My friend was a big guy by normal standards, but Krueger had him by five inches. The power forward smirked and threw a roundhouse left. The former bouncer blocked it with his right, pounded Krueger's midsection with a left hook, and finished him with a right cross to the jaw.

Krueger folded like a bad poker hand and crumpled to the hardwood.

It took the coaches twenty seconds to revive him. When he came to, they grabbed him by the armpits and pulled him to his feet.

"You're done for today," Coach Martin said. "Go take a shower and head on home."

When the excitement was over, Martin asked me to work on jump shooting with Benton and Jefferson while he ran the remaining seven players through some drills at the other end of the court. I didn't ask, but I figured Martin saw things the way I did — that Benton and Jefferson were the real deal and that the rest of us were along for the ride.

I fetched a spare hoop I'd found in the locker room, laid it upside down on the sideline, and handed each player a basketball.

"Set them down inside the rim," I said.

So they did. Both balls both fit snugly inside the iron.

"What does this tell you?" I asked.

"That a shot doesn't have to be perfect to go in," Benton said.

"That's right," I said. "A regulation basketball is a hair over nine inches in diameter, and the hoop is twice that size. That means you've got plenty of room for error. I like to keep that in mind. It gives me confidence. Helps me stay relaxed."

Then I had them pick up the balls and get on their knees. I stood four feet in front of them and raised the rim over my head.

"If you toss the ball straight up at the hoop, what's going to happen?" I asked.

"Come on, man," Jefferson said. "You think we're eight years old or somethin'. We know what's gonna happen."

"So tell me."

"It's going to hit the front rim and bounce the fuck off," Jefferson said.

"Right," I said, "so why do you do that?"

"I do?"

"Not exactly," I said, "but your arc is inconsistent. Sometimes you don't get enough air under the ball. When your arc is shallow, the rim looks like a narrow oval from the ball's point of view. This makes the target smaller, increasing the likelihood that your shot will clang off the rim and bounce out. But when the arc is right, the ball rises above the rim and comes almost straight down, doubling or tripling the odds that the shot will go in."

"We know this shit, grandpa," Benton said.

"Sure," I said. "Both of you do. But knowing and doing aren't the same thing."

"Is my arc inconsistent, too?" Benton asked.

"No," I said. "You've got that part down. Your problem is your release."

"Oh, yeah? What's wrong with it?"

"Sometimes your right elbow flies out," I said. "You need to practice keeping it tucked close to your head. And remember not to rush your shot. Always take a fraction of a second to get both feet squared to the basket."

"When the defense is all over me, I don't have time for that."

"That's what passes are for," I said.

He thought about it for a moment, then nodded.

"Now just sit there for a few minutes and watch my form," I said.

I dragged two carts full of basketballs over and started firing them up from twenty-five feet. Fourteen swished through the strings. Three others hit the back rim, bounced straight up, and came down through the hoop.

"Why did the shots that hit the rim go in?" I asked them.

"Because you put a lot of rotation on the ball," Jefferson said.

"Do we need to work on that, too?"

Benton asked.

"It's not a big issue for either of you," I said, "but you could both be a bit more consistent."

Together, we collected the loose balls and returned them to the carts.

"Okay," I said. "Start shooting. And Benton?"

"Yeah?"

"Don't rush, okay?"

Forty minutes later, we were still at it.

"How long are we going to do this?" Jefferson asked.

"Until Coach tells us to stop," I said. "You should both take a hundred jumpers every day. Pay attention to your form on every shot, and eventually muscle memory will take over. Then you won't have to think about arc or spin or whether you're square to the basket anymore."

"A hundred shots *every* day?"

"Ray Allen's the best jump shooter in NBA history, guys, and he *still* does that."

"If we do, think we'll get as good as Allen?" Benton asked.

"Don't talk crazy," I said.

"As good as you, then?" Jefferson said.

"Of course not," I said, and they both laughed. "As far as I can tell, the jump shot is the only flaw in your games. Work on that, and maybe, just maybe, you won't have to sling burgers anymore."

After I showered and dressed, I called Yolanda from the locker room.

"How about dinner tonight?" I asked. "I've got something to celebrate."

"Don't tell me you made the team!"

"Not that."

"What, then?"

"The story you said I should write? It's leading the Sunday paper tomorrow."

"Great. Hope I'm right about it getting the Providence cops to ease up on you."

"So where shall we eat?"

At first, she didn't say anything. I wasn't sure if she was sorting through a mental checklist of restaurants or deciding on the best way to let me down.

"I do want to see you again," she finally said, "but I'm not sure I'm ready yet. How about a rain check?"

"It's not raining, Yolanda. It's a beautiful spring day. But it would be more beautiful if I could spend some of it with you. Besides, if we wait, I probably won't be in a celebratory mood."

"Why not?"

"Because once the story hits the streets, I'm probably going to get fired."

286

"What? Why would they fire you for writing a page-one story?"

"I'll explain over dessert."

The maître d' at Andino's seated us at a table for two with a view of Atwells Avenue, the main thoroughfare in the city's Italian district. Beside us was a pastel mural depicting the great little restaurant in a row of other eateries. I'd spruced up for the occasion, dragging a comb through my hair and donning a blue blazer over my Dustin Pedroia Red Sox T-shirt. Yolanda was sheathed in a low-cut, yellow silk dress designed by someone who knew how to make me lose my mind. She was still wearing the scales-of-justice pendant I'd given her. It fell in the valley between her breasts, as if I needed another reason to look *there*.

"I've missed you," I said.

"It's been less than a week."

"The state I'm in, that feels like a long, long time."

"Don't," she said.

"I shouldn't tell you how I feel?"

She dropped her eyes to the table and drew a breath.

"At least wait till we have some wine."

She ordered a bottle of something white and expensive to go with our meal, a snail salad appetizer and linguini in clam sauce for her, clams Giovanni and shrimp fra diavolo for me. When the first course arrived, she helped herself, as usual, to a morsel from my plate.

Yolanda steered the conversation to safer territory, her work and mine, so I filled her in on why my story was sure to cause trouble at the paper. One bottle of wine led to another, and by the time the waiter cleared our plates away, both of us were a little drunk.

As we sipped our after-dinner cappuccinos, she finally got around to talking about us. But not in the way I hoped.

"People are staring," she said.

"At you?"

"At the two of us."

"I haven't noticed. I've been concentrating on you."

"I hate it," she said.

"Hard to blame them, don't you think?"

"What do you mean?"

"If we were in Miami or New York City, nobody would look at us twice," I said, "but in Providence, you and I are a sight."

"I know *why* it happens," she said. "But that doesn't make me comfortable with it."

I tore my eyes away from her and took a look around. A couple of tables away, an elderly gentleman, dressed for dinner in a tailored black suit, was eating alone. He glanced at us, saw that I'd caught him looking, smiled warmly, and turned back to his pasta. To his right, two young people on a date were stealing furtive looks at us and whispering to each other. A few yards to our left, three men in suits, probably here for a business meeting, couldn't keep their eyes off Yolanda. Halfway across the room, a middle-aged couple dining with their three preteen children were staring with open hostility. Nobody else seemed to be paying us any attention.

"The old guy over there approves of us," I said. "The young couple, the ones giggling now, are just curious. And the three businessmen to our right aren't looking at *us*. They're looking at you because you're beautiful."

"What about the couple with the three kids?"

"They think we're an abomination."

Yolanda turned in her seat and locked eyes with them. The woman averted her gaze, but her husband didn't look away. I pushed my chair back from the table, strolled over to where they were sitting, and loomed over them.

"Got a problem?"

"What? No," the husband said.

"Because if you do, I'll be happy to drag you outside and teach you some manners."

His face reddened, and his hands curled into fists. I'd embarrassed him in front of his family. Now he was trying to decide whether he had the stones to do something about it.

"Honey, don't," his wife said.

He started to get up anyway, then thought better of it and settled back into his seat.

"Wise move," I said. I stood over them for another ten seconds. Then I turned my back and returned to our table.

"What did you say to him?" Yolanda asked.

"I asked him if he had a problem. He assured me he didn't."

"They're not looking at us anymore."

"I'll bet."

"If we keep seeing each other, this is going to keep happening."

"It's just two assholes in a restaurant full of people, Yolanda. Don't let them get to you."

"Doesn't it bother you?"

"I'm having dinner with the most beautiful woman in New England," I said. "I couldn't care less about what a couple of morons think."

"That's because it only happens to you

when you're with me. You've never felt the whole attitude of a room change just because you walked into it. Store detectives follow me around when I shop. Cashiers call my bank to check on my credit card because they think I probably stole it. People look astonished when I open my mouth and actually speak the King's English. They expect me to sound like Prissy from *Gone with the Wind.*"

I didn't know what to say about any of that. I just reached across the table, took her hand, and caressed her palm with my thumb. She took another sip of her cappuccino. Then she looked at me over the rim of her cup, and something inside of me melted.

"You're getting to me, Mulligan. I think about you all the time now."

"And you're stuck in my head like a wrong song." I stroked her palm again. "So what are we waiting for?"

"You know."

"Didn't I tell you? I'm black Irish."

"Not the same thing."

"Then maybe you could just close your eyes."

"Stop with the jokes."

"I'm not joking. Close them, Yolanda. Do it right now."

She looked at me curiously, then did as I asked.

I rose from the table, went to her, and kissed her mouth. Her eyes flew open, and she pulled away. Then she put her hands behind my neck, closed her eyes again, and tugged me back down. Our lips met, and this time they parted. I'm not sure how long the kiss lasted, but I didn't stop until she pulled away again. Everyone was staring now, and this time we'd given them a reason. I think I was actually blushing as I sat back down across from her.

"Damn," she whispered.

"Was that a good damn or a bad damn?"

"Good," she said, her voice slurring a little.

"I could kiss you like that every day."

She picked up her cup, stared out the window, and finished her cappuccino. Then she leaned forward and gave me that look again.

"Mulligan?"

"Um."

"Finish your coffee and take me home."

"Then what?"

"Then you can help me out of this dress."

34

Johnny Arujo had been a newspaper security guard for a dozen years. Each morning, he'd always greeted me by name when I entered the lobby. But Monday morning, he rose from behind his desk to give me a high five.

"Hell of a story yesterday," he said. "I didn't think *The Dispatch* did that kind of thing anymore."

"Neither did I."

"Gonna be more where this one came from?"

"I'd like to think so," I said, "but I doubt it."

I rode the elevator to the third floor, punched the newsroom time clock, and saw Twisdale beckon me from his office door. He looked glum. I dropped into the chair across from his desk and said, "What's the damage?"

"Herald Price Beauregard, one of the five corporate vice presidents for news, called me at home Sunday night. Sounded mad as hell."

"I'm not sure I heard right. Did you say *Harold*?"

"It's Herald. As in "Hark! the Herald Angels Sing."

"There's an actual person named Herald Price Beauregard?"

"There is. He's flying in from corporate HQ in Tulsa tonight, and he's bringing a company lawyer and a VP for advertising with him. They're meeting with me and our advertising director in the boardroom upstairs at eight tomorrow morning. Beauregard ordered me to bring you along, so be on time for a change."

"Swell."

"And for God's sake, behave. Let me do most of the talking. Don't speak unless you're asked a direct question. And please, none of your wisecracks. Oh, and wear a jacket and tie for a change, okay?"

Later that morning, my buddy Mason rang me up.

"Great story yesterday," he said.

"Thanks."

"I'm calling to thank *you*. You just made me a nice piece of change."

"I did that how?"

294

"That super PAC, Americans for the Preservation of Free Enterprise? The one your story says is funded by New Jersey gambling interests?"

"Yeah?"

"They dropped their account with *The Dispatch* and started running a banner ad on *The Ocean State Rag* site this morning."

"I figured they'd be dropping us," I said, "but why'd they turn to your little website? I thought they'd just start spending more on local radio and television."

"Because we're growing like crazy," Mason said. "As of the first of this month, I've got more eyeballs than the four local broadcast TV affiliates combined."

"Really?"

"Yeah."

"Good for you."

"The super PAC will probably pull its ads from us, too, once they get a load of the coverage I've got in the works," he said. "But for now, I'm delighted to take their money."

Tuesday morning I got up early, showered, shaved, and put on a white dress shirt, my blue blazer, and my best black Reeboks — the pair without any holes or bloodstains. I punched the newsroom clock at a quarter to eight and stepped into Twisdale's office.

"Didn't I tell you to wear a tie?"

"I'm sure I've got one around some-where," I said, "but I couldn't find it this morning."

"You only have *one* tie?"

"One is usually more than I need."

"Couldn't find your hard shoes either?"

"When you gave me the dress code," I said, "you didn't say anything about foot-wear."

He scowled and shook his head. Then he reached into a desk drawer, pulled out a red-and-black checkerboard tie, and threw it at me.

"Here. Put this on." After I knotted it, he shot his cuffs and glanced at his watch. "Time to head upstairs."

When we arrived, the boardroom was dark. Twisdale flicked a switch, illuminating twenty carved chairs arranged around an enormous meeting table. The furniture was as old as the newspaper and was said to be the only thing the Mason family had sal-vaged when they sold their crumbling Victorian headquarters on Washington Street and moved to these new digs on Fountain Street in 1934. For a century and a half, generations of Masons had gathered around this slab of Ecuadorian mahogany to talk business, politics, and public service. I wondered why the family had decided to abandon it here. Perhaps the castles they lived in weren't spacious enough for a table that could serve as a landing strip for military aircraft. Or maybe they just weren't as sentimental about mahogany as they were about power and money.

Twisdale and I took adjoining chairs, our backs to a row of high windows that looked down on a McDonald's restaurant and a shuttered strip club. Across from us, dusty glass trophy cases lined the wall. Inside were scores of plaques, framed certificates, and medals the newspaper had won for its journalism over the decades. Five of them were Pulitzer Prizes. Since our new owners took over, nothing new had been added.

A couple of minutes later, Butch Martin, our advertising director, trudged in. He'd supplemented the dress code with a pocket handkerchief and a funereal expression. Martin was trailed by a cafeteria worker who wheeled in a cart full of pastries and jugs of coffee. The three of us sat in silence as the guy set the table.

The three emissaries from corporate, each toting a leather briefcase, strode in fashionably late at quarter past eight. They took a moment to run their eyes over the trophy cases, claimed the seats directly across from us, and introduced themselves. Twisdale, playing host, poured the coffee. Then Beauregard, the VP for news, opened his briefcase, removed a copy of the Sunday paper, and angrily slapped it on the table.

When he spoke, his voice startled me. Subconsciously, I'd been expecting a man named Herald Price Beauregard to speak in the manner of an effete southern patrician. Like South Carolina senator Lindsey Graham, maybe, or actor Will Patton: "Ah am *so* disappointed in these heah goin's-on. And ta think ah had *such* high regahd fo you fine gentlemen."

But when he growled, "You three douchebags got some splainin' to do," he sounded more like a character from *Goodfellas*. I couldn't help myself. I laughed out loud.

"You think I'm funny? I'm talkin' ta *you,* jerk-wad."

"Yeah, I do," I said. "Ever done any stand-up? That Joe Pesci impression would knock 'em dead at the Comedy Store."

Beauregard gave me a hard look. I returned it with a disarming smile. Twisdale frowned and dug an elbow into my ribs. Martin fussed nervously with his tie. For what felt like a full minute, no one spoke. Then Martin plucked the handkerchief

298

from his jacket pocket, wiped a sheen of sweat from his brow, and broke the silence.

"Mr. Beauregard, I didn't know a thing about any of this until I read the paper Sunday morning."

"Why the fuck didn't you?" Beauregard snapped.

"It's not his fault," Twisdale said. "I never told him about the story."

"That right?"

"Yes, sir."

"How many times I gotta tell ya, Twisdale? Any story affecting an advertiser has gotta be run past the ad director."

"The story was written before the super PAC became an advertiser," Martin said.

"But it *ran* three days after they placed their first ad," Dwight Freeley, the corporate advertising VP, put in.

"I realize I should have consulted with Mr. Martin at that point," Twisdale said, "but I was distracted by the work required to prepare the story for publication."

"You were *distracted*?" Beauregard said. "That's your fuckin' excuse?"

"I'm not making excuses," Twisdale said. "I'm merely telling you what happened."

This is where Pesci would have pulled a revolver and started blasting. Beauregard wasn't packing, but his dark eyes drilled us with hollow-points.

"So what's the bottom line, here?" Free-ley asked. "How much is this fuckup going to cost the company?"

"The super PAC, Americans for the Preservation of Free Enterprise, called me yesterday afternoon to announce they were dropping us," Martin said.

"They were running daily, four-color, full-page ads?" Freeley asked.

"That is correct," Martin said. Again with the tie.

"We get eight grand for a full page, is that right?"

"And ten thousand for the Sunday edition," Martin answered.

"How long were they planning to continue the campaign?"

"At least another two weeks," Martin said. "After that, I'm not sure."

"So this lack of communication between news and advertising will cost us" — Freeley pulled an iPhone from his pocket and worked the calculator — "at a minimum, we're talking one hundred and sixteen thousand dollars."

"Only a hundred thousand, actually," Martin said. "*The Dispatch* doesn't publish on Saturdays."

"Only?" Beauregard said. He raised an

eyebrow and turned to Freeley. "Did that fucking toad actually say *only* a hundred thousand dollars?"

Martin slumped in his chair and tried to make himself smaller. Freeley started to ask another question, but Beauregard raised his hand for silence, wanting the enormity of the dollar figure to sink in.

"Okay, then," he finally said. "Let's turn to our legal department's concerns about this piece-of-shit story."

Todd Grissom, the corporate lawyer, opened his briefcase, pulled out his copy of *The Sunday Dispatch,* and laid it gently on the table. I noticed that he'd used a red pen to fill the front-page margins with angry notes.

"Why didn't you see fit to have this story vetted by legal, Mr. Twisdale?" he asked. "It obviously presents a number of significant libel risks."

"Mr. Mulligan and I went over it all line by line, and we determined that it does not," Twisdale said. "Therefore, I decided it would be prudent to save the company unnecessary legal expenditures."

"You think *you* possess the legal expertise to make such a determination?" Grissom asked.

"Sure he does," I butted in.

Twisdale gave me another shot in the ribs. I ignored it.

"The Alfanos are both dead," I said, "and Mario Zerilli's reputation as a thug was already public knowledge. The only other people the story potentially libels are the New Jersey gambling interests, but that phrase doesn't identify them. It's more than vague enough to protect us from legal action."

"Do you have a law degree, Mr. Mulligan?" Freeley said.

"I've been writing investigative stories in Providence for more than twenty years, Mr. Freeley. I bet I know more about Rhode Island libel law than you do."

Freeley was briefly taken aback.

"Well," he huffed, "I do concur with your assessment of our legal exposure, Mr. Mulligan. However, company policy requires that stories of this nature must be run past the legal department. In the future, I trust the two of you will follow the proper procedure."

Beauregard whacked his palm on the table. The sound made Martin flinch.

"There ain't gonna *be* any more stories like this," he said. "No more running around pretending you're the cast of *Law and Order*. Ya get me?"

302

"Now that was inspiring," I said. "I think Ben Bradlee once gave the same speech to Woodward and Bernstein."

For that, Joe Pesci would have put a bullet in my brain. I figured Beauregard would fire me on the spot. Instead, he laughed out loud.

"You might have a future in stand-up yourself," he said. "But you sure as hell ain't got one in the newspaper business."

"Nobody does," I said.

Beauregard nodded in agreement. "On my way in," he said, "I saw your name on one of them Pulitzer medals. I think I saw it on a Polk Award, too. You have my respect for that, Mr. Mulligan. But the economics of the news business have changed, and we gotta change with it. If Ben Bradlee himself walked through that fuckin' door and begged for a job, I wouldn't hire the bastard. And if Woodward and Bernstein were working here, I'd fire both their asses. The age of newspaper heroics is over. Today, the only job of the news department is to fill the holes between the ads. Do I myself clear?"

I didn't say anything.

"Mr. Twisdale?" Beauregard said.

"Yes, sir. I understand."

"Okay, then," he said. "One last thing." He picked up his copy of the Sunday paper and waved it in Twisdale's face. "I'm told you never sent this story to our copy center. Is that right?"

"It is."

"Why the fuck not?"

"Copyediting this story properly required an extensive knowledge of Rhode Island law and politics. That is something the professionals at our copy center do not possess. Under the circumstances, I thought it best to do the job myself."

"You're the managing editor, pal," Beauregard said. "I don't pay you to be a goddamned copy editor."

"I understand, sir."

I should have left it alone, but as usual, I couldn't help myself.

"The clowns you *are* paying to be goddamned copy editors are useless," I said. "They edit in more errors than they fix."

"Oh, is that so?" Beauregard said.

"Yeah, it is. If you're hankering to recoup the hundred grand that's got your jockstrap in a bunch, the copy center would be the place to start."

"I'll take that under advisement, Mr. Mulligan. Meanwhile, I believe we can realize some immediate savings. When I leave this room, I'm taking somebody's head with me."

He swept his eyes across the three of us, hoping to make us squirm. Only the ad director did.

"Mr. Martin," Beauregard said, "get the fuck out and don't come back. Security will pack up any personal crap in your office and ship it to your home address."

35

"Why do you suppose he singled out Martin and not me?" Twisdale asked.

"Because Martin was a nervous wreck," I said. "The poor bastard couldn't stop sweating. You stayed cool, and I think Beauregard respected that."

"I came off as cool?"

"You did."

"Inside, I was shaking."

He rested his elbows on his desk and clasped his hands in front of him.

"So we live to fight another day," he said.

"We do. Should I tell you where I'm going next with this investigation, or would you prefer that I keep you in the dark?"

"You heard Beauregard. No more stories like this."

"Yeah, but 'like this' is pretty vague," I said. "That gives us some wiggle room, don't you think?"

"No, I don't."

I chose to ignore that and pressed on.

"We know that Pichardo, Longo, and Templeton refused the bribes," I said, "but I'll bet at least a few of our thirty-eight state senators and seventy-five House members took money from the Alfanos. I want to find out who they are."

"Oh, hell no. You want to go through another meeting with Beauregard the Destroyer? Next time, he'll fire the both of us."

"Until he does," I said, "I'm gonna keep doing my job. How 'bout you?"

Twisdale folded his arms across his chest. "Easy for you to say, but I've still got a wife and kids to support." He paused, self-interest and self-respect at war on his face. "But just for the sake of argument, how would you propose to go after this?"

"Most legislators are successful lawyers and businessmen," I said, "so if they suddenly started installing swimming pools or buying new luxury cars, no one would think anything of it. But about two dozen of them live paycheck to paycheck. Lovellette paints houses for a living. Parkinson is a sixth-grade teacher. Franklin is a prison guard. Berube got laid off by the Post Office last March and hasn't worked since. For people like them, twenty grand would be hard to resist."

"If they were smart," Twisdale said, "they'd sit on the dirty cash for a few years and wait till the heat dies down."

"Sure," I said, "but most of them aren't smart. And some of them need the money right now."

"Yeah, I get that. But what would you do, exactly? Drive around and look for new SUVs in their driveways or front-end loaders digging up their backyards?"

"For starters, I'd ask a P.I. friend of mine to tap his bank sources, find out if there's been unusual activity on their credit cards."

"Spending sprees?" he said.

"Or paying off large balances."

"Wouldn't it be illegal for the P.I. to do that?"

"Only a little."

He leaned back and stared at the ceiling, thinking it over.

"I'm not comfortable with this," he said. "Besides, I don't see how it would help us. You might find something that looks suspicious, but it wouldn't prove anything."

"No, but it would tell us which legislators we should take a closer look at. Once we start asking questions and digging deeper into their finances, there's no telling what might shake loose."

"I don't know, Mulligan. I mean, how long

would all this take?"

"Maybe three or four weeks if I work it full-time."

"Uh-uh. No way I can spare you that long."

"Come on, Chuck. It's an important story. If the Masons were still running the paper, they'd put three or four people on it."

"But they're not, so it would have to be just you — and mostly on your own time again."

"That would take me two or three months," I said. "By then it will be too late."

"How do you mean?"

"The governor's going to send the gambling bill to the legislature this week. There'll be hearings in both houses, but it will probably come up for a vote in about a month."

"So?"

"So once the votes are counted, all we'll be able to do is expose a few sad sacks for taking bribe money. That would cause them a world of hurt, but what good would it really do anybody? The sleazebags who've been spreading money around already will have gotten what they paid for. The damage will have been done."

"I guess that's how it's going to have to be, then," Twisdale said.

He'd grown some balls in the last week, but Beauregard had snipped them off.

"Fuck you, Chuckie," I said.

I pulled myself from the chair and stomped out.

A fresh stack of press releases was waiting on my desk. Still fuming, I sorted through them and identified the winner of the day's stupid press release challenge:

"We are proud to announce that East Bay Exotic Animals of Johnston, Rhode Island, has been designated the official pet store of the Providence Vipers."

The team wouldn't have been all that proud if they'd bothered to check the store owner's criminal record. Over the last five years, he'd been fined three times for violating the federal prohibition against the importation and sale of endangered species.

I added the salient fact to my story. It was an empty gesture of defiance. The Vipers and the pet store were both advertisers. Twisdale would feel compelled to show the story to our acting ad director, who would insist that the unflattering details be removed.

36

Early Wednesday morning I jumped out of bed, rummaged through yesterday's clothes, located my cell phone, and called the paper. The managing editor was already at his desk.

"I'm feeling poorly again, Chuckie-boy. Looks like I'll have to take another sick day. Who knows? If I can't shake what ails me, I might be out the whole damn week."

"Bullshit, Mulligan. Get your ass in here."

"No can do."

"You're pissed off about the Vipers' press release, aren't you?"

"I don't give a rat's ass about press releases," I said, and that was more or less the truth.

"You're really not coming in?"

"I'm not."

He paused, then said, "I'll need another doctor's note."

I ended the call and turned the phone off.

Then I stepped into the shower and let the hot water wash the tension from my shoulders. Now that I had the day free, I wasn't sure what to do with it. I was eager to hunt down bribe-taking legislators; but to pull that off I'd have to fake illness for a month. Chuckie-boy would, never let me get away with that. Twenty minutes later, I was still pondering my next move when the water turned cold.

After I toweled off, I pulled on a fresh pair of jeans and sniffed the Red Sox T-shirts in my laundry basket. The one with Shane Victorino's name on the back was the least offensive, so I put it on. Completing the ensemble with a Red Sox cap, I walked into the living room and roused Joseph from the couch.

"Got anything planned for today?"

"No."

"Good. Let's take a drive."

"Where we goin'?"

"Nowhere in particular," I said.

"Okay, but can we get some breakfast first? I had too much to drink last night and barfed up my dinner. I'm fuckin' famished."

Ten minutes later, we were seated in a booth at Charlie's diner. By the time I finished my bacon and eggs, Joseph had consumed two stacks of pancakes and was making short work of an egg and sausage sandwich.

"Hey, Joseph?"

"Umf?"

"How closely do you follow the NBA?"

"Ask me fuckin' anything."

"I'm thinking of putting a bet down on the Indiana Pacers to go all the way. What do you think?"

Joseph plopped the last morsel in his mouth, swallowed, licked the plate, and washed everything down with a swig of coffee. Then he launched into a soliloquy about matchups, odds, and point spreads that was worthy of Jimmy the Greek. I filed the information away for future reference. When Charlie came by with the check, Joseph asked for two corn muffins and a large coffee to go.

As we crossed the Providence River and turned south on Route 114, Joseph asked again where we were going.

"A reporter needs to know what's happening on the streets," I said, "but most days my boss keeps me cooped up in the office. It's been months since I've had a chance to take a good look around, so I want to make a circuit of the state and see what's changed out there."

"Fine with me," he said, "long as we can

stop for lunch."

We were cruising through the bedroom suburbs that line the eastern shore of Narragansett Bay when I noticed a black SUV keeping pace with us three car lengths back. I couldn't be sure, but I thought I'd seen the same car behind us as we crossed the river.

In the little bayside town of Warren, Route 114 becomes Main Street, with shabby World War I–era storefronts, some of them empty, lining both sides of the street. There, something piqued my interest, so I backed Secretariat into a metered parking space.

The display windows of a store that had once sold baby clothes were plastered with campaign posters for a Democrat seeking reelection to a third term in the state House of Representatives. A freshly painted sign stretching across the storefront proclaimed: "Concerned Citizens for Gus Lovellette."

Campaigns for the Rhode Island state legislature are normally small-time, retail politics. The candidates hand out fliers at strip malls and glad-hand old folks at nursing homes. They knock on doors and ask homeowners for their votes. Occasionally, some of them scrounge enough campaign contributions to run a few radio ads. But usually, that's about it. Now and then, when unions representing teachers or state employees get worked up about a piece of pending legislation, a few key committee chairmen can accumulate war chests of fifty grand or so. But as a rule, most legislative campaigns cost less than ten thousand dollars.

So why did Lovellette have his own campaign office? Usually the best someone like him could hope for was a poster in the local Democratic Party headquarters, which was located in another storefront just across the street. Lovellette was a struggling house painter. I doubted he was paying for this himself.

As Joseph and I climbed out of Secretariat, the black SUV slowly rolled by. The windows were tinted, so I couldn't see the driver. Was Mario stalking me again? The car continued on for half a block and then backed into a parking space.

"Looks like we picked up a tail," Joseph said.

"I think you're right."

I opened the passenger-side door, popped the glove box, and fetched the Kel-Tec the cops had reluctantly returned to me. I tucked it in my waistband and pulled my T-shirt over it.

"Want I should drag him out and ask why

he's screwin' with us?" Joseph asked.

"Not just yet. Let's keep an eye on him and see what he does."

"So what the fuck are we doing here?"

"We're gonna go into that campaign office and pretend we're trying to decide whether to vote for Lovellette," I said. "Ask some questions about his stand on the governor's gambling bill. Think you can do that?"

"Duh."

Inside, a young man with a phony smile plastered on his face was standing at a counter, waiting to greet walk-ins. Behind him, two middle-aged women were working the phones. From their chatter, it sounded as if they were making cold calls to voters.

"Welcome," the young man said. "Are you registered voters?"

"We are," I said.

"Great. Are you familiar with Representative Lovellette's stands on the issues?"

"That's what we come to find out," Joseph said.

"Well then, let me give you our new flier. It outlines his thoughts on the major issues facing our state and points you to a website where you can find his detailed position papers."

He handed us the fliers, and we took them.

"Main thing I care about is the gambling

316

bill," Joseph said. "What's Lovellette got to say about that?"

"Representative Lovellette believes that legalized sports betting is the best way to alleviate the state's fiscal crisis without raising taxes," the young man said. "However, he opposes having the state Lottery Commission take the bets. He wants to turn that responsibility over to private enterprise. Mr. Lovellette is a firm believer in our capitalist system, and he opposes anything that would make big government bigger."

"Cool," Joseph said.

"So can we count on your vote?"

"You bet."

With that, the young man turned to me.

"And what about you, sir?"

"I'm still thinking on it," I said as I flipped through the flier. "Huh. At the bottom here, it says, 'Paid for by Americans for the Preservation of Free Enterprise.' What the heck is that?"

"We are an organization that raises money to support candidates who share our position on sports gambling."

"You mean this isn't Mr. Lovellette's campaign office?"

"No, sir, but we are doing everything we can to support his reelection."

"How long have you been at this location?" I asked.

"We had our grand opening on Saturday. Would you two like some bumper stickers? How about a couple of lawn signs?"

We smiled gratefully and carried them to the car with us, even though we didn't have a lawn.

I pulled out of the parking spot and cruised past the SUV. It waited until two other cars fell in behind us and then followed at a discreet distance. I kept tabs on it in the rearview mirror as I led our little convoy south toward Bristol.

There, we found another new campaign office in a Hope Street storefront, this one promoting the reelection of veteran Republican state senator Ralph Cummings. According to the fliers the staff was handing out, Cummings was courageously bucking the Republican leadership's stand for legalized, privately run sports gambling. He was morally opposed to any form of legalization. The small type at the bottom of the fliers read "Stop Sports Gambling Now" — the super PAC funded by the NCAA and the professional sports leagues.

It was still morning when we crossed the Mount Hope Bridge and drove south through Portsmouth, but it wasn't too early for Joseph to start whining about lunch. I'd been daydreaming about the Reuben Cuban sandwich at Newport's White Horse Tavern; but when Joseph spotted the McDonald's on East Main Road in Middletown, he drooled the way Homer Simpson does whenever somebody says "doughnuts."

Inside, we took our orders to a booth that looked out on the parking lot. The grilled chicken club sandwich and a medium Coke for me. Three Quarter Pounders, two large fries, and a strawberry shake for Joseph.

"Keep this up," I said, "and you're gonna regain all those pounds you lost."

"I weigh myself every fuckin' day," he said. "Don't worry, Mom. I'm keepin' an eye on it."

We'd just started eating when the black SUV rumbled into the lot and braked to a stop two parking spaces from Secretariat. The driver sat behind the wheel for about five minutes. Then he climbed out and came inside. He waited at the counter for his Big Mac, fries, and Coke, carried them to a booth in back, and studiously avoided looking at us.

I put him at forty-five years old with thick gray hair, a lantern jaw, and a slight paunch. Six feet tall and wide in the shoulders, he had the look of a former athlete who still worked out but had developed an unhealthy

319

fondness for fatty food and beer.

"Recognize him?" Joseph whispered.

"No. You?"

"Uh-uh."

We finished our meal, bused the table, and headed outside.

"What now?" Joseph asked.

"We sit in the car and wait for him to come out."

"And then?"

"We roust him and find out who he is."

" 'Bout fuckin' time."

Fifteen minutes later, we were still sitting there while our quarry nursed a second cup of soda and made a show of not watching us through the window.

"How 'bout I go back inside and drag his ass out?" Joseph said.

I shook my head and cranked the ignition. I backed out of the parking space, rolled slowly past the front of the restaurant, made a quick right turn, and braked beside the windowless south side of the building.

"Get out of the car, stay out of sight, and grab him when he comes out," I said. "I'll circle the building and meet you out front."

I got there just in time to see Joseph rush our stalker from behind and bull him against the hood of his SUV. As I climbed out of Secretariat, Joseph kicked the guy's legs

320

apart and started to frisk him.

"What the hell!" the guy said.

Joseph smacked him hard on the back of the head and jerked a semi-auto from the small of his back.

"Who are you," I said, "and why are you following us?

"Go fuck yourself."

"Empty your pockets."

"No."

Joseph gave him another smack.

"My buddy here's going to get annoyed if I have to ask you again," I said.

"You can't make me do shit. You two assholes aren't cops."

"No, we ain't," Joseph said. "Cops probably wouldn't do this."

He shoved a paw between the guy's legs, grabbed his scrotum, and squeezed. The guy yelped like a dog getting neutered without anesthesia. Then he dug into his pockets and tossed the contents onto the hood. A set of car keys, a cell phone, a handful of change, and a brown leather wallet.

The cell looked like a prepaid that couldn't be traced, but even burners were vulnerable to my expert sleuthing. I turned it on, checked the list of recent calls, and jotted the numbers in my notepad.

Then I opened the wallet and slid out his

driver's license.

"Jesus!" I said. "How many Alfanos are there in New Jersey, and how many of you have to get killed before you learn to stay out of Rhode Island?"

He didn't say anything. From the set of his jaw, I figured he wasn't going to unless we roughed him up some more, and I lacked the stomach for that.

Instead, I returned his phone and wallet, and he put them in his pockets.

"What about the Glock?" he asked.

"You're joking, right?" Joseph said.

The guy turned to pluck his car keys from the hood, but I snatched them first and shoved them in my pocket.

"Whaddaya 'spose he was after?" Joseph asked as we cruised south toward the Newport waterfront.

"The people he works for must have been mad about my bribery story," I said. "They probably asked him to find out what I'm going to do next."

"What *are* you gonna do next?"

"We're doing it," I said.

In Newport, we stumbled on another new legislative campaign office, this one paid for by the super PAC working for privatization of sports gambling. After we talked up the staff and walked out with more fliers and lawn signs, I told Joseph to take the wheel and head west.

As he drove across the majestic Claiborne Pell Bridge, I asked him to hand me the Glock. I slid my window down and tossed both the gun and Alfano number three's car keys over the railing into Narragansett Bay's East Passage. Then I pulled the cell out of my pocket and called Judy at *The Atlantic City Press.*

"Hey, Mulligan. What's up?"

"There's another Alfano in town."

"Which one?"

"How many are there?"

"Two more brothers and maybe a dozen uncles and cousins."

"All of them connected?"

"That's what I hear."

"Is Marco Alfano one of them?"

"Another brother."

"According to his driver's license, he's from Somers Point, New Jersey. Where's that?"

"Just south of Atlantic City. How the heck did you get a look at his driver's license?"

"By asking politely. So what does Marco Alfano do for a living?"

"Other than help out with the illegal family business?"

"Yeah. Other than that."

"He owns a chain of escort services."

"So he's a pimp."

"He is, but in Atlantic City you don't get arrested for that. You get a plaque from the chamber of commerce."

"I've heard."

"So what was he doing in Rhode Island?" she asked.

"Tailing me. Probably will be again once he figures out how to start his SUV without his car keys."

She chuckled at that. "Why? Because of the story you wrote?"

"That's how I figure it. Probably wants to find out what I'm up to now."

"Think he's also spreading money around?"

"Wouldn't surprise me."

"He might also have a personal reason for being in Rhode Island," she said.

"Because Mario Zerilli probably killed his brother?"

"Yeah. The Alfanos aren't the kind to leave something like that to the authorities."

"If he wants Mario," I said, "he'll have to get in line."

After we hung up, Joseph gave me a nudge.

"I think we picked up another tail."

I glanced in the side mirror.

"Where?"

"Four car lengths back. The gray Honda Civic."

It followed us for a dozen miles, but when we turned north on Route 1, it peeled off.

I fetched my laptop from the backseat and used a reverse directory to check the phone numbers from Marco Alfano's cell. Three of them were New Jersey landlines belonging to women who shared his last name, probably a wife and daughters. One was the number for Party Hearty Escorts in Atlantic City. The other six were unlisted. Probably more untraceable burners. When I called them, each was answered by a male voice that said, "Yeah?" When I asked who was speaking, they said, "Fuck you," and clicked off.

It was still light, but well past Joseph's dinner hour, by the time we rolled into Central Falls and decided to call our tour to a halt. We'd cruised through nineteen of the state's thirty-nine cities and towns and found freshly opened, super-PAC-run legislative campaign offices in twelve of them.

On the drive back home, Joseph grumbled every time I passed a fast food joint. As we approached Providence on I-95, I spotted another gray Honda Civic in my rearview. I told myself that it was the most common car on the road.

Still, it worried me.

37

Shortly before eight the next morning, I stepped off the newsroom elevator, turned to punch the clock, and couldn't find my time card. I strode to Twisdale's office to complain, but first I wanted to fill him in on what I'd learned during yesterday's tour of the state.

"Super PACs have started pouring a ton of money into the House and Senate races," I said as I settled into the leather visitor's chair. "By law, they have to report those expenditures to the Campaign Finance Division, so I should be able to get some hard numbers for you by the end of the week."

Twisdale glowered.

"I'm surprised you had the gall to show up here this morning," he said.

"Huh?"

"You're fired."

"I'm *what*? Why? Because I called in sick again?"

"Like you don't know. You've gone too far this time, Mulligan. You'll never work in the news business again. Gather your personal belongings and get out."

Puzzled and angry, I got up, stomped to my cubicle, and slumped into what used to be my chair. I rummaged through the desk and didn't see anything worth taking home. Then I stood and took one last look around at the newsroom where I'd spent my entire working life.

It was here that I'd learned how to write, exposed corrupt judges and politicians with front-page headlines, and forged a handful of friendships that would last a lifetime. It was here that I'd discovered my calling as an investigative reporter — and where I'd learned most of what I know about life.

And death.

I'd seen the brains of shotgunned mobsters spattered on barroom walls, smelled putrefied cadavers pulled from polluted rivers, watched medical examiners paw through the remains of dismembered bodies, witnessed firemen carrying charred corpses from smoking ruins, and stared into the dead eyes of abused children. I'd been struck dumb by what remained of human beings who'd been run through wood chippers, crushed by automobiles, fed to pigs, and smashed in aircraft accidents. Once, I'd even stood on the Amtrak ties on the outskirts of the city as rescue workers plucked bits of a fifteen-year-old named Tommy Santos out of the trees minutes after he'd stumbled into the path of a speeding train.

Good times.

As I trudged to the elevator, Frieden approached, a pen and an open notebook in her hands.

"Mulligan?" she said, her voice a tentative whisper. "Twisdale assigned me to write the breaking story about you and the governor, and I was hoping you could give me a comment."

A story about me and the governor?

"Sorry, Kate," I said. "In my twenty-two years in the news business, I've learned one important lesson. *Never* talk to a reporter."

The rest of the staff stared at me as I trudged to the elevator. Nobody said goodbye.

Outside, I stood at the curb for a moment and looked up at the red-brick newspaper building. Nearly fourteen feet above the sidewalk, a brass plaque marked the high-water mark of the flood that had inundated downtown Providence during the 1938 hurricane. Meteorology was a primitive science when that storm formed in the Atlantic, so it had slammed into the New England coast without warning. But why hadn't I seen today's storm coming?

I pulled the cell from my pocket and realized I hadn't turned it back on since I shut the power off last night. There were two dozen new messages. Three from the governor insisted that I call her right away. A couple from McCracken and my buddy Mason at *The Ocean State Rag* asked if I was all right. The rest were from Iggy Rock and from reporters at the Associated Press, *The Pawtucket Times,* and the state's TV affiliates, each of them asking me to call back with my comment on "the scandal."

I turned toward the street and whistled for Secretariat. When he didn't come, I went looking and found him grazing in a nearby parking lot. I slumped behind the wheel and wondered whom I should call first. Mc-Cracken, Mason, or the governor? I decided not to call any of them.

Instead, I spurred the Bronco toward Chestnut Street, where *The Ocean State Rag* occupied half the second floor of an old jewelry factory that recently had been renovated for office space.

■ ■ ■ ■

Mason greeted me with a furrowed brow
and a bear hug.

"Jesus, Mulligan. Are you all right?"

"I don't know," I said.

He ushered me into a leather chair across
from his desk. Then he turned to his bar,
poured some bourbon into a glass, and
handed it to me.

"Really?" I said. "It's awfully early for
hard liquor, don't you think?"

"Not today, it isn't."

"Maybe so," I said, and gulped half of it
down.

"I assume *The Dispatch* fired you this
morning."

"Yeah."

"Well, you've got a job here, Mulligan.
But not just yet. I can't bring you on board
until this bullshit gets straightened out."

"And what bullshit is that?"

"You mean you don't know?"

"Apparently I'm the only one who doesn't.
Twisdale just told me to get out. Never gave
me a reason."

"You haven't seen the TV news this morning?"

"No."

"Didn't listen to Iggy Rock or check the news online?"

"Uh-uh."

He drew a deep breath and blew it out through his nose.

"Okay, then. Step over here and have a look at this."

He tapped at his keyboard and called up The *Ocean State Rag* website. The top headline screamed ALLEGED SEX SCANDAL ROCKS R.I. GOVERNOR.

"What the hell?"

Accompanying the story was a color photograph of the governor and me sitting together at a table at Hopes. Two bottles of beer, both half empty, stood on the table between us. I was holding Fiona's hand.

"The photo was e-mailed to every news outlet in the state early this morning," Mason said. "With it, there was an audio file."

He clicked on it and let it play.

Fiona's voice: "I'm disappointed. I was hoping you were going to stroll in wearing those black-and-yellow Bruins boxers."

My voice: "I could drop my pants if you want to have a look at them."

Fiona: "I better lock the door first. It wouldn't do to have anyone walk in on us."

Me: "Do it. I've always wanted to fool

332

around in the governor's office, but until now, the opportunity never came up."

Fiona: "How come?"

Me: "Because we never had a girl governor before."

Fiona: "If you keep teasing me, I might not be able to keep my hands to myself."

The audio stopped there, leaving the rest to the listener's imagination.

"Our story suggests this could be just playful banter between old friends," Mason said, "but all the other outlets are treating it as gospel."

"Where'd this come from?" I asked, although I thought I already knew.

"It was sent anonymously."

"Swell."

"Give me a statement denying that you slept with the governor," he said, "and I'll stick it in the story right up top."

"I'm thinking about it."

"What's there to think about?"

"Tell me what the governor said about it first."

"So far, she has refused to comment."

"Huh. I wonder why she hasn't issued a denial."

"Me too," Mason said. Then he paused and gave me a quizzical look. "I mean, it's not true, right?"

"Are you asking as a friend or as a journalist?"

"Both."

"To a journalist, I have no comment."

"To a friend, then?

"Of course it's not true."

I walked back around the desk, flopped into the visitor's chair, and swallowed the rest of the bourbon.

"So what's the play?" Mason asked.

"First, let's see if we can prove where this crap came from," I said. "Would you mind if I ask McCracken to look at the e-mail? He might be able to track the IP address."

"Call him," Mason said.

The first thing McCracken said was, "How are you holding up?"

"I'm fine and dandy."

"Really?"

"Yeah."

"Get fired yet?"

"Of course."

"It's for the best, buddy. You don't belong there anymore, anyway. You can start work here tomorrow morning. I'll have Sharise mount the nameplate on your door soon as we hang up."

"You don't want to wait until this thing blows over?"

"What for? Clients like to believe private

detectives are at least a little bit shady. Makes 'em think we won't hesitate to bend the rules for them." And then he chortled. "You gotta admit, this is pretty funny. I mean, you and the governor? The woman's built like a twelve-year-old boy."

When he finished trying to cheer me up, I told him Mason had offered me a job, too, and that I needed time to consider my options. Then I told him why I'd called. He said he'd be right over.

With that, I pulled myself out of the chair, thanked Mason for handling the story responsibly, and headed for the door.

"Where are you going?" he asked.

"To the statehouse to talk dirty with the governor."

But first, I had an urgent call to make.

38

"McDougall, Young, and Limone. How may I direct your call?"

"Yolanda Mosely-Jones, please."

"One moment, sir."

And then, as if the day hadn't already gone badly enough, I slumped behind the wheel in Secretariat and suffered through a minute or two of Kenny G's nausea-inducing "Forever in Love."

"Miss Mosley-Jones's office."

"Is she in?"

"Who may I say is calling?"

"Mr. Mulligan."

"Liam Mulligan?"

"Yes."

"I'm sorry, sir, but Miss Jones asked me to inform you that she is not accepting your calls."

I clicked off, twisted the rearview mirror, and took a hard look at myself. Same Sox T-shirt that was pressed into duty five years ago. Same lanky guy with a rakish lock of hair that wouldn't stay off his forehead. Same sucker who'd married badly and suffered through a contentious divorce. Same damned fool who'd stumbled so badly with love that he'd all but given up on it. Same bastard who'd resorted to treating his infrequent overnight guests as conquests. But the lady who'd finally welcomed him into her bed a few days ago was a revelation. This time, it was the guy in the mirror who'd been conquered.

Poor bastard.

I readjusted the mirror and tried Yolanda's personal cell. It went straight to voice mail. I didn't leave a message.

If Yolanda didn't trust me, what good would a message do?

39

For once, Fiona didn't keep me waiting. I was ushered straight into her office, where I found her sitting primly on the couch of infamy. The one where our "scandal" began.

She looked up at me and burst out laughing.

At first, I was too worried about what Yolanda was thinking to appreciate the humor in the situation; but once I seated myself beside the governor, the hilarity proved to be infectious. I don't know how long we sat there, arms wrapped around each other, our bodies shaking.

"Oh, my God!" she finally said. "I haven't laughed that hard in years."

"It's not *all* funny. I got fired this morning. And Yolanda isn't speaking to me."

"I'm so sorry. If I could have debunked the story before it got out, I would have; but once Iggy Rock went on the air with the audio file this morning, it was too late."

"Has Parisi figured out who bugged your office yet?"

"No, but he bullied Channel 10 into giving him the IP address the audio file and photo were sent from, and he's trying to trace it."

"I've got McCracken working on that, too," I said, "but we already know who's behind this."

"Yeah. The same person who took our photo at Hopes."

"Cheryl Grandison," I said. "She's trying to destroy you so you won't be able to get the gambling bill passed. The NCAA and the pro sports leagues will probably give her a bonus for this."

"But as always, Mrs. Grandison, if you or any of your Stop Sports Gambling Now super PAC force should be caught or killed, the commissioners will disavow any knowledge of your actions."

And we both laughed again.

"So what now?" I asked.

"I'm leaving for Trenton tomorrow."

"Trenton? What for?"

"To confer with Governor Christie."

"Why?"

"To see if we can come up with a joint strategy for derailing the opposition to our gambling bills. But mainly to duck reporters for a few days."

"Duck them? Why? The move here is to tell them that the audio file is harmless kidding between friends and that your enemies obtained it by illegally bugging your office. You've got to act fast to change the narrative, Fiona. If you don't, this thing is gonna get a lot worse."

"That's exactly what I want, Mulligan. Let the scandalmongers have their fun for a few more days."

"Why?"

"Because this so-called scandal is going to guarantee my reelection."

She shot me a sly smile.

"Okay, Fiona. What's up your sleeve?"

When she laid it out, I had to admit it was worthy of her nickname. The plan was both brilliant and diabolical.

40

While Fiona was out of town, I spent my time ducking reporters, applying for unemployment insurance, listening to Iggy Rock rant about our slut governor and her disgraced boy-toy, following the news about the legislative hearings on the gambling bill, trying unsuccessfully to reach out to Yolanda, and getting drunk with Joseph. We turned the TV news into a drinking game. Every time somebody said "disgraced boy-toy," we each chugged a 'Gansett.

Reporters had staked out the front of my tenement building, so whenever we went on a pizza and beer run, we sneaked down the fire escape, jumped the back fence, and jogged to Joseph's truck. Almost everywhere we went, a gray Honda Civic was lurking. I figured I was getting paranoid. I wasn't an investigative reporter anymore. Except for the press, no one had a reason to tail me now — unless Mario or Marco Alfano still held a grudge. And the last I time I saw Alfano, he was driving a black SUV.

Each night, I lay awake in bed and wondered about the same few things.

Would Yolanda ever speak to me again?

Was there life after journalism?

Should I give it up and take a job with McCracken?

Should I stick with it and go to work for Mason?

Or should I go for the money and take over for Whoosh if the gambling bill failed?

It was nearly a week before I stopped obsessing about myself and started wondering about more important things.

Would McCracken or Parisi be able to trace the source of the e-mail?

Would the cops find Mario before Marco Alfano put a bullet in his head?

Did Mario kill Romeo Alfano and make off with the two hundred grand? Despite what Whoosh had told me, I still thought yes. But if Mario didn't do it, who did?

Then something else occurred to me. What the hell had been in that grocery bag the Providence cops had lugged out of my apartment?

On Friday, McCracken called with one of the answers. The IP address belonged to a computer in the Providence Public Library reading room. After we hung up, I rang Parisi.

"What now, lover boy?"

"I hear the IP address is a dead end."

"No comment."

"The governor told you who snapped the photo of us at Hopes, right?"

"So?"

"Is that enough to make an arrest?"

"For what? Last I checked, photography isn't illegal."

"It ties Grandison to the audio file. They were both in the same e-mail."

A ten-second delay. And then, "It's not probative."

"Why not?"

"All it tells us is that she, or maybe somebody she gave the picture to, sent the e-mail. Doesn't prove she planted the listening devices."

"Any leads on the money from Romeo Alfano's briefcase?"

"No comment."

"Why do you keep saying that? I'm not a reporter anymore."

"The answer to my prayers."

"I got a guy who swears Mario doesn't have it."

Ten seconds this time. "That so?"

"Yeah."

"What guy?"

"I'm not saying."

Five seconds. "Seen Whoosh around lately?"

"All the time."

Ten seconds. "Any idea who *else* could have the money?"

"No."

"I've been wondering if maybe it's you," he said. And then he clicked off.

There was no reason to keep going to the Vipers' tryouts. I wouldn't be writing about that for *The Dispatch* anymore. But what the hell. I didn't have anything better to do on Saturday.

In the locker room, the players weren't calling me "grandpa" anymore. Now it was "sexy grandpa" — and a few other things that were pornographic in nature. The ribbing was good-natured, so I took it in stride.

As we staggered onto the court, Coach Martin pulled me aside.

"I was worried you weren't going to show this morning."

"Almost didn't."

"When the news broke, management ordered me to cut you, but I talked them out of it."

"Why would you do that?"

"Because you've been doing a great job with Jefferson and Benton. I also talked them into giving you this," he said, and handed me an envelope.

I tore it open. Inside was a check for twelve hundred dollars.

"What's this for?"

"Compensation as a temporary member of the coaching staff. It covers what you've done so far and for working with the guys today and next Saturday."

"That's the last day?"

"It is."

"Told Jefferson he's made the team yet?"

"Not yet."

"What about Benton?"

"We're still talking that over. With Cartwright on the shelf, we need a backup point guard, but the kid's awful small."

"So's Nate Robinson," I said, "and he's been in the NBA for years."

Before getting down to work, I slipped back into the locker room and folded the check into my wallet. It was more than enough to cover my next rent payment. That gave me a few weeks of breathing room to ponder what the hell I was going to do with the rest of my life.

41

Tuesday morning, Fiona and I huddled in
her office. Just outside the door, the press
assembled in the State Room, a spacious
hall where Rhode Island governors conducted bill signings and addressed the
public. It had been more than a week since
the sex story broke. More than a week
without a word from the governor. More
than a week in which the scandal was allowed to swell to Clintonesque proportions.

With nothing but the photo and video to
sustain them, media outlets, both local and
national, had kept the story alive with a
frenzy of absurd interviews and speculation.
Fox News assembled a panel of psycholo-
gists to discuss the supposed sex addiction
that had caused the governor to throw away
her promising political career. Providence
TV reporters hunted down my ex-wife and
former girlfriends and pestered them with
questions about my sexual history. CNN

padded its coverage with still pictures and video of other political sex scandals from JFK's Mob moll to Anthony Weiner's dick pix. Iggy Rock went on the air with a rumor that Fiona had presided over weekly orgies with hookers and lobbyists, and he dared the governor to come on the air and deny it. An "Impeach the Whore Governor" Facebook page swelled with followers. And Rush Limbaugh crowed that Attila the Nun was now Attila the Slut.

Only the wiser heads at *The Daily Show* and *The Colbert Report* exercised restraint, directing their mockery at the journalism feeding frenzy.

To stir the pot, Fiona directed an underling to phone Channel 10's Logan Bedford with a not-for-attribution tip that I'd gotten her pregnant and that she had sneaked off to Trenton for a secret abortion. The reliably unreliable Bedford went right on the air with it. Laura Ingraham, the syndicated talk-radio shrew, and Reverend Crenson, a Republican gubernatorial candidate, promptly denounced Fiona as a baby killer. Devereaux, the GOP front-runner, declined to comment, preferring to let the press do the dirty work for her.

According to a new *Providence Dispatch/ URI* opinion poll, the governor's previously record-high approval rating had plummeted to a record-low 22 percent.

Shortly before ten A.M., the governor's administrative assistant stuck her head in the door to tell us that the stage was set. Reporters for *The Providence Dispatch, The Pawtucket Times,* the local Associated Press office, and eight Rhode Island radio stations were present. Others from *The Boston Globe, The Washington Post, The New York Times, Time, Newsweek, The Huffington Post,* and *The Drudge Report* had shown up from out of town. And CNN, MSNBC, Fox News, and the four local network TV affiliates would be broadcasting the press conference live.

"Ready for the show?" Fiona asked.

"You bet."

I took her arm, pushed the door open, and escorted her toward a lectern that had been placed in front of the State Room's dominant feature, a life-size Gilbert Stuart portrait of George Washington. TV lights clicked on. The lectern bristled with microphones. We walked slowly through the room, giving the reporters ample time to shout their questions:

"Do you admit the affair?"

"Is it true that you had an abortion?"

"Are you going to resign?"

"What's your boy-toy doing here?"

And a cacophony of others I couldn't make out.

Fiona took her place behind the lectern with me at her side. She didn't speak, letting the questions wash over her. And then she beamed, looking at once chic and businesslike in a forest-green tailored suit. After a minute or so, she finally bent to the microphones and said, "Shhhhhhhh."

The shouts gradually subsided.

"Thank you all for coming," she said. "It's especially gratifying to see so many members of the national press here this morning. We don't often get this much attention in Little Rhody.

"What's *not* gratifying is that none of you are asking the important questions. You ought to be asking when the legislature is finally going to pass my gambling bill, which is essential to restoring the financial stability of our state government. You ought to be asking who illegally bugged the governor's office and distributed the infamous audio file to the media.

"But it is apparent that you have something else on your minds." She smiled slyly and paused for dramatic effect. "So, since you asked — and because you are plainly obsessed with the subject — let's talk about sex.

"I can't tell you how much I've enjoyed your salacious news reports over the last five days. They've been more entertaining than an entire season of my favorite TV show — *Scandal.* The saga of Olivia Pope's affair with the president of the United States is riveting fiction, and the show deserves its huge following. But lately, the fiction about my affair with a newspaper reporter has been giving it a run for its money, driving up both newspaper circulation and TV news-show ratings. I've always been a strong supporter of a vigorous press, so I'm sorry to be the one to spoil your fun, but perhaps you are ready to hear the truth."

Another pause.

"Liam Mulligan and I have been close friends since high school, and we're both big kidders. What you heard on the audio file was me joshing him about his choice of underwear, which, frankly, I find mystifying. I understand why a guy would wear a Red Sox cap or Bruins jersey, but darned if I get why he'd wear his favorite teams' colors where only that special someone gets to see them. After all, nobody who gets that close is thinking about baseball or hockey, so what's the point?

"Mulligan? Would you care to explain?"

I bent to the microphones and delivered my line: "I've been supporting my teams for years, Governor. Seems to me it was time they gave me some support where I need it most."

That drew some laughs. It also prompted an indignant shout from Iggy Rock.

"Do you think this is a *joke,* Governor?"

"I do," she said. "Just not as big a joke as you are, Iggy."

With that, reporters started shouting questions again. Again the governor shushed them.

"Mr. Mulligan and I do not have, never have had, and never will have a sexual relationship."

"*Never* will?" I said, ad-libbing a line and pouting in mock disappointment.

"Sorry, darling, but I am immune to your boyish charms."

I gasped, my feigned shock drawing more chuckles.

"For the record," the governor continued, "Mr. Mulligan did not get me pregnant, and I did not recently have, and have never had, an abortion. Any more questions?"

More shouts.

"One at a time, please. Mr. Bedford?"

"We've all seen the photo and heard the

351

audio. Why should we believe your denial?"

Fiona paused again for dramatic effect.

"Because I'm gay," she said.

That stunned the room into silence.

"At the conclusion of this press conference," Fiona said, "my administrative assistant will distribute notarized copies of a medical examination that was conducted yesterday afternoon by Dr. Martin Philbin, the chief of staff at Rhode Island Hospital. It will confirm that I have never been pregnant. And to satisfy your impertinent, prurient, and entirely inappropriate obsession with my private life, it will also confirm that my hymen is intact.

"I trust that when you report this earth-shattering news, your stories will be accompanied by the appropriate apologies to me and to Mr. Mulligan. Now, if you don't mind, I'd like to turn to some matters of actual importance.

"Two weeks ago, a routine, monthly sweep of my office by statehouse police uncovered several listening devices. These devices illegally intercepted the infamous conversation that was subsequently edited to remove its innocent context and then e-mailed to dozens of news outlets. The Rhode Island State Police traced the IP address and discovered that the e-mail was sent from a computer in the reading room of the Providence Public Library. The state police then examined video from a surveillance camera mounted beside the library entrance and observed Cheryl Grandison, vice president of the Stop Sports Gambling Now super PAC, entering the library just ten minutes before the e-mail was sent. That alone would not be sufficient evidence of guilt. However, the state police also interviewed two witnesses who observed Mrs. Grandison using the computer in question and five witnesses, including me and Mr. Mulligan, who saw her take the photograph that was included in the same e-mail.

"At six o'clock this morning, Mrs. Grandison was arrested at her room in the Omni Hotel. She has been formally charged with violating Chapter 11, Section 35-21, of the Rhode Island General Laws, which prohibits both the willful electronic interception of oral communications and the disclosure of the contents of such communications to third parties. The crime is punishable by five years in the state prison, where the accommodations, I assure you, are not up to the Omni's standards. Mrs. Grandison was arraigned in Providence District Court and released after posting a thirty-thousand-dollar bond.

"According to press reports, the super PAC Mrs. Grandison represents is funded by the National Collegiate Athletic Association and the five major professional sports leagues, which vigorously oppose all forms of legalized sports gambling. We believe her intention was to create a scandal that would derail the gambling bill by forcing my resignation. The five sports organizations have disavowed any knowledge of her actions.

"One last point," the governor said. "State law also prohibits anyone from willfully disseminating the contents of an intercepted conversation if they know, or have reason to believe, that it was illegally obtained. Since it was apparent on its face that my playful conversation with Mr. Mulligan was illegally intercepted, every news organization represented in this room could face criminal charges, and the reporters and editors directly responsible could spend the next half decade behind bars."

More shouted questions.

"One at a time, please. Mr. Hardcastle of *The Dispatch*?"

"Are you are seriously considering prosecuting news outlets?"

"That's up to the attorney general."

More shouts.

"Mr. Rock?"

"Are you currently in a lesbian relationship, and if so, can you tell us the name of the lucky girl?"

"None of your fucking business. Thanks for coming, and have a nice day."

42

"How do you think it went?" Fiona asked.

"Are you kidding? You slayed 'em."

We were sitting on the couch of infamy again, a chilled bottle of Dom Pérignon White Gold, two Waterford crystal goblets, and a corkscrew laid out for us on the coffee table.

"Pop the cork," she said.

So I did, filling the goblets and handing her one. We clinked glasses and drank.

"One thing, though," I said. "Could coming out hurt your reelection chances?"

"If anything, it'll help," Fiona said.

The population of Rhode Island was 44 percent Catholic, the Bishop of Providence was fervently anti-gay, and the state had lagged behind the rest of New England on the gay marriage issue. But here, like elsewhere in the country, there had been a stunning change of heart. Two years ago, the state legislature had finally legalized gay marriage. The vote wasn't close. Fifty-six to fifteen in the Senate. Twenty-six to twelve in the House. According to the opinion polls, the new law had overwhelming support among every demographic group except thugs named Mario.

"I was surprised you called on Iggy," I said.

"It was part of the plan," she said. "I was fishing for that final question, and I figured he'd have the bad taste to ask it."

"Did you mean to say 'fucking,' or did you just blurt it out?"

"I was hoping to work the f-word in at the end."

"Why?"

"Remember what David Ortiz said when he addressed the crowd at Fenway Park a few days after the Boston Marathon bombing?"

"Yeah. He said, 'This is our fucking city.' "

"He struck just the right note of determination and defiance," she said. "The crowd loved him for it. After what I've been through the last few days, I think the public will love me for it, too."

And so they did.

Two days later, a new *Dispatch*/URI poll put the governor's favorability rating at 73 percent and showed her surging to a twenty-five-point lead over Devereaux and a forty-point lead over Crenson.

By week's end, the hottest item at the Providence Place Mall was a sweatshirt emblazoned with the words "None of Your F★★king Business."

43

Saturday morning, there was no more locker-room ribbing about sexy grandpa. Instead, the guys laughingly offered to hook me up with their maiden aunts and older sisters.

Coach Martin assigned me to work with Jefferson and Benton again while he and his assistants ran the rest of the players through some perfunctory drills at the other end of the court. When that was done, we chose up teams for a final five-on-five. The play was sloppy, the players tight, knowing this was their last chance to impress.

About twenty minutes in, Krueger took a bounce pass in the post, drew the defense with an up-fake, and fed a wide-open Sears at the top of the circle. As the shot went up, Jefferson and I crashed the boards. The ball hit the rim and bounced out. We both leaped for it. Jefferson leaped higher and came down with the basketball. I came down on the back of his right heel.

Jefferson dropped the ball, toppled to the floor, grabbed his foot, and screamed. In the stands behind the bench, his wife screamed, too. Then she jumped up and ran to him with their son in her arms.

Martin and his two assistants bent over Jefferson. I got out of the way and cursed under my breath. When they pulled the kid off the floor, he couldn't put any weight on his right leg, so they lowered him back onto the hardwood. Martin walked to the bench, pulled his cell phone from a gym bag, and called for an ambulance.

When Jefferson's wife began to weep, my heart sank.

"Hey, Mulligan," Jefferson shouted. "It's not your fault."

But that's not the way it felt.

After the EMTs carted Jefferson away, his wife and son trailing behind, the somber coaches assembled the players on the sideline and told Benton that he'd made the team. They wished the rest of us well and told us it was time to go home.

As the others filed into the locker room, I remained behind on the bench, holding my head in my hands. Martin wandered over and sat beside me.

"How bad?" I asked.

"Real bad. It's his Achilles."

"Snapped?"

"Yeah."

"Oh, Jesus."

He draped an arm over my shoulder.

"Don't blame yourself, Mulligan. Shit happens."

This particular shit that had happened meant surgery and a year's worth of painful physical therapy. Keenan Jefferson's dream of a basketball career was almost certainly over. He could look forward to a lifetime of flipping burgers now.

By the time I shuffled into the locker room, the other players had already showered and were getting dressed. Krueger, furious that he hadn't made the team, shouted "Fuck" a dozen times and dented a locker door with his fist.

Benton came over and sadly shook his head.

"I guess I'm supposed to be happy," he said, "but I feel like shit. I think I got the spot that was gonna go to Jefferson."

"That's not what happened," I said. "Both of you were going to make it."

"You think?"

I wasn't sure about that, but what I said was, "Absolutely."

He looked at the floor and thought it over.

361

"Either way, I owe you big time," he said. "I'd never have gotten this far without your help."

And then he grabbed my hand and shook it.

A minute later, only Sears and I remained behind.

"Too bad about Jefferson," he said as he stuffed his Converse All-Stars into his gym bag. "That was a tough break."

"It was."

"When he went down, my first thought was that my chances were better with him out of the way. And then I felt like such an asshole."

"Um."

"So, listen," he said. "The guys have had a good time playing together. We talked it over and decided to meet for a regular pickup game at Begley Arena every Saturday morning. Can we count you in?"

"I don't think so, Chris. I don't know if I'll ever want to play basketball again."

Late that afternoon, Joseph and I pulled on hooded sweatshirts and walked the mile and a half to Hopes. My plan was to get shit-faced on Bushmills shots and Killian's. Knowing how Joseph liked to pound 'Gansett, I didn't want either of us behind the wheel tonight.

As the empties piled up on our table, my mind wandered to Yolanda. I was angry and hurt that she hadn't trusted me — or at least given me a chance to explain. I'd expected her to call me after the governor's press conference, but she hadn't. I resisted the urge to call her. I figured it was her move. I kept glancing at the door, longing to see her stride in on those long legs and scan the sparse crowd for me. But she didn't.

Instead, shortly before nine, it was Twisdale who wandered in. He took a quick look around and then headed straight for us. It was the first time I'd ever seen him in the place.

"Mind if I join you?"

"Suit yourself."

He dragged a chair across the grimy linoleum and sat beside us.

"Are you okay?" he asked.

I smirked and cocked one eyebrow at him.

"You know the hot new catchphrase that's on everyone's lips, right? None of your fucking business."

"I heard about what happened with you and Jefferson. A real shame."

"I don't want to talk about it."

"Okay. I can understand that." There was

363

an uncomfortable pause. "So, have you found work yet?"

I looked away and studied the label on the Killian's bottle. "I've decided to loaf for a while and catch up on my drinking."

"Any prospects?" he asked.

"Oodles of 'em. I'm a hot commodity."

"Given the sorry state of the news business, I really doubt that."

"I don't give a shit what you think, Chuckie-boy."

"How about coming back to *The Dispatch*?"

I raised my eyes from the bottle and gave him a hard look. "You gotta be shittin' me." I was suddenly aware that I was slurring my words.

"I'm serious."

"Ain't gonna happen."

"Corporate has authorized me to offer you a forty-dollar-a-week raise."

"Not interested."

"And a formal apology."

"You know where you can shove that."

He sighed and got to his feet. "I'm trying to help you out, here, Mulligan. When you sober up, give me a call."

With that, Twisdale turned for the door. Joseph's eyes flashed laser beams, boring a pair of holes in his back.

"Fuckin' jerk," he said. "Want I should punch his lights out for you?"

"I've got a better idea."

I yanked the cell phone from my jeans, fumbled it, dropped it on the floor, got down on my knees, found it under the table, and called for a cab. Ten minutes later, the driver pulled up out front and honked.

"Sit tight," I said. "I'll be back in a half hour."

Joseph nodded. He didn't ask where I was going.

I directed the cabby to the Walmart on Silver Spring Street. When he pulled into the parking lot, I asked him to keep the meter running and wait.

Inside, I grabbed a shopping cart and rummaged through the hardware aisles. I'd planned on buying tubes of silicone sealant, but when I squinted at the print on the packaging, I learned that the stuff took twenty-four hours to cure. I didn't have that kind of time. I interrogated the other suspects on the shelves and learned that epoxy sealant cured in four hours. Still on the long side, but I could work with it. I swept twenty tubes into the cart. I also tossed in two caulking guns, a forty-foot garden hose, and two pair of cotton work gloves. On my way to checkout, I passed through the toy section and, on impulse, picked up a dozen red, blue, and yellow plastic fish.

Ten minutes later, I lugged my shopping bags into Hopes and plopped them on the floor next to our table. Joseph didn't ask. He just waved at the waitress and ordered another round. And then another. And another.

At closing time, Joseph bullied the bartender into illegally selling us a half-dozen bottles of beer to go. We staggered out of the place with our purchases and walked three blocks to *The Dispatch.* There, the big garage doors on the northeast side of the building were raised so the box trucks could roll in to load bundles of the final edition.

We tugged the sweatshirt hoods over our heads and averted our faces as we passed the building's surveillance cameras. Once we slipped inside, we walked swiftly toward an unlocked steel door that opened onto a concrete and steel staircase. We climbed two flights and emerged inside the newsroom. It was empty, only a couple of overhead lights left burning.

The aquarium, my pet name for Twisdale's office, stood in the middle of the vast newsroom. Its four glass walls were eight feet high, leaving a gap between them and the newsroom's ten-foot ceiling. We dropped our bags beside it, pulled on the gloves, loaded epoxy tubes into the caulking guns, and set to work.

Sealing the seams at the corners and along the tile-covered concrete floor took about twenty minutes. When we were done with that, we sealed the door, laying the epoxy on thick. I'd overbought. We had three tubes left over.

"Now what?" Joseph said.

"We wait until it cures."

"And if somebody walks in on us?"

"We hide in the toilet stalls. Probably won't happen, though. The morning shift isn't due in until eight."

We slumped into chairs at the horseshoe-shaped desk where the copy editors used to work, popped open a couple of bottles, and got back to serious drinking. After my second beer, I turned my cell on and started playing Angry Birds. In my inebriated state, it didn't go well. Joseph got up, rummaged through the reporter cubicles, emerged with a crime fiction short story collection, and sat down beside me to read. After a half hour or so, the book slipped from his hands. He began to snore.

At quarter past five, I roused him.

"It's time," I said.

For years, I'd imagined how funny it

would be if someone sealed the aquarium and filled it with water, but it had taken a night of heavy drinking to make me realize what a brilliant idea it really was.

Pulling on the cotton gloves again, I uncoiled the garden hose, tossed the business end over the aquarium wall, and dragged the other end into the men's room. There, I screwed it onto the threaded faucet in the custodian sink and turned the water on. Then I turned to the urinal and emptied my beer-swollen bladder.

When I emerged, Joseph was standing in front of the aquarium, hands on his hips.

"Think it'll fill by the time the morning shift comes in?" he asked.

I watched the water gush from the hose, spread over the floor, and begin to rise.

"Should be half full, at least."

We'd worn gloves when we worked with the hose, caulking guns, and epoxy tubes, but somehow, I had the presence of mind to remember that I'd plucked them from the Walmart shelves with bare hands. I went back into the bathroom and came back out with a stack of paper towels. Together, we went to work wiping away my prints. When that was done, we did the same with the twelve empty beer bottles. Then, for no good reason I can think of now, we cleaned up after ourselves, tossing all the refuse into a trash can.

We were wiping down the desk and chairs we'd used when something occurred to me.

"Oh, shit," I said.

"What?"

"I almost forgot the best part."

Where was that other shopping bag? Had I left it behind at Hopes? Then I spotted it under the copy desk next to the chair I'd spent much of the night in. I opened it, took out the plastic fish, and tossed them one by one into the aquarium.

Joseph giggled. I did, too.

"Time to go," I said.

It was all we could do to stifle our laughter as we dashed down a different interior stairway and pushed through a steel exterior door. As soon as we burst outside, the burglar alarm went off. We ran across the street, ducked into an alley, and turned toward home.

Later that Sunday, I rose well after noon. My head was pounding. I pulled on some clothes, stumbled into the kitchen, and found Joseph stirring a pitcher filled with his vile hangover remedy. He poured the mixture into two tall glasses and handed me one.

"I may be a drunk," I said, "but I'm not crazy."

A hangover is a symptom of alcohol withdrawal, so the surest cure is more booze. I poured myself a shot of Bushmills and threw it down. Together we wandered into the living room, collapsed on the couch, and snapped on the TV. We watched the Red Sox all Sunday afternoon before switching the channel to ESPN. Our stomachs begged us to leave them alone, and for once we listened. Sometime during the third or fourth replay of *SportsCenter,* we fell asleep.

Monday morning I got up late again, stumbled down the stairs, and collected my mail from the box in the hall. Then I opened the outside door and fetched the daily paper from the stoop. Upstairs, I tossed four frozen sausage, egg, and cheese sandwiches into the microwave and started a pot of coffee. When I dropped the sandwiches on the kitchen table, the smell roused Joseph from the couch. He trudged in and snagged the sports page. I scanned page one and spotted a two-deck, one-column headline at the bottom of page one.

VANDALS ATTACK DISPATCH NEWSROOM.
It was accompanied by a photo of Twisdale's office, where plastic fish bobbed in what looked like about six feet of water.

According to the story, the damage was estimated at seven thousand dollars.

I slid the front page to Joseph. He glanced at it and laughed. Now that I'd sobered up, I didn't find our escapade all that funny.

"Think they suspect you?" he asked.

"Oh, sure," I said, "along with the forty other people the company let go in the last year and everybody who's got a beef with anything they printed."

"A lot of suspects, then?"

"Hundreds."

I finished the paper and turned to the mail. A credit card bill, three offers for more credit cards I didn't want, and a little package. I didn't remember ordering anything. Puzzled, I tore it open and found a pale blue box with gold lettering. Inside were a gift card and a heavy sterling chain, each link in the shape of an old-fashioned typewriter. It looked expensive. I flipped the card open.

I'm sorry. I was wrong to doubt you. Please call me. — Yolanda.

I draped the chain over my head and let it settle on my neck. I liked the way it felt.

"Sweet," Joseph said. "Is it from her?"

"It is."

I snatched my cell from the table and placed a call.

"Good morning, beautiful."

"Hi, Mulligan. Did you get my peace offering?"

"I did. Not sure it's appropriate, though."

"What do you mean?"

"I'm not a writer anymore."

"Baby, you'll always be a writer. Nobody can ever take that away from you."

"Thanks for saying that."

"How about coming over tonight and giving me a look at those infamous Bruins boxers? I'll cook for you."

I hesitated. One glance in the mirror this morning told me that my lost weekend had done some damage.

"Can we make it Tuesday? I've got some things I need to do today."

44

Tearing Jefferson's Achilles had cost me
more than heartache. I'd lost fifty bucks betting he'd make the team. Then again, my
winning wager on Benton was worth two
bills, so Whoosh owed me a hundred and
fifty dollars. Leaving Joseph behind in the
apartment, I skipped down the stairs and
fetched Secretariat.

I'd just cranked the ignition when it occurred to me that Mario Zerilli and Marco
Alfano were out there somewhere and probably still nursing a grudge. I went back
upstairs for my nine mil, stuck it in my
waistband, and headed out again. Ten
minutes later, I pulled up to Zerilli's Market
and parked on the street a few car lengths
in front of an unoccupied gray Honda Civic.
Christ! The damned things were everywhere.

The store lights were burning; but the
place was locked up tight, a "Closed" sign

hanging on the front door. That was odd. I shaded my eyes with my right hand and peered through a gap in the beer and cigarette advertising posters plastered all over the front window.

At first, I saw only Doreen, the latest in a series of gum-chomping high-school dropouts Whoosh had hired to man the register. She was standing halfway down the center grocery aisle. She looked terrified. Then Whoosh appeared and beckoned her to follow him. They turned left at the end of the aisle, and I lost sight of them. I shifted to look through another gap in the window and spotted them climbing the short flight of stairs to Whoosh's private office. A tall, scrawny guy in jeans and a black T-shirt followed them up. He had a silver pistol in his hand.

I pulled the cell phone from my pocket and called 911.

Unless a patrol car was in the area, it was going to take the Providence cops at least ten minutes to get there. I sprinted around the building to the back door and tried the knob. It wouldn't turn, but the lockset looked cheap. I slid a credit card from my wallet, shoved it between the door and the frame, and felt the lock give. But if the dead bolt was thrown, I was sunk.

It wasn't. I pulled my gun, pushed the door open, and stepped into a storage room piled high with cartons of cheap beer and boxes of Doritos, Ding Dongs, and cigarettes. I tiptoed through it, found another door, nudged it open, and emerged just a few feet from the stairs to the office. At the top, the steel door stood slightly ajar. Angry voices floated down, but I couldn't make out the words. I put my foot on the first step and started up.

I was halfway there when I heard a grunt. Then, in quick succession, a thump, a growl, a shriek, and a single gunshot. A heartbeat later, a woman screamed. Leading with my gun, I burst through the door.

Doreen was standing beside the keyhole desk, her face contorted as if she were about to scream again. Whoosh was sprawled on the carpet, bleeding from a gash on his head. The man who'd held the gun was doubled over in pain, the weapon lying uselessly on the floor. Shortstop, his jaws locked on the man's gun arm, dug his back paws into the carpet and dragged the creep down.

Mario Zerilli's head made a cracking sound as it hit the thin carpet. I pointed my pistol at him and kicked him once in the ribs. Hard. When he didn't react, I knew he was out cold, embarked on an exciting new career as a canine chew toy. I looked closer and saw that he was also bleeding from what appeared to be a bullet wound in his right foot.

I squatted, grabbed the silver pistol, and slipped it in my back pocket. Then I went to Whoosh, helped him up, and deposited him in his desk chair.

"Are you okay?"

"I don't fuckin' know."

"Want to call off your dog?"

"Why the hell should I?"

"He's gonna kill Mario if you don't."

Whoosh took a couple of seconds to decide whether he gave a shit.

"Shortstop! Come here, boy."

The big mutt unlocked his jaws from Mario's arm, loped over, and rested his bloody maw in his master's lap.

My first words to the homicide twins: "Believe me now?"

"Believe what?" Wargart said.

"That Mario's still alive."

"Barely," Freitas said. "He's got a hairline skull fracture, a painful gunshot wound, and a dog bite that nicked an artery. The punk lost a lot of blood."

"He gonna make it?"

"The docs at Rhode Island Hospital say yeah."

We were drinking coffee in that same interrogation room. By now, I was a regular, so they knew how I took it.

"Start at the beginning," Wargart said, "and tell us what happened."

"I don't know much," I said. "By the time I got there, it was all over but the bleeding."

It was midafternoon by the time they were done with me. A squad car gave me a lift back to my vehicle, which was still parked in front of Zerilli's Market. Just down the street, Patrolman Bobby Santo, one of the few Providence cops I remained on good terms with, was pawing through the trunk of that gray Honda Civic.

"Hey, Bobby."

"Oh, hi, Mulligan. Nice work in there today."

"Not really," I said. "All I did was call 911."

"And maybe saved two lives."

"Not me. Shortstop did that."

"Who's Shortstop?"

"Whoosh's dog."

"His *dog* took the shooter down? I hadn't heard that. The dicks have been in and out of there all day, but they aren't telling me shit."

"The mutt woulda killed him if Whoosh hadn't called him off."

"Too bad he didn't let the pooch finish the job."

"This Mario's car?"

"Not exactly. It was stolen from a Stop and Shop parking lot in Johnston last week."

"Find anything interesting inside?"

"Dirty clothes, a dozen empty Pabst cans, and a bunch of fast food cartons. Judging by the stink, I think maybe he's been living in it."

"No bundles of hundred-dollar bills stuffed under the seats?" I asked. "No briefcase with two hundred grand in it concealed in the trunk?"

"Two hundred grand? If I'd found that, I'd already be on my way to Brazil."

I thanked him, saddled up Secretariat, and pointed him toward Rhode Island Hospital. Turning onto Olney Street, I spotted another gray Honda Civic. It trailed me for a couple of miles, but when I crept through the congestion in downtown Providence, it dropped off and backed into a parking space.

I told the hospital receptionist I was Dominic Zerilli's grandson, learned that he had been admitted, and rode the elevator to his room on the fourth floor. There, I peeked inside his door and saw him sitting up in bed, a fresh bandage covering the gash on his temple. His wife sat at his side, fingering her rosary beads.

"Stop being so stubborn," she said. "Next time, you might get yourself killed. It ain't worth it anymore, honey. We got all the money we need. Why don't you just walk away?"

"I can't, sweetheart. You know Arena ain't gonna let me leave till I find somebody to take over."

"Mulligan to the rescue," I said as I stepped inside.

Whoosh looked up at me and managed a smile.

"That mean you're gonna take the job?"

"Sort of," I said. "Unless the governor's bill passes and puts us out of business."

"*Sort* of? What the hell's that mean?"

"It means you two lovebirds can move to Florida," I said. "We'll hash out the details when you're feeling better. How's he doing, Maggie?"

"He's got a mild concussion," she said. "If he was younger, they woulda sent him home already, but they want to keep an eye on the old coot for a coupla days."

"Who you callin' an old coot?"

"You," she said. "It's time you started actin' your age."

Whoosh dismissed that with a wave of his hand.

"So what happened this morning?" I asked.

"Mario came into the store waving a pistol and demanding money. Said he needed at least fifty grand to start a new life out of state. I told him no fuckin' way. That the ten grand I already gave him was all he was gonna get. So he locked the front door, herded me and Doreen into the office, and ordered me to open the safe. I worked the combination and showed him there wasn't nothing in it but my Walther, my coded record book, and maybe twelve grand in cash."

"Then what?"

"I gave him the twelve grand and closed the safe. He asked where I kept the rest of the money. 'The Caymans,' I told him, and that's when the fucker pistol-whipped me."

"Sweetie," Maggie said, "you know I don't like that kind of language."

"And when he hit you, Shortstop jumped him?" I asked.

"Yeah. Leaped through the air like he was

Michael Fuckin' Jordan and chomped down like he was Mike Fuckin' Tyson."

Maggie scowled and wagged her finger. I wasn't keen on Whoosh's choice of words either. Jordan *had* played a little baseball, but neither he nor Tyson had ever been a shortstop. I would have gone with "leaped like Ozzie Smith," but I couldn't come up with a shortstop who'd ever bitten anybody. Ty Cobb was mean enough to have done it, but he'd played the outfield.

"And that's when the gun went off and shot Mario in the foot?" I asked.

"Served the cocksu—" Whoosh hesitated and glanced at Maggie. "Served him right."

After I left them, I called the Providence cops and asked what Mario was being charged with. They wouldn't tell me anything.

45

I was stuffed, but I didn't know how to unsnap my jeans in a way that wasn't suggestive.

"Yolanda, that was the best soul food I ever tasted."

"How many soul food meals have you had?"

"Counting tonight?" I asked.

"Counting tonight."

"One. But damn, it was good."

"The smothered chicken was my mama's recipe. It was the first thing I ever learned to cook."

"If this keeps up, I'll need my own ZIP code."

Her dining room table was scattered with china we'd scraped clean of the onions-and-gravy-lathered chicken, the fried okra, the collard greens, and the sweet potato pie. I helped her clear it and load the dishwasher.

"Go get comfy in the living room," she

said. "I'll be there in a sec."

I sank into the sofa in a room that was all mint green and light, the setting sun burning gold through the open mullioned windows. Yolanda strode in, set a birdbath-size glass of white wine on the glass coffee table, and handed me a tumbler half filled with amber liquid.

"Gimme one more minute, baby," she said, and turned back to the kitchen.

I rolled the drink around on my tongue and knew instantly that it was better than my brand of Irish whiskey. She returned with an open bottle of Locke's Single Malt and placed it on the table. Then she flopped down beside me, tucked those long legs under her, picked up her wineglass, and laid her head on my chest.

"Now that's what I'm talkin' about," she said. "I definitely could get used to this."

"I know I could."

She dropped her hand to my thigh.

"Are you really wearing Bruins boxers?"

"No. I don't have any. That was just a joke."

"Actually, I picture you in Blackhawks briefs. Maybe I'll get you some."

"I've already got what I need," I said. And then I kissed her.

"You know I'm breaking a rule here,

right?" she said.

"The one about not dating white guys?"

"The one about not dating clients."

"I'm a client?"

"You gave me a five-dollar retainer."

"Give it back. I don't need a lawyer."

"Oh, yes you do."

'What? Why?"

"Because I think you've got a solid wrongful termination case."

"I never thought of that."

"Let me ask you a couple of questions," she said, her voice suddenly lawyerly. "Did *The Dispatch* give you an opportunity to explain before they fired you?"

"No. My boss never even told me *why* I was being fired. He just ordered me to collect my personal stuff and get out."

"He offer to hire you back?"

"Yeah. With a raise, too."

"What did you say?"

"I don't remember. I wasn't exactly sober at the time."

"But you didn't accept?"

"No."

"That's good. We can show damages."

"Huh," I said. I was warming to the idea.

"I've already done my homework on General Communications Holdings International," Yolanda said. "Over the last decade, three dozen wrongful termination complaints have been brought against them. Only eleven had merit, and they were all settled out of court."

"For how much?"

"The amounts varied, but the average was a hundred and forty thousand."

"Sounds like a lot."

"It's nowhere near what the legal costs would have been if the cases had gone to trial."

"How do you know about this?" I asked. "There's no public record of out-of-court settlements."

"One of my law school classmates used to work for the firm that represents them. He quit a couple of months ago when they didn't come through with the partnership he'd been promised, so he was more than willing to rat them out."

"You really think I should sue the paper?"

"I do. I'll take the case on a contingency basis."

"Meaning what, exactly?"

"The firm gets twenty-five percent if they settle before we file."

"And if they don't?"

"If we file and they settle before trial, our fee goes up to thirty-five percent."

"And if they don't settle?"

"They will," she said.

I took a moment to mull it over.

"I got fired because of Grandison," I said. "Isn't that a conflict of interest for you?"

"Not anymore. I've informed her that her actions created a conflict with another client and that she will have to seek other representation."

"Okay, Yolanda. Let's do it. After I collect, will you marry me for my money?"

"My annual salary is four times what you're likely to get."

"Can I marry you for *your* money?"

"I don't think my money's what you've got your eye on."

She rose, slipped out of her dress, took me by the hand, and pulled me into the bedroom.

46

When I stepped into McCracken's suite in the Turk's Head Building, I observed that Sharise had chosen a very short skirt today. Or maybe it was just a very wide belt. I also saw that the "Shamus Mulligan" nameplate had been mounted on one of the interior office doors.

"Mr. McCracken is expecting you," Sharise said. "You can go right in."

He greeted me with his customary bone-crushing handshake, and we seated ourselves on the leather couch. The coffee table had already been set with a fresh pot and all the fixings, and this morning, there were also doughnuts. I snagged a leaking jelly as the P.I. poured us each a cup.

"So," he said, "when can you start?"

"Look," I said, "I'm not ready to give up writing just yet. Any chance I could work for you part-time?"

"Full-time would be better, but if that's

what it takes to get you started. For now, I'll pay you sixty bucks an hour for the time you put in on each case. How's that sound?"

"Works for me."

"As an operative of McCracken and Associates, you can work under my P.I. license, but you ought to have your own. Sharise has done the paperwork, so sign the forms on your way out. . . . Oh, and is it okay if I keep your name on the door?"

"Sure thing. So what's my first case?"

"You know Brian Annunzio?"

"The criminal lawyer?"

"That's the one," McCracken said. "He's hired us to help prepare the defense for his latest client."

"What's the charge?"

"The guy's ready to cop to attempted robbery, assault and battery, and possession of an unregistered firearm; but the Providence cops are also looking at him for two murders and for stealing two hundred grand from one of the dead guys."

I turned and stared at him.

"Are you talking about *Mario*?"

"I am."

"If Mario can afford Annunzio, he must have Alfano's money stashed somewhere."

"He claims he doesn't."

"Then how's he paying the lawyer?"

"Whoosh is footing the bill."

"You've got to be kidding."

"I'm not," McCracken said. "He isn't springing for bail, though. Says he doesn't want the punk running around loose for a while."

"I'll bet. Are you sure you want *me* on this one? I haven't exactly been getting along with Mario lately."

"Me either," McCracken said. "As you may recall, the last time I ran into him I popped him in the nose."

"Did you tell Annunzio about this?"

"Didn't have to. Mario gave him the whole story."

"And he still wants us?"

"It's *why* he wants us. We already know the case. Anybody else would be starting from scratch."

"Have you talked to Mario yet?"

"I have."

"What's his story?"

"Says he didn't shoot Templeton. Claims he never even heard of the guy."

"What's he saying about Romeo Alfano?"

"Says he didn't kill him either."

"Bullshit."

"The way Mario tells it, he did get pissed off at Alfano."

"When I spilled the beans about what his

boss was really up to?"

"Yeah. After you and I left the hotel room, he told Alfano he was quitting and demanded payment for services rendered. Alfano pulled a gun on him. Said that if Mario had been any good at his job he wouldn't have let us get the drop on him."

"And then?"

"Mario says he scooped his empty revolver off the floor, turned tail, and beat it out of the hotel. When he heard that Alfano was dead and that the cops thought he'd shot him, he just kept on running."

"Don't tell me you believe that," I said.

"Could be the truth," McCracken said. "The cops ran ballistics on the gun Mario used to pistol-whip Whoosh, and it's not a match to the one that killed Alfano."

"So they can't tie him to either murder," I said.

"Not yet, anyway."

I'd given up cigars during the Vipers tryout, but I was jonesing for one now. I drew two Cohibas from my shirt pocket and clipped the ends. McCracken stuck one in his teeth, and I set fire to it with my torch lighter. Then I got mine going. We smoked in silence until I tapped two inches of white ash into my empty coffee cup.

"Mario's not the only one who had motive and opportunity to kill Alfano," I said.

"Freitas and Wargart like him for it," McCracken said, "but I hear they still think it could have been you."

"What about you?" I asked.

"I've been wondering about that. Think the desk clerk saw me leave the hotel with you that day?"

"Could have," I said. "And if he told the homicide twins —"

"Then they might suspect both of us."

"You know what I'm thinking?" I said.

"What?"

"That it could have been them."

McCracken nodded. "When we left the hotel, the first thing you did is call Wargat. You pointed him and his partner right to that hotel room."

I took a moment to think it over.

"I called Parisi, too," I said.

"Uh-huh."

"If he was at state police headquarters when he answered his cell, it would have taken him a good forty minutes to get to the hotel," I said. "In that case, the homicide twins would have beat him to the scene."

"But was he?"

"I don't know."

McCracken shook his head. "Parisi's a straight arrow," he said. "But Wargart and

391

Freitas have been on the pad for years."

"Really? I hadn't heard that."

"Oh, fuck yeah. I wouldn't trust those two assholes with their own kids' lunch money."

That afternoon, the House finally voted on the governor's gambling bill and defeated it by twenty-three votes. It then took up the Republican version, which called for sports gambling to be run by private enterprise, and passed it with a solid majority. The next morning, the House bill passed the Senate with a margin of seventeen votes. Whoever the Alfanos had been working for had gotten something for their money.

That evening, Fiona and I met to commiserate over brews at Hopes.

"The tax on private sports gambling will amount to only six percent of the revenue we could have brought in if the Lottery Commission had been authorized to take the bets," she said.

"Twelve million a year is better than nothing," I said.

"You think?"

"You don't?"

"No, I don't," she said. "We'll have to spend most of the first year's proceeds just to fight the federal lawsuits the NCAA and the professional sports leagues are going to file against the state. Besides, the whole thing is tainted now."

"By the bribes that got handed out?"

"And by all the super PAC money," she said. "The way I see it, that's just *legal* bribery."

"So what are you going to do?"

"I'm going to veto it."

"Told anybody else yet?"

"Just you."

"Mind if I give the story to Mason?"

"So you can rub *The Dispatch*'s face in it?"

"Of course."

"I'm all for that."

Next morning, I slipped into Mason's office at *The Ocean State Rag* and found him hunched over his computer, his fingers flying over the keyboard.

"Give me a sec," he said, "and I'll be right with you."

Edward Anthony Mason III was no longer the slim, naive, fresh-faced Columbia University J-School grad I'd met six years earlier when he strode into *The Dispatch*'s newsroom. He'd put on a few pounds; I could see it in his face. He'd grown wiser in the ways of the world. And he'd recently gotten engaged to Felicia Freyer, the drop-dead-gorgeous attorney he'd met when we worked the Diggs case together a couple of years back. Once, he'd been a callow, privileged youth who thought the publisher's chair at *The Dispatch* was his birthright. But when the family patriarchs sold the paper out from under him, he hadn't sulked. He'd started his own business, and it was growing. He *was* a publisher now.

He rose from the computer, shook my hand, waved me into a visitor's chair, and settled back down behind his desk.

"So," he said, "are you ready to start?"

"Sort of."

"What does that mean?"

"It means I've agreed to work part-time for McCracken. I'm thinking maybe I could do the same for you."

"Figure on trying out both jobs to see which suits you best?"

"Something like that."

"Reporter or private detective? Interesting life choice."

"It is."

"Tell you what. For now, I'll add you to our stringers list and pay you by the piece."

"Sounds good."

"You'll be on your own for health insurance, Mulligan."

"I understand."

"So, then. Got any story ideas?"

"I already have a scoop for you," I said. "Show me where to sit, and I'll bang it out."

47

If the homicide twins were guilty of robbery and murder, proving it was going to be a bitch. I didn't know where to start. The next morning, I kicked it around with Joseph for a couple of hours. He wasn't any help.

At noon, I drove to the Omni and cornered the desk clerk who'd been on duty when Romeo Alfano was killed. Had he seen anybody who looked like a cop walk out of the hotel with a briefcase that day? He didn't remember. When I slipped him forty bucks, he still didn't. The concierge was no help either.

The hotel detective was a retired Providence police sergeant named Ferguson Conklin. I found him sitting in a cramped office near the reception desk, his eyes scanning the hotel's surveillance monitors.

"How ya doin', Fergie?"

"Been better. Murder ain't good for business."

"I assume you've gone over all the video from the day of the murder."

"Of course I have. Freitas and Wargart did, too."

"They show anything?"

"Nothing helpful."

"No intruder sneaking into the murder room before the cops showed up?"

"There aren't any surveillance cameras in the hallways."

"What? Why not?"

"Our guests value their privacy."

"But the cameras cover the stairwells and elevators?"

"Of course."

"Anybody go up to the ninth floor shortly before the cops arrived?"

"Just a couple of the housekeeping staff. And one guy who knew how to avert his face from the cameras. Could have been the killer. Could have just been some guy cheating on his wife. Happens all the time. Of course, the cameras also caught you and McCracken coming down. Wargart and Freitas seemed real interested in that."

"Did the homicide twins go up before Parisi arrived?"

"I don't remember."

"Mind if I take a look at the tape?"

"Sorry. The Providence dicks took it with them."

I went back to my car and tried to think things through. A couple of weeks ago, I was an investigative reporter hell-bent on exposing massive political corruption in the state legislature. Now I'd been reduced to trying to clear a violent punk, and myself, of a murder rap. The sense of mission that had driven me for more than two decades as a journalist was gone, but my new task did come with a sense of urgency.

When I couldn't think of anything better to do, I decided to try talking things over with Parisi — even though he was never much for talking.

"I hear you're a private dick now," he said through his rolled-down driver's-side window.

"I am."

"I hate private dicks."

"That's funny. Last time we talked, you said some nice things about McCracken. And he always speaks well of you."

"Of course he does."

"Mario Zerilli claims he didn't shoot Romeo Alfano," I said.

"What else would you expect him to say?"

"He also says he doesn't have the two

398

hundred grand."

"Umpf."

"Know what I'm wondering?" I asked.

"No idea."

"I'm wondering if the homicide twins took it."

A ten-second delay, and then, "You're thinking they found Alfano dead and grabbed the money before I got there?"

"Or maybe scooped it after they shot him."

Five seconds. "Interesting theory. Only one problem with it."

"And what would that be?"

Ten seconds this time. "That grocery bag the Providence cops confiscated when they executed the warrant on your apartment?"

"Yeah?"

"You know what was in it?"

"No idea. I didn't notice anything missing."

Five seconds. "Hundred-dollar bills bundled with blue bank bands."

"What?"

"You heard me."

"How much?"

"Seven grand."

"Jesus!"

He gave me a hard look and held it.

"Want to tell me where you and McCracken stashed the rest of the cash?"

I studied his face, trying to figure out if he was serious. It didn't tell me anything.

"Come on, Captain. Freitas and Wargart must have planted a few bundles to set us up. You know we didn't do this."

"Do I?"

"Otherwise, you'd already have us in handcuffs."

Ten seconds. "Not my decision. It's Providence PD's case."

With that, he rolled up his window and roared out of the parking lot.

At first, I was too shocked to think straight. When I finally calmed down, my mind flooded with questions. If the homicide twins had me in a frame, why was I still running around loose? If they thought McCracken was involved, why hadn't he been brought in for questioning? Why hadn't his home and office been searched? For that matter, why hadn't they searched my car?

None of it made sense.

I was halfway back to Providence when I spotted another gray Honda Civic in my rearview. This one tailed me all the way to Federal Hill, then kept going straight on Atwells Avenue when I turned onto America Street. I parked in front of my tenement building and spotted another one parked two blocks away on the other side of the street. I was getting paranoid about them again. The damned things were everywhere.

I turned off the ignition and fished the cell out of my pocket to tell McCracken what I'd learned. Just before I hit the call button, I was struck by a frightening thought.

After I'd tipped Parisi and the homicide twins that they could find Romeo Alfano and Mario Zerilli at the Omni, McCracken and I had parted ways in front of the hotel. The P.I. could have slipped back inside before the cops arrived, waited until Mario shot Alfano, and then grabbed the money. Or he could have killed Alfano himself.

Was my old friend capable of that?

I didn't think so. But his agency wasn't in the black yet, and two hundred grand was a lot of money. McCracken certainly had the skill to break into my apartment without leaving a trace and plant a few bundles of cash for the homicide twins to find.

The more I thought about it, the more paranoid I got.

48

I spent the next few days brooding and hiding out in my apartment. No matter how I looked at it, I couldn't see a way out of the mess I was in.

Every morning, I caught up with the local news in *The Ocean State Rag:* Family of three shot dead in Pawtucket carjacking. Murder of state legislator remains unsolved. Sports gambling veto dooms state employee pension system. Providence Vipers release regular season schedule. State cheerleader championships at the Dunkin' Donuts Center on Saturday. Fried calamari crowned official state appetizer. When had I started getting my daily dose from Mason's website instead of the newspaper? I couldn't remember, but it was definitely before I started stringing for him. In fact, it was well before Chuckie-boy fired me.

Yolanda called early Wednesday morning, and this time she had news.

"GCHI settled," she said.

"Already?"

"I met with their attorneys in our conference room yesterday afternoon. I gave them a figure. They huddled and made a counteroffer. We haggled for about an hour and then agreed to split the difference."

"Just like that?"

"Just like that."

"How much?"

"A hundred and thirty-five thousand. If you accept the offer, they'll cut the check this week. After our fee, you'll get a hundred and one thousand dollars and change."

"I need to think about it."

"It's the best deal you're going to get without going to trial, Mulligan, and we don't want to do that."

"I agree."

"What is it, then?"

"Do you think you could let me have twenty-five grand this week and hold on to the rest of the money for a while?"

"Sure, I can do that. But may I ask why?"

"I'll explain over dinner Saturday."

After we hung up I spent another hour or so feeling sorry for myself, wondering if I'd have to spend the settlement on a criminal defense. But self-pity didn't suit me, so I stopped. Either I was going to get arrested for robbery and murder, or I wasn't. The thing to do was hope for the best and continue making plans for life after *The Dispatch*.

Those plans included Yolanda, of course, but they also involved Joseph.

The smell of eggs and coffee roused the big guy from the couch again. He wandered into the kitchen in nothing but yellowed boxers and sat down at the table. He had a sour look on his face.

"My fuckin' truck broke down again yesterday," he said. "Had it towed to the Shell station on Broad. Dwayne took one look under the hood and said the engine's blown. Piece of shit ain't worth fixing."

"Want the Bronco?" I asked.

"Sure, but I ain't got no money to buy it from you."

"Give me a dollar, and I'll sign the title over to you."

"Why would you wanna do that?"

"I'm buying a new ride later this week."

"You ain't trading it in?"

"No dealer wants a fifteen-year-old gas guzzler with body damage," I said.

"Still drives pretty good," Joseph said.

"True, but you won't have to drive it long. You'll be able to afford a hot new set of wheels soon enough."

"What the hell you talking about?"

When I told him what I had in mind, his eyes got huge.

That afternoon, Zerilli buzzed us both into his inner sanctum. I didn't need to make introductions.

"Joseph?" Whoosh said. "Ain't seen you around for months."

"That's cuz I'm fuckin' broke."

"I don't take no bets on credit, pal."

"Not why I'm here," Joseph said.

"So why are you?"

"Let Mulligan tell it."

Whoosh raised an eyebrow. I smiled, pulled a rawhide strip out of my pocket, lured Shortstop out of the visitor's chair, and sat down.

" 'Bout time you showed up," Whoosh said. "Maggie and I are flyin' to Fort Myers next week to look at condos, but I can't make an offer on anything till you and me settle our business."

"That's what we're here for," I said.

"We?"

"Uh-huh."

"What's this palooka got to do with it?"

"A lot," I said. "I can't see myself spending every day taking bets in this cramped little office. I want Joseph to handle that

405

end for me."

"You're shittin'."

"I'm not."

"What the fuck does *he* know about makin' book?"

"He's standing right here. Why don't you ask him?"

Whoosh tossed me a skeptical look, then started lobbing questions at Joseph, challenging his knowledge about sports, betting lines, and odds-making. Nearly an hour dragged by before he was satisfied.

"Okay. Looks like he can handle the day-to-day. But you still gotta be responsible for overseeing things, Mulligan."

"I understand."

"Joseph," Whoosh said, "boot Mulligan out of that chair and drag it over here. You and me gotta go over some details."

I listened in as Whoosh reeled off the percentage that had to be kicked up to Arena each month. When he started to explain how to write the bets down in code, I turned to leave. I didn't need to hear that part. I told Joseph I'd be back for him in an hour, skipped down the stairs, and ducked out of the store.

For a government form, the application to create a Rhode Island corporation was

surprisingly simple. Even a former newspaper hack could tackle it without consult-
ing a team of Harvard-trained attorneys. I
filled in the blanks standing up at the
counter in the secretary of state's office.

COMPANY NAME: Tuukka & Associates
Insurance Underwriters of North America
PURPOSES OF INCORPORATION: Retail life
and liability insurance
PRESIDENT: Tuukka Mulligan
VICE PRESIDENT: Joseph DeLucca
SECRETARY: Yolanda Mosley-Jones
DIRECTORS: Steve Dillard, Rick Miller, Ted
Cox, Doug Griffin, Tom House

Tuukka was dead, and the directors all
played on losing Boston Red Sox teams in
the 1970s, but it wasn't like anybody was
going to check.
I handed a clerk the papers and the
hundred-and-fifty-dollar filing fee and was
informed that the application would be
processed in seven to ten days.

"So," Joseph said when I picked him up.
"Can we get somethin' to eat? I'm fuckin'
starving here."
At four in the afternoon, Charlie's diner
was nearly empty. We claimed a corner

booth and talked about the Red Sox while the short-order cook scorched our cheeseburgers and fries. After they were delivered, we got down to business.

"How'd it go with Whoosh?" I asked.

"Fine."

"Any details I need to know?"

"Uh. Let's see. He said he wants to put the store in your name, but he's gonna hold on to the real estate."

"And charge us rent?"

"A dollar a year."

"It should be in your name," I said. "I'll talk to him about it."

"Okay."

"Anything else?"

"If any problems come up, he don't want me talkin' to Grasso or Arena. He says you gotta handle that."

"And?"

"He's gonna have his accountant show me how to pad the store revenue."

"To make it look like you've got a legitimate source of income?"

"Yeah. Oh, and I told Whoosh I'm gonna stop selling those illegal tax-free cigarettes he stocks behind the counter. I heard on the news the fuckin' feds are cracking down on that shit. It only brings in a few grand a year, so it ain't worth the risk."

"Good thinking," I said. "By the way, did Whoosh tell you which cops we gotta pay off?"

"He said to put five grand in a paper grocery sack the end of every month for a coupla bent dicks named Fatass and Widget."

"You mean Freitas and Wargart?"

"I guess so, yeah."

"That's odd. I heard they were on the pad, but those two pricks work homicide."

"Whoosh said they started coming around with their fuckin' hands out years ago when they was workin' vice. The cash ain't all for them. They just collect it and spread it around the department."

"To whom, I wonder."

"Whoosh didn't say. So, Mulligan?"

"Yeah?"

"You never did tell me what my cut's gonna be."

"You'll be working on commission, Joseph."

"Commission? How's that gonna work?"

"After expenses, Whoosh generally clears at least three hundred and fifty grand a year," I said.

"He told me."

"But some years are better than others."

"He told me that, too."

"Each month, I'll be wiring half of the profits to Whoosh's bank account in the Caymans."

"Okay."

"And I'll expect you to hand me six grand in cash the end of every month."

"That's all?"

"My needs are small."

"That comes to, uh, seventy-two thou a year. What about the rest of it?"

"It's yours."

"Jesus! That could be over a hundred grand a year."

"Maybe more," I said, "if you run things right."

"I get a bigger cut than you?"

"You do."

"Why?"

"You'll be doing all the work and taking most of the risk."

"Holy shit! I'm fuckin' rich."

"Not really, but it's a lot more than you're used to."

"What the hell am I gonna do with that much money?"

"I'm sure you'll think of something. Just don't be conspicuous with it, okay?"

"Whadda ya mean?"

"Don't do anything to draw attention to yourself. You don't want the IRS to come sneaking around asking questions."

"No Dodge Vipers. No diamond pinky rings. I get it. But can I get a new truck?"

"Knock yourself out."

"Probably need to pick up a gun for the office, too."

"Ask Whoosh to get you one."

Joseph flopped his head back against the booth cushion, stunned by his sudden good fortune. Then he bent over the table, finished his burger, and ordered another.

"I just thought of somethin' else," he said. "Whoosh ain't gonna be around forever. What happens when he croaks?"

"We keep sending his share to the Caymans account as long as Maggie's alive. That's probably going to be a long time, Joseph. She's in good health, and she's ten years younger than he is."

After Yolanda transferred the first twenty-five thousand from the settlement to my bank account, it had twenty-five thousand three hundred and sixteen dollars in it. But it didn't stay there long.

The day dawned hot and humid, the temperature soaring to eighty-six degrees, by the time Joseph pulled Secretariat into a customer parking space at Tasca Automotive Group in Cranston. I climbed out, glanced across the vast lot of used cars, and burst out laughing. About a quarter of them were Honda Civics. And a lot of them were gray.

We'd just turned toward the showroom when a slim blond woman in a crisp tan business suit and a fat man in a white dress shirt with sweat stains at the armpits both broke into a run. The woman was faster but the fat man was closer, so he beat her to the new mark.

"Burt Silva," he said. "Welcome to Tasca."

He stuck out his hand, and I shook it. Then he bent over, grabbed his knees, and took a moment to catch his breath.

"Thinkin' of tradin' this old gal in?" he asked.

"It's a he," I said, "and his name's Secretariat."

"Ha! Great name for a Bronco."

"I think so."

He took in my jeans and my faded Red Sox T-shirt, sizing me up.

"In the market for somethin' used?"

"No," I said. "We're heading for the showroom. Stay the fuck out of our way, okay? When I need you, I'll let you know."

"Okay, okay. Just remember to ask for Burt."

Stepping into the air-conditioned showroom felt like getting trapped inside a refrigerator. As we walked by the Fusion, the Focus, the Escape, and the Explorer, Burt kept an eye on us and tried not to hover. Joseph stopped dead beside a black F-150 pickup and tried not to drool. I left him there and headed for the Mustangs.

I gave the V6 coupes a quick once-over and then popped the hood of a red Mustang GT convertible. Aluminum block, 420 horsepower, five-liter V8 engine. Six-way power drivers. Stainless steel dual exhausts. Six-gear automatic transmission. I opened the door, slid the seat back, sank into the saddle-leather upholstery, and admired the eight-speaker Shaker sound system. Sticker price, $42,640.

After five minutes or so, I climbed out and gave Burt a wave.

"Wanna take this baby for a spin?" he asked.

" 'S'what I'm here for."

"Got one just like it in Ingot Silver out back," he said.

Five minutes later, I was behind the wheel at the edge of the street, Burt squeezed into the passenger seat at my side. I pushed a button and powered the roof down.

"Zero to sixty in four-point-eight seconds," he said.

"Let's see," I said.

Burt squealed like a girl when I floored it out of the lot. A moment later, he regained his composure and launched into his canned spiel about the car's features.

"Burt?"

"Sir?"

"Do us both a favor and shut up."

He did, but a couple of minutes later he started in again.

I punched on the sound system, flipped through the radio channels, caught the first few bars of Stevie Ray Vaughan's "Crossfire," and cranked the volume. Try talking over that.

A half hour later, I pulled back into the lot and parked beside the showroom doors.

"So, whaddaya think?" Burt said. "Is that a sweet ride or what?"

"Only two things I don't like," I said.

"What?"

"The sticker price and the color."

"You want the red one in the showroom?"

"Does it come in a dark blue?"

"Deep Impact Metallic Blue," he said, as if that was supposed to mean something to me.

"Show me."

He pointed out a Taurus in that color. I liked it fine.

When we stepped back into the show-room, Joseph was still lingering by the F-150.

"Ought to test-drive the Toyota Tundra before you decide," I said.

"The Dodge Ram and the Chevy Silverado, too," he said. "But I ain't in no hurry. Gotta wait till I get title to the store first so I can write it off as a business expense."

"Good thinking."

A moment later I sat across Burt's desk for the negotiation.

"Are you trading the Bronco?" he asked. "Cuz I can only give you scrap value for it."

"No."

"Well, I can give you a small break off the sticker price," he said. "But you gotta understand, the new Mustangs are really moving."

"Bull," I said. "The local economy sucks, and your sales are in the crapper. I want an out-the-door price of thirty-nine five including dealer costs and registration fees. And Burt? Say one more word about the price and I'm out the door to another dealer."

He leaned back and looked me over again.

"How much are you thinking of putting down?"

"Fifteen grand," I said.

"We can arrange financing for you."

"I might have a problem with that."

"What?"

"When dealers arrange financing, they like to tack on a thousand-dollar fee for themselves. I'm not paying that."

"Okay. Let me have a word with my supervisor, and I'll see what we can do."

Ten minutes later, he waddled back with his boss, a Cheshire cat named Edwin who tried to squeeze another grand out of me, gave it up as a lost cause, and slinked off to do the paperwork.

If the homicide twins were going to arrest me now, I thought, they'd have a devil of a time catching me.

49

The plunging neckline of the sleeveless, lime-green dress Yolanda wore on Saturday night made it difficult to keep my eyes on the road.

"I love your car," she said. "Is this what the twenty-five grand was for?"

"You betcha."

"Going to miss Secretariat?"

"Not really. I gave him to Joseph, but I retained visiting privileges."

"Decided on a name for the new one yet?"

"Mr. Ed, after the talking horse on that old TV show."

"Ha! Why not something noble like Citation or Seabiscuit?"

"I named my first car Citation after the three moving violations I got the first week I owned him. He was a used Yugo. When I named the Bronco, I was still in my ironic period. I decided to give the Mustang a name that actually suits him."

"Mister Ed suits him? I don't get it."

"This baby talks to me."

"He does? What's he say?"

"Whenever I obey the speed limit, as I am now, he gets pissed off," I said. "Listen to the engine. He keeps growling 'Chicken!' "

I was searching for a rare parking space within walking distance of Andino's when blue flashers lit us up. There was no place to pull over, so I stopped in front of the restaurant, blocking traffic. In the rearview, I watched Wargart and Freitas climb out of an unmarked Crown Vic. Wargart swaggered toward us on the driver's side, and Freitas approached the passenger side. Their right hands rested on the butts of their Beretta .40 semi-automatics.

I waited until they rapped their knuckles on the side windows before I powered them down and let the evening heat in.

"Sweet ride," Wargart said.

"It is."

"Must've set you back more than forty grand."

"Not quite."

"Where'd you get the money?" Freitas said.

"None of your business."

"Bet I know," she said.

"Bet you don't."

"That's one hot-looking broad sitting next to you, too," Wargart said.

"I think you meant to say hot-looking lady."

"This what you're blowing Alfano's cash on, Mulligan? Fast cars and high-class hookers?"

Beside me, I felt Yolanda's whole body stiffen as she prepared to tear the officer a new one. I squeezed her hand, signaling her to let me handle it.

"Fuck you, Wargart. Want to take that badge off so I can teach you some manners?"

"Maybe some other time. For now, why don't you two lovebirds join us at the station so we can discuss your newfound affluence?"

"Affluence?" I said. "Who bought you a dictionary?"

This had been fun, but I decided it was time to put an end to it.

"I just collected a six-figure wrongful termination settlement from *The Dispatch*," I said.

"Oh, really?" Wargart said.

"Ask my attorney."

"And who would that be?"

"You're looking at her."

He'd met Yolanda several weeks ago when

she burst into the interrogation room to rescue me. Maybe he didn't recognize her in her party duds. Or maybe he was just being an asshole.

After a little more bluster, Wargart wrote me a ticket for blocking traffic and let us go on our way. Ten minutes later, the maître d' seated us at a table by the front window. Andino's was becoming our place.

"Detective Wargart is a goddamned bigot," Yolanda said as we waited for the waitress to take our drink orders. I was surprised her language wasn't stronger.

"He's got his faults," I said, "but I don't think that's one of them."

"What are you talking about?"

"He's married to a nurse who works at Rhode Island Hospital."

"So?"

"She's half Dominican."

"Oh."

"The prick was just trying to get a rise out of me, Yolanda."

After my Killian's and her carafe of white wine were delivered, Yolanda started looking uncomfortable.

"People are staring at us again."

"They're just curious," I said. "You mind if I give you a word of advice?"

"What?"

"I know I'm not you. I know I'll never feel what you feel. But if you keep looking this hard for signs of racism, you're always going to find them. Whether or not they're actually there."

"So I should let my guard down?"

"No. But you shouldn't jump to conclusions either. It'll drive you nuts."

She sat silently for a moment, trying to decide whether to get angry. She chose against it.

"Why are the cops still pestering you about Alfano's money?" she asked. "Don't they think Mario Zerilli took it?"

"They haven't found it yet," I said, "so they're keeping their options open."

"If they bring you in for questioning again, you'll call me, right?"

"Of course."

When the appetizers were served, she turned the conversation to business.

"What am I supposed to do with the seventy-five grand I'm holding for you?"

"Seventy-six thousand two hundred and fifty, to be precise," I said.

She smiled. "That's correct. What did you think? That I was skimming?"

I reached into my blazer, extracted an unsealed business envelope, and passed it to her. The address on it read: *Keenan Jeffer-*

421

son, 17 Willard Ave., Providence, RI. She opened it and found a business letter I'd created on my laptop. The letterhead said: *Tuukka & Associates Insurance Underwriters of North America.*

I watched her face as she read the text.

Dear Mr. Jefferson,

We are pleased to inform you that we have approved payment on a policy the Providence Vipers Basketball Club purchased on your behalf. The policy insured you against any physical injury incurred during the team's recent open tryouts. Enclosed you will find our check in the amount of $76,250.

If you have questions regarding this policy, or if we may be of future service, do not hesitate to contact our legal representative, Yolanda Mosley-Jones, at McDougall, Young, & Limone in Providence, Rhode Island.

Yours truly,
Joseph DeLucca/Vice President and
Director of Benefits

Yolanda laid the letter on the table and slowly shook her head.

"Does this company actually exist?" she asked.

"On paper, it does. I filed incorporation papers last week."

"You really want to do this?"

"I do."

"It wasn't your fault."

"So everybody keeps telling me. But I feel responsible, Yolanda. I destroyed his dream. This is the least I can do for him and his family."

"What will you do for money?"

"The work I'm doing for McCracken and the stories I'm writing for *The Ocean State Rag* will pay more than I was making at *The Dispatch*. It's enough to keep the sheriff from my door." Of course, I was also in business with Whoosh and Joseph. I hated keeping secrets from Yolanda, but I decided she didn't need to hear about that.

"You're really sure?"

"I am."

"Maybe you're not really this much of an angel. I'm going to give you another week to think about it. If you haven't changed your mind by then, I'll send the check by registered mail."

"Okay, then."

So far, this wasn't the romantic evening I'd envisioned, but by the time the entrees arrived, things took a turn for the better.

"I downloaded Brian McKnight's old

423

Back at One album yesterday," she said.

"Love songs?"

"Yes. I love that man's voice."

"Does he put you in the mood?"

"Wanna find out?"

"Let's skip dessert," I said.

And this time, she let me stay the night.

In the morning, I awoke to an empty bed. Norah Jones's "Come Away with Me" floated in from the next room. Beneath the music, I heard Yolanda rattling pans in the kitchen. I rose, stepped over the clothes we'd hurriedly shed the night before, and stepped into the shower. I was lathering up when she opened the shower door and stepped inside. I grinned and wrapped my arms around her.

"There's nothing finer than a wet woman," I said.

"Any wet woman?"

"Pretty much, but I've got a crazy thing for this one."

"Maybe this will make you crazier," she said. She smiled mischievously and slid to her knees.

After we toweled off, we slipped into terry-cloth robes, sat at the kitchen table, and devoured the cheese omelets she'd prepared.

"This is wonderful," I said, "but you know what would be better?"

"What?"

"If we moved in together. Then every morning could be like this one."

She fell silent. I held my breath.

"You haven't said the words," she said.

"I love you, Yolanda."

"I think maybe I love you, too."

"What will it take to get you to hit the delete button on maybe?"

"I don't know."

"I'll wait," I said.

"How long? They say black women are stubborn."

"However long it takes."

50

I was helping Yolanda clear the dishes when Johnny Rivers's "Secret Agent Man," my ringtone for McCracken, started playing on my cell phone.

"Haven't seen your face for more than a week," he said.

"I've been busy."

"Think you could drop by the office Monday? We should talk."

So shortly after noon on Monday, I pushed through the door to McCracken & Associates.

"Good morning, Mr. Mulligan," Sharise said. "Mr. McCracken is with a client now, but he'll join you in your office momentarily."

I opened the door with my name on it and stepped inside. A large butcher block desk, a black leather office chair, two matching visitor's chairs, and two oak file cabinets were tastefully arranged on a maroon carpet that looked as if it had never been trod on.

I sank into my chair and examined the items on the desk. A new HP desktop computer with a twenty-inch flat screen. A humidor with twenty Ashtons inside and plenty of room for more. An unopened box containing a 9-millimeter Walther PPQ M2, the latest update on the PPK — James Bond's gun. And two boxes of ammunition. I left the semi-auto in the box. Until I found time to get comfortable with it, I was going to carry the Kel-Tec.

"Like your new digs?" McCracken asked as he stepped into the office.

"A lot nicer than I'm used to."

We shook hands, and he dropped into one of the visitor's chairs.

"Been working the Mario Zerilli case?"

"I have," I lied.

"And?"

"I'm not getting anywhere."

"I was afraid you were going to say that."

"Any ideas? I'm fresh out."

"Well," he said, "you could always confess to shooting Romeo Alfano and stealing the two hundred grand. *That* would certainly make the client happy."

I cocked an eyebrow.

"Hey! I was just kidding."

"Were you?"

He drew in a deep breath and blew it out through his nose.

"I have to confess, Mulligan. The possibility did occur to me."

"Because I could have returned to the hotel room after we parted ways in front of the Omni," I said.

"You could have."

"You could have, too," I said.

"Fuck you, Mulligan. The cops didn't find any of Alfano's cash in *my* apartment."

"You heard about that, huh?"

"From a source in the detective division."

"It was planted."

"Probably," he said, "but you'd say that either way."

"Of course I would."

"I wonder why the cops haven't arrested you yet."

"I've been wondering the same thing."

He leaned back in the chair and laced his big hands behind his head.

"Maybe the homicide twins think we're in this together," he said.

"Have they brought you in for questioning?" I asked.

"Not yet."

"Seems odd."

"It does."

"Occam's razor says the simplest answer

is the right one," I said.

"Meaning Mario is guilty."

"Yeah."

"Not what our client wants to hear."

"He probably doesn't give a shit," I said. "Annunzio gets paid either way."

McCracken nodded.

"This isn't getting us anywhere," I said.

"No."

"Something I should tell you."

"What?"

"I bought a new Mustang convertible this week."

"You know I gotta ask."

"Go ahead."

"Where'd the money come from?"

"Yolanda got me a fat wrongful termination settlement from *The Dispatch*."

"Really?"

"Go ahead and ask her."

"Aw, fuck," he said. "We're both getting paranoid."

"No way to start a partnership," I said.

"No it's not. We need to trust each other."

"But we don't," I said.

"So what are we going to do?"

"I don't know about you," I said, "but I'm gonna take another crack at the hotel staff. Ask if any of them saw somebody go into Romeo Alfano's room before the cops arrived. Or maybe saw one of the homicide twins sneak out with a briefcase before Parisi showed up."

"Grab photos of Freitas and Wargart off the *Dispatch* website and show them around," McCracken said.

"Good idea."

"And Mulligan?"

"Yeah?"

"Go ahead and take a snapshot of me with your cell phone. You might as well show that around, too."

51

I'd already struck out earlier with the desk clerk, the concierge, and the hotel dick, so this time around I tried my luck with the housekeeping staff. That didn't get me anywhere either. Most of them were Mexicans who didn't understand English. Or maybe pretended they didn't. They probably thought I was from the INS. I couldn't even get them to *look* at the photos.

I was striding through the hotel lobby, heading for the exit, when Fergie, the hotel detective, stepped into my path and put a hand on my chest.

"I'd like a word," he said. "Please step into my office."

Fergie wedged his rump into his swivel chair and plunked his Buster Browns on his desk. I plucked a stack of manila file folders off the visitor's chair, dropped them on the floor, and sat. Behind him, a citation for bravery he'd earned when he was a Providence detective was mounted on the wall.

"You've been questioning our housekeeping staff," he said.

"I have."

"Why?"

"I think you know why."

"You're not a reporter anymore, Mulligan. How come you're still sticking your nose into this?"

I pulled out my wallet and flashed my P.I. credentials.

"Who are you working for?" he asked.

"Bruce McCracken."

"I meant, who's the client?"

"Mario Zerilli's lawyer."

"Humpf."

He removed a soft pack from his shirt pocket, shook out a Marlboro, and lit it with a Bic. I took that as permission to clip the tip from an Ashton.

"There's no smoking in here," he said.

"Could have fooled me."

"I make an exception for the hotel detective."

I put my lighter away, shoved the cigar in my mouth, and gnawed the tip.

"The maids tell you anything?" he asked.

"No."

"Pretended not to speak English, did they?"

"That they did."

"Haven't told me a damned thing either," he said.

"Think they know something?"

"No, but I suppose it's possible. I get the feeling a couple of 'em are scared. Like maybe somebody threatened them with deportation."

"They don't have green cards?"

"Of course they do, but I don't look too hard at them. Some of the documents could be phony."

"I hope you're gonna keep letting that slide."

"Long as the INS doesn't come snooping," he said.

"Any chance one of the housekeepers grabbed the money? Maybe stuck it under some towels and rolled it downstairs in a laundry cart?"

"Anything's possible."

"I don't suppose one of them up and quit recently."

"Didn't happen."

"Okay, then. Are we done? Your second-hand smoke is thin on nicotine. I need to go outside and light this baby."

"One last thing," he said.

"Yeah?"

"Remember asking me whether the Providence dicks or the state cop got here first?"

"I do."

"I been thinking about that. Might be that Parisi beat the homicide twins by a few minutes."

"But you're not sure?"

"No."

The hotel surveillance video would tell the story, but Freitas and Wargart had made off with it, and they weren't the kind to share.

"The first cop on the scene could have shot Alfano and stolen the money," I said.

"I doubt that happened."

"But you've got to be wondering."

"I'm still pretty sure Mario did it," he said, "but the thought has crossed my mind."

I left Fergie's office and strolled slowly across the lobby. Was the hotel dick trying to make me suspicious of Parisi to divert my attention from his old Providence PD pals? I wouldn't put it past him.

By the time I pushed through the hotel door, the sun had fled to its hideout in the west. The downtown streetlights were burning. I turned right on the sidewalk and was startled to find Parisi leaning, arms crossed, against a new, unmarked Chevy Cruze — the model his department had chosen to phase out the Crown Vics. Why GM decided to spell *cruise* wrong, I had no idea.

"Good evening, Captain."

"Not for you, it isn't. Turn around and place your hands on the wall."

52

Across the street, a yellow North Kingstown School District bus was disgorging a swarm of squealing teen girls. The pom-poms they carried told me they'd come to town for the state cheerleader competition at the Dunkin' Donuts Center.

"What's this about, Captain?"

"Do as you're told, Mulligan. I'd hate to have to shoot you in front of the kids."

"I'd prefer it if you didn't shoot me at all."

I turned and laid my palms flat on the hotel wall. Before I could spread my legs, Parisi kicked them apart, patted me down, and jerked the Kel-Tec from the small of my back. I glanced over my left shoulder and saw the cheerleaders staring wide-eyed at the big-city drama as their handlers tried to hustle them away down the sidewalk.

"Empty your pockets."

I pulled out my keys, wallet, and cell phone.

"Drop them," he said, so I let them clatter to the pavement.

Parisi grabbed my right wrist, twisted it behind my back, and cuffed it. Then he did the same with my left.

"I thought this wasn't your case," I said.

"Shut up and get in the car."

He grabbed me by the cuffs, bulled me toward the Cruze, opened the back door, and shoved me inside. After locking me in, he retrieved my belongings from the sidewalk, stuffed them in his pockets, and got in behind the wheel.

I expected him to turn right at the first intersection and work his way toward Route 10 for the dreary forty-minute drive west to state police headquarters in Scituate. Instead, he blew straight through the light.

"You haven't told me that I'm under arrest."

He didn't speak. Ignoring the next opportunity to turn, he kept driving east through downtown Providence.

"You haven't read me my rights."

Nothing.

"Hey, Captain?"

Still nothing. I was starting to get a bad feeling about this.

"Where are you taking me?"

No reply.

As we crossed Francis Street, a gray Honda Civic pulled in behind us, but when Parisi swung south onto Dyer, it peeled off. Just south of downtown, Parisi picked up Eddy Street, drove past the entrance to Point Street Bridge, and swung left at the Eddy Street–Allens Avenue split. To our right, a low-end strip club and a few shabby retail stores, some of them boarded up. To our left, the docks, oil tanks, and warehouses of the Port of Providence. Behind us, just a couple of cars on the road now. I couldn't make out the models or colors through the glare of their headlights.

"Are you planning to shoot me?"

Nothing again. But this time, nothing sounded like an answer.

"You'll never get away with it, Captain."

More silence. And then, "Of course I will."

"At least twenty people saw you scoop me up."

"I've got that covered."

"How are you going to tell it? That you shot me for resisting arrest? For trying to escape? It won't pass the smell test, Captain. Too many witnesses saw me cuffed and secured in the backseat."

Silence.

"Can you at least tell me why?"

Nothing.

"Too bad about your pension, Captain."

No response.

"But I guess Alfano's two hundred grand will make up for it."

So it wasn't the homicide twins who'd stolen Alfano's money and set me up to take the fall. But why had Parisi targeted me? Wasn't Mario a more credible suspect? Oh, wait. When Mario was on the run and living out of stolen cars, there was no way to plant evidence on *him*. I saw all that clearly now. What I didn't get was why Parisi needed to kill me to make his plan work.

He drove in silence for another minute, maybe two. Then he said, "How did you figure it out?"

"I didn't. Except for Pope Francis, you were the last one I suspected."

Ten seconds, and then, "If you didn't, you would have eventually. You're way too persistent for your own good."

Your life is supposed to flash before your eyes in a moment like this, but what I flashed on was the things I'd never done. I'd never strolled the streets of Paris. Never danced at Mardi Gras in New Orleans. Never researched my family tree. Never climbed an active volcano. Never learned to ski. Never swam with dolphins. Never walked on the Great Wall of China. Never fathered a child. But it was too late for a bucket list.

"You don't want to do this," I said. "It violates everything your life has stood for."

Ten seconds, and then, "I know." His voice was a mix of regret and determination.

"Let me out, and we can both walk away. I don't have a thing on you. Nothing I can prove, anyway."

Silence.

"I'll never mention my suspicions to anyone."

Five seconds. "Sure you will."

"No I won't," I said, and I might even have meant it. "The state screwed you out of your retirement by mismanaging the pension system. You saw a chance to secure your future, and you grabbed it. I'm *glad* you took that money, Captain. It's not like it belonged to somebody who deserves to get it back."

Nothing.

Had Parisi found Romeo Alfano dead? Probably. Had he killed him for the money? Until now, I wouldn't have believed he was capable of murder.

I twisted around in the seat. As usual, Allens Avenue was nearly deserted at this time of night. Only one car was behind us now, and it had fallen back about a hundred yards.

Parisi turned left into a cluster of unlit waterfront warehouses. Some of them were abandoned, and at this hour, all of them were empty. He punched the headlights off and drove slowly toward the water, the car rocking over pavement riddled with pot-holes.

"You haven't thought this through," I said.

"I think everything through."

Not this time, I thought, but I kept that to myself.

It was a black night, so dark that I could barely see the outlines of the warehouses against an overcast sky. Parisi braked to a stop, shoved the car into park, opened his door, and climbed out. It was so quiet that I could hear the waters of upper Nar-ragansett Bay lap against the shore.

He pulled my Kel-Tec from his jacket pocket and opened the back door on the driver's side. He was going to shoot me with my own gun.

I was on the verge of panic now. I took two deep breaths, and it helped a little.

"Get out of the car."

"No."

"Do it!"

I retreated to the passenger side and

swung my legs onto the backseat, my cuffed hands trapped beneath me.

"If you're going to shoot me, you're going to have to do it right here."

"You think I won't?"

"I think you'll have a hell of a time explaining the blood spatter on the backseat."

"I'll clean it up."

"You'll never get all of it, Captain. There'll always be a trace."

"Get out of there, or I'll drag you out."

I had a dozen years, four inches, and thirty pounds on him. I didn't think he was up to it. He hesitated a beat, then decided that he was. He transferred my gun to his left fist, leaned in, and grabbed my left ankle with his right hand.

I kicked him square in the face with my right foot.

His nose exploded.

The gun discharged.

For a moment, I thought I was dead; but the round had gone wild, crashing through the window behind me.

Suddenly, two flashlight beams lit us up.

"Providence PD. Drop your weapon."

The order resonated in two-part harmony, the sweetest sound I'd heard since Yolanda played Norah Jones for me.

"Down on your knees, hands behind your head."

I swung my feet to the floor, stuck my head out the door, and saw Parisi kneeling on the pavement. Freitas and Wargart stood over him, their guns drawn. Wargart swung his pistol my way.

"Get out of the car and drop to your knees."

"He was going to kill me," I said.

"That's a lie," Parisi said.

"Just do it, Mulligan," Freitas said. "By and by, we'll all pop into the station for a nice little chat. See if we can get this thing sorted out."

Freitas covered us while Wargart cuffed Parisi. Ten minutes later, a squad car with two patrolmen inside pulled up. Wargart shoved Parisi into the backseat, and we watched it roll away. The homicide twins holstered their weapons, gripped my arms, and led me through the gloom, lighting the way with their flashlights. They'd left their car near the street.

It was a gray Honda Civic.

Wargart shoved me into the backseat and climbed in beside me as Freitas took the wheel.

"Where's your Crown Vic?" I asked.

"At the station," Wargart said.

443

"Where'd you get this heap?"

"Borrowed it from impound. Been using it for undercover."

"For tailing me, you mean."

"From time to time."

"Why?"

"We thought you'd eventually lead us to the rest of Alfano's money."

"So why were you following Parisi tonight?"

"We weren't. We were sitting on your Mustang outside the Omni. When Parisi grabbed you, we decided to tag along. See what was up."

"Lucky for me," I said.

At the station, the homicide twins escorted me to an interrogation room, removed Parisi's handcuffs, and recuffed me with my hands in front. Then they nudged me into a chair, locked me inside the room, and swaggered off to get Parisi's side of the story. I figured they'd be gone for an hour or two. But in five minutes they were back.

"Parisi must have lawyered up," I said.

"Good guess," Freitas said.

"Going to read me my rights?"

"Why would we do that?" Wargart said. "I thought you were claiming to be the victim here."

"I've got nothing to say until I speak with my lawyer."

Yolanda stormed in a half hour later, kicked the homicide twins out, sat across the interrogation table from me, and took notes as I spilled my story. When I was done, and she finally looked up, her face was a battlefield of fear and suppressed rage. She reached into her bag for a tissue to wipe tears from her eyes.

"I almost lost you tonight."

"You can't get rid of me that easily."

She reached across the table and held my cuffed hands in hers for a moment. Then she regained her composure, summoned the homicide dicks, and stood in the corner while I answered a barrage of hostile questions.

"That's quite a tale," Wargart finally said.

"It's not a tale," Yolanda said. "Charge him or release him."

"We're gonna need more time to sort this out," Wargart said. "So for the time being, we're charging him with possession of stolen goods."

"Stolen goods?" Yolanda said. "What stolen goods?"

"The money we found in his apartment," Freitas said.

"That was planted," Yolanda said.

"We don't know that," Freitas said.

"Can you hold Parisi as well?" Yolanda asked.

"For illegally discharging a firearm," Freitas said. "It's a bullshit charge, but it will have to do for now."

I spent the next three days in a holding cell.

Late Thursday afternoon, the homicide twins cut me loose without an explanation or apology. When I walked out of the station house, I found Yolanda waiting at the door. She hugged me hard and drove me to the Omni to pick up Mister Ed. Three parking tickets were tucked under the wipers.

That evening she cooked for me again. This time, the music was by Michael Bublé, but the dinner conversation was all business.

"Parisi has been charged with kidnapping and attempted murder," she said.

"Can they make it stick? It's just my word against his."

"They've got more than that," she said. "For one thing, he broke into your apartment before he scooped you up and left a suicide note on your computer."

"How can they be sure *he* wrote it?"

"One of your neighbors spotted him

sneaking down the fire escape. The time stamp on the note is a match for the time and date."

"Have you seen the note?"

"No, but Freitas pulled me aside and described what was in it."

"Tell me."

"You confessed to killing Romeo Alfano and stealing the two hundred grand. You knew the cops had found some of the money in your apartment, and you felt the walls closing in. You didn't see any way out. So you decided to take your own life."

"Anything else?"

"He included a sorrowful farewell to the woman you love."

"That would be you," I said.

"So I've heard."

"Okay," I said. "Now I get how he was planning to get away with it. He was going to say that he picked me up for questioning and then cut me loose. His questions panicked me, so I wandered down to the waterfront and shot myself with my gun."

"Sounds about right."

"Has he confessed?"

"No. But there's more."

"What?"

"Freitas and Wargart got a court order to open Parisi's safe deposit box at Citibank.

Inside, they found nearly two hundred grand in hundreds. Romeo Alfano's prints were on a few of the bank bands."

"They're charging him with that, too?"

"With grand larceny."

"What about Alfano's murder?"

"They still don't know if it was Parisi or Mario Zerilli," she said. "From the sound of it, they may never find out."

"But chances are, Parisi's going to die in prison," I said.

"Yes."

"It's a shame, really."

"Why on earth would you say that?"

"Stephen Parisi was a damned good cop, Yolanda. For thirty years, he was relentless and flat-out incorruptible. And how was the state of Rhode Island prepared to reward him for his years of faithful service? By slashing the pension he and his wife were going to retire on. He didn't plan his crime. He just walked into a hotel room *I* sent him to and stumbled on two hundred grand in cash. And in a moment of weakness, he took it. Under the same circumstances, I might have done the same thing."

"He was going to *kill* you, Mulligan."

"It wasn't personal. He needed a patsy to pin the crime on, and I happened to be handy. I'll never forget the tortured expres-

448

sion on his face when he pointed the gun at me and ordered me out of the car. Maybe I'm reading too much into it, but I can't help but wonder, when it came right down to it, if he could have pulled the trigger."

"I guess we'll never know," she said.

"I bet he doesn't know either."

Whatever Mario Zerilli's part in the drama had been, he was apparently going to get away with most of it. He may not have shot Romeo Alfano, but he probably killed Templeton. Yet the only charges pending against him were last spring's gay-bashing outside the Stable and the assault and gun charges from the incident at Whoosh's store. He'd probably serve less than ten years for all that. And when he gets out, I thought, he'll be back to making trouble for me about the bookmaking business.

I was relieved that it was all over for now, but nothing about the way things had turned out felt right.

After I helped Yolanda clear the dishes, she put Tony Bennett on the stereo. We held each other on the couch for a while, but when Bennett started crooning "Tender Is the Night," we got up and danced.

That night, she wasn't the tender lover I had grown accustomed to. This time, she responded with urgency. She even bit me.

449

53

"You look like you could use a drink," Mc-Cracken said.

I made a show of looking at my watch. "It's still morning."

"But you had quite a scare this week."

"Aw, you know me. Nerves of steel."

He smirked, got up from behind his desk, and strolled to the bar.

"What's your poison?"

I turned and ran my eyes over the options.

"Knob Creek," I said. "But if you want to keep me working here, you better lay in some Irish whiskey."

"Bushmills, right?"

"That's my usual, but Locke's Single Malt would be better."

"Done."

He poured and handed me the bourbon. For now, it would have to do.

"How are you with the way things turned out?"

"Happy to be alive. Otherwise, everything pretty much sucks."

"A shame about Parisi," he said.

"Templeton, too."

"At least our client's happy."

"I'll bet," I said. "No way the cops can hang murder and robbery charges on Mario now."

"Thanks to you."

"Um."

"Annunzio sent over a check, and he threw in a thousand-dollar bonus."

"How nice."

"He's putting us on retainer, too."

"Good to hear."

"Do you need a few days off, or can I toss you another case?"

I took a moment to think about it, then said, "I'd like to stay busy."

"But nothing too heavy?"

"For now, I think that would be best."

"Got a call from Walmart yesterday. Somebody's been pilfering electronics from their store on Silver Spring. The manager will set you up with a job in the storeroom next week."

"I dunno. Someone's bound to recognize me."

"Shear off that mop and shave your head," he said. "And I'll get you a pair of horn-rims with window-glass lenses. Not even Yolanda will recognize you then."

"Unless I take my pants off," I said.

I wandered into my office, opened the box containing the new Walther, and dry-fired it, testing the trigger pull. Then I fired up the computer, logged on to *The Ocean State Rag,* and caught up on the local news I'd missed while I was in lockup. Parisi's arrest had been the main story for three days running. I picked up the desk phone and dialed.

"Mulligan? I was hoping you'd call."

"Hi, Mason."

"Are you okay?"

"It was touch-and-go for a while, but I'm fine now."

"Are you up to writing a first-person account of your ride with Parisi?"

"I was on a case for McCracken when it happened," I said. "He can be a sticker for confidentiality. I'll have to check with him first."

After we signed off, I wandered into Mc-Cracken's office.

"I'll have to clear it with Annunzio," he said.

Ten minutes later, he popped his head into my office and gave the okay. I spent the rest of the day pounding out the story. After

I checked it over, I e-mailed it to Mason. Then I leaned back in my chair and allowed myself to dream a little.

After a half hour or so, I bent over the keyboard and searched the real estate listings for Jamestown, the town that occupies the largest island in Narragansett Bay. In a year or so, I'd have enough cash from Joseph to make a down payment. Something cozy and secluded with a view of the water. If Yolanda relented and let me move in, I wouldn't need it, but it could be our place to slip away for romantic weekends. Putting it in my name would be a risk, but Tuukka & Associates Insurance Underwriters of North America could hold the title. Nobody had to know that I was the sole stockholder.

Life after *The Dispatch* was coming into focus now, and I was starting to like the way it looked.

Whenever I visited Rosie at Swan Point Cemetery, it had nearly always been raining, but Saturday morning dawned clear. The sky was alive with Canada geese getting an early start on their annual pilgrimage from Hudson Bay to the Chesapeake.

I opened my gym bag, pawed through my basketball shoes and gym shorts, and found the Manny Ramirez jersey. I draped it over the gravestone, squatted in the grass, and gave Rosie a hug.

"No, I don't think I'm going to miss news-paper work, Rosie. *The Dispatch* isn't worth working for anymore anyway. Besides, wasn't twenty-two years as a reporter enough? It's time for me to start a new chapter. The truth is, I'm not sure how much good I ever did there anyway. . . . Yeah, I know. I exposed a lot of bad people over the years. But most of them were just errand boys. The real corrupters always got clean away.

"Well, look at how things worked out this time, Rosie. Two of the Alfanos ended up dead, but the people who hired them keep getting richer. Cheryl Grandison will do time for bugging Fiona's office, but I never laid a hand on the deep-pocket organiza-tions that tried to buy our state legislature. The state budget is still in the crapper, the best cop I ever knew is behind bars, and *Citizens United* is still the law of the land.

"America is being poisoned by big money, Rosie. Casino money. Oil money. Big Pharma money. Wall Street money. It makes a mockery of our elections. It cor-rupt our cops and politicians, even some of the ones who entered public service for the right reasons. And somehow, the fat cats and their acolytes have convinced half the population that the avaricious pursuit of wealth is a virtue.

"What's that? . . . What am *I* going to do about it?

"I'm heading to Begley Arena, Rosie. The guys who failed the Vipers' tryouts are gathering for a pickup game, and they need one more to play five-on-five."

ACKNOWLEDGMENTS

Whatever is right about this book can be attributed largely to three remarkable women who were with me every step of the way. Susanna Einstein, my agent, is one of the best story doctors in creation. Claire Eddy, my editor at Forge, is both supportive and an exacting taskmaster. And Patricia Smith, one of the finest poets working in English, edited every line, adding musical notes to my sometimes toneless prose. Of the three, only Patricia sleeps with me.

ABOUT THE AUTHOR

Bruce DeSilva's crime fiction has won the Edgar and Macavity Awards, has been listed as a finalist for the Shamus, Anthony, and Barry Awards, and has been published in ten foreign languages. His short stories have appeared in Akashic Press's award-winning noir anthologies, and his book reviews have appeared in *The New York Times Sunday Book Review, Publishers Weekly,* and scores of other publications.

DeSilva was a journalist for forty years, most recently as worldwide writing coach for the Associated Press, editing stories that won nearly every major journalism prize, including the Pulitzer. He has worked as a consultant for fifty newspapers, taught at the University of Michigan and the Columbia University Graduate School of Journalism, and lectured at Harvard University's Nieman Foundation. He and his wife, the poet Patricia Smith, live in New Jersey with two enormous dogs named Brady and Rondo. Find him online at www.brucede silva.com.